The Forgotten
ITALIAN
RESTAURANT

BOOKS BY BARBARA JOSSELSOHN

SISTERS OF WAR SERIES

Secrets of the Italian Island

The Lost Gift to the Italian Island

LAKE SUMMERS SERIES

The Lilac House

The Bluebell Girls

The Lily Garden

The Cranberry Inn

BARBARA JOSSELSOHN

The Forgotten
ITALIAN
RESTAURANT

bookouture

Published by Bookouture in 2024

An imprint of Storyfire Ltd.
Carmelite House
50 Victoria Embankment
London EC4Y 0DZ

www.bookouture.com

ISBN: 978-1-83525-767-8
eBook ISBN: 978-1-83525-766-1

To Miss Clarson and to all the Teachers

PROLOGUE
OCTOBER 26, 1943

There were no stars.

Emilia pulled the wooden door shut behind her, gently, so she wouldn't wake Signora Jorelini. She stayed still for a moment, the door at her back. It was not a pretty night. Not like the gorgeous nights of last summer, often starry and utterly breathtaking, the sky a rich shade of bluish-black that all but defied description. Tonight the sky was gray and patchy with clouds. But Emilia knew it was better this way. For staying hidden. The cloud cover made the night darker. Still, she'd have liked to see stars.

Gathering the collar of her brown cloth coat closer to her neck, she began to walk, quickly but gingerly. It was best not to run, though the urge to do so was strong. Rapid footsteps would make noise. And even though it was nearly midnight, someone could be awake. Someone who'd look out their window and spot her. Nobody rested well these days, that was what Signora Jorelini had said. Everyone slept with one ear open for unexpected noises.

Like the sound of a motorcar in town late at night. That was the one people most worried about. It could lead to the sound of an engine turning off. Then the slamming of one or more car doors, the click of brisk, efficient footsteps on the cobblestones, and the hurl of German, the tone harsh and syllables clipped. Few drove in this neighborhood. Nobody Emilia knew even had a car. Everything was close enough to walk to: the school, the library, the shops. Meeting neighbors on the street was how people stayed in touch, how they found out who was sick and needed groceries delivered, whose daughter had just gotten engaged, who had a new baby and could use some outgrown toys or clothes.

But Nazis had their own way of doing things.

Emilia studied the road ahead. Thanks to the flickering streetlamps, the cobblestones were glistening, still wet from the earlier drizzle. She hoped the dampness wouldn't seep through the new lace-up shoes Signora Jorelini had bought her. She hadn't brought another pair. She hadn't known what to bring. Nightgown? Toothbrush? Extra barrettes? She'd pinned the sides of her hair back as best she could when she'd climbed out of bed a little while ago, since there'd been no one to help her pull it back more neatly. She'd dressed in the trousers and warm sweater she'd placed on the chair last night, trying to move silently in the darkness.

How long would she wear these clothes? When would she change next, and where? She'd slipped some garments—skirts, sweaters, underwear—into her small suitcase, which she now grasped by its worn handle as she walked, finding comfort in the rhythm of her footsteps.

The code color was green today, she reminded herself. That meant there would be guides in the woods beyond the town border. At least that's what she'd been told. She hoped it was true, because what else could she do but go there? She was only fifteen. She shouldn't be making choices like this. She shouldn't be out here in the middle of the night by herself. And yet she was alone. Her father gone. Her sisters gone. Her home gone. Her friend Corinna, Signora Jorelini's daughter, now gone too. How far was the edge of town? Maybe another twenty minutes? Maybe less if she quickened her pace? She'd never needed to keep track before.

She continued on, staying away from the streetlamps, grateful for the shadows that the buildings cast onto the sidewalk. To her right was the Simona house, where a Jewish family had stayed last week. There were three of them—a mother, father, and five-year-old son. The mother had such a pretty name, Emilia remembered. Ariella. Emilia had gone with Corinna one evening to bring food for them. Signora Simona had called Emilia and Corinna the supper club angels. Emilia was struck by how worn the family looked. How sunken their eyes, how drawn their faces. Even the little boy.

As Signora Simona hurried off to the kitchen with the basket, fragrant with the dishes packed inside, Ariella had come closer to the doorway to describe what was happening in the north.

"It's getting worse," she'd said. "They know where we are. Hiding won't be good enough."

Signora Simona had returned to the door to draw Ariella back. "It's dangerous," she'd told the young woman. "You might be seen."

Ariella had let herself be pulled away, but not before extending a warning to Emilia. "They'll be coming here soon. Do you have somewhere to go? You can come along with us..."

Emilia had been stunned. She had no idea how the woman knew she was one of them.

"Don't worry," Corinna had said. "I have a plan for Emilia."

Emilia had been so relieved. It was all she needed to hear, that Corinna had a plan. She'd never imagined what the plan was. Or that she would have to tell Corinna no.

Emilia wiped her nose with the back of her hand and

continued forward in the darkness. How she would miss this town. So pretty, with its stone buildings and cobblestone roads, the purple wisteria and pink oleander blossoms that saturated window boxes and balconies from one end of town to the other each spring. The courtyards that overlooked the dazzling blue of the Tyrrhenian Sea below. It was the town where she'd been born, the youngest living daughter, the baby. *Do you have somewhere to go?* Ariella had asked. The people who lived here, the neighbors, the family friends in this town that was her home—now so many of them were different. As Signora Jorelini had told her many times, it was hard to know whom to trust.

Suddenly she heard a whooshing sound, growing larger and louder. It was them. They had entered the town, as Ariella had predicted. They knew she was here, a Jewish girl, the daughter of the town's Jewish tailor. They knew everything. She froze, her breath stalled in her chest and her heart pounding so hard that she could feel it in her temples. She had to move away from the street. But her legs wouldn't go. They felt weak, as though her bones had turned into the elastic strips her father would sew into the waistlines of dresses for women with babies growing inside. *I have to move*, she whispered to herself, her breathing stuttered. *I have to.*

Ahead was the carved arch above the stone stairway that led to the other side of town. Emilia forced in a deep breath and somehow found the strength to dart beneath it. Standing on the bottom step, she waited to hear the motorcar come closer, the men approach. What would they do to her? She closed her eyes, but couldn't stop the images from filling her head: women and men dragged from apartment buildings wearing only their nightclothes. People being thrown into cars or the backs of trucks. Being driven to... where? Nobody knew. Or they didn't want to say.

Emilia stayed hidden under the archway, crouching down,

listening to the sound of her shallow breath, closing her eyes and lowering her chin, biting her bottom lip so she wouldn't scream. But then the sound subsided. It hadn't been a car at all. Just the wind kicking up from the sea.

Sinking onto the bottom step, Emilia waited for her breathing to normalize. She couldn't stay where she was. She had to keep walking, to make it to the woods before another whooshing sound approached, this time signaling a car for real. Forcing herself to stand, she climbed up the narrow stone stairway until she emerged again into the open air. Ahead of her was the line of shops she knew so well: the shoemaker, the dress shop, the dry goods store, the *pasticceria*, the butcher. Some had been closed for a while. There was so little to be had these days.

She kept walking, and that's when she saw it, on the corner just past the dress shop. It was her house, her family's house, with her father's tailor shop on the ground floor and the kitchen, sitting room, and bedrooms upstairs. Such a nice house, simple white stone with a green door and bushes that grew lush in the spring. It was the house and shop her father had been forced to sell. Now there was another family living there. The De Luca family. Running her father's shop. Cooking meals in her family's kitchen. Sleeping in her family's beds.

She sighed and looked up, and that's when she noticed a few dim stars. Three... no four. It made her think of the story her father used to tell her as he tucked her into bed, a tale he'd learned as a young Jewish boy. It was about a man forced to leave his home, who finds purpose in the multitude of stars above. It was a story of courage and faith. The man was compelled to go forward, and so he did.

Her father had told her that story often. He'd wanted her to remember it.

She took one last look at the house, *her* house. "I'll be back," she whispered. She *would* return to this house, this neighborhood, this town, to turn everything back to the way it used to be. One day.

Grasping her suitcase tighter, she proceeded down the street.

The woods were not far ahead.

ONE

OCTOBER 2019

Monday

From inside the black sedan, Callie looked out the window at her childhood house. It felt as though she was seeing an old friend after many years. A friend whose face was recognizable— the shape of the eyes, the tilt of the head, the splash of freckles around the nose or faint scar beneath the eye from a tumble as a child—and yet who still seemed a stranger. Of course, it was because she hadn't been back in so long. The familiar features only made the feeling of separation more acute.

The driver parked, and Callie climbed out of the car. Behind her, the parents of her brother-in-law, Joe, exited, and then she heard Chloe, her fourteen-month-old niece, sweetly chatter as Joe maneuvered her out of her car seat. The graveside service had been simple, just as her sister would have wanted it. The only fanfare came from the brilliant yellow glow of the afternoon autumn sun and the rustle of the orange and gold leaves on the branches of the large oak tree that would shade Pam's headstone, as it now sheltered those of their parents and grandparents. Joe had been the only family member to speak.

He talked about how much Pam had loved this town, her house. She'd lived there all her life and never wanted to leave.

"So of course, when we became a couple, the only choice I had was to move in with her," he'd said with a sad chuckle.

Tucking a strand of her chin-length brown hair behind her ear to keep it from blowing across her face, Callie had looked at the many people sniffling and dabbing their eyes at his words. She was struck by how many people had shown up—neighbors and childhood friends and colleagues from the town's elementary school, which she and Pam had attended and where Pam had taught third grade. She'd always assumed—erroneously, evidently—that Pam and Joe lived a quiet, isolated life. Boring, even. Stifling. Maybe that was because Pam had always been such a homebody. Or maybe it was because Pam had been so hard on Callie these last few years.

"What are you fleeing from?" she'd ask when Callie found time to return her phone calls. "What are you afraid will happen if you slow down for a bit?"

"I'm not fleeing anything," Callie would answer, hating how she sounded, like a petulant child caught with the cookie she'd been told not to eat. Pam liked to mother her. It was a role she'd spent years practicing. Ten years old when Callie was born, Pam had always been more like a parent than a sibling. The two had been raised by their grandparents from the time they were young, and when both Nonna and Nonno passed away the year Callie turned twelve, it was Pam who took care of her.

Still, from the time she left for college, Callie had resented Pam's advice. Pam didn't know any more about the world than she did.

But now Callie wondered how she would manage without Pam. What if Pam's involvement was the one thing that had been keeping her life from spinning completely out of control?

She walked up the slate path that led to her childhood house, the deep-green juniper shrubs seeming to glow in the afternoon sun. It felt like a lifetime since that awful phone call from Joe last Tuesday. The next morning, she'd boarded a train from Philadelphia to Connecticut, moving in a daze. She, Joe, and Chloe were staying in the guest cottage, where Joe's parents lived. Neither Callie nor Joe had wanted to sleep in the big house without Pam.

Now, though, Callie was glad to be the first one inside, to have a moment to herself in the house before guests began arriving. Already she could hear cars turning onto the quiet street. Looking over her shoulder, she watched drivers park by the curb and passengers start to exit, the men's dark slacks and women's black dresses peeking out from beneath their fall outerwear.

Opening the unlocked front door, Callie stepped inside and hung her coat in the hall closet, feeling this regular task disquieting on a day so far from routine. To her right, Mrs. Greenbaum and two other women were arranging platters of cold cuts, salads, cheeses, and fruit, and baskets of bagels, sliced bread, and mini pastries, on the dining room table. It was covered in her grandmother's fancy white tablecloth, the one always reserved for special occasions. The three women had left the cemetery early, having volunteered to set up the post-funeral reception. Callie considered going to thank them, but changed her mind. She'd been away from home for so long and hated the thought that, aside from Mrs. Greenbaum, the women might not even recognize her. Besides, she was feeling shaky and shocked, and didn't know if she was capable of uttering a coherent sentence. She'd declined Joe's invitation to say a few words at the cemetery for these same two reasons.

Starting to kick off her black pumps, she thought better of it. It seemed more respectful to keep them on. Still, she couldn't help but think how strange it was to be here in a black dress and tights. As a kid, she'd rarely worn anything in the house but sweatshirts and sweatpants or tee shirts and terrycloth shorts, depending on the season. It had always been that kind of house.

Pam had updated some of the furniture over the years, but the feel of the place, its vibe, its voice, was just as it had always been. As was the neighborhood. The houses were all similar, split-level in style and fronted by neat lawns. The school was down the block, and a small shopping strip with a café, a dress store, a fruit market, an Italian bakery, and a pizza place was a few blocks further. Back when she was in high school, she'd found the simplicity of the town stifling. She'd promised herself she would leave as soon as she could.

Grasping the banister, she started up the stairs, feeling as though she were walking through mud. It was so heavy, the weight of all her memories. So many life-changing events had taken place, so many consequential discussions had been had, so many impassioned decisions had been reached in this house. And Pam had been a part of them all: Pam working with Callie to learn her lines when she was chosen to play Elle in the middle school production of *Legally Blonde*. Pam helping her pack for her semester abroad in Vienna when she was a college junior. Pam popping open a bottle of champagne when Callie got her first job, as a publicity assistant for an off-Broadway theater. Pam sitting next to her on the living room sofa last winter, pointedly asking why Callie, now thirty-two, never seemed to get serious with any of the men she dated. Pam as a beautiful bride, a joyful soon-to-be mom, an exhausted but happy new mother holding Chloe in her arms as if a hole she'd always felt in her heart had finally been filled.

Pam on the phone with her three weeks ago, begging her not to move to Philadelphia. Even now, Callie could picture Pam stroking Chloe's head as she slept soundly in her crib, could see Pam's dark, fine hair parted in the middle and pulled away from her makeup-less face, could hear her voice, distressed but soft, so as not to disturb the baby. "You're far away in New York City already—an hour's train ride is a lot. How can you move even further? What's in Philadelphia, anyway?"

"It's a fun city. Why not?" Callie had answered. The truth was, she needed to get as far away from New York as she could. She'd have preferred to go abroad, and would have done precisely that, except that she'd misplaced her passport. She thought she might have left it somewhere in this house, as she'd made a quick visit here last March after taking an impromptu trip to Iceland to see the Northern Lights. She hadn't wanted to wait to replace her passport once she'd noticed it missing last month, because she wanted to get out of New York right away. So she'd chosen to move to a nearby big city where she hoped she could build a new life.

"We have no family on our side, Callie, except you and me," Pam had said, and Callie could feel the force of Pam's entreaty through the phone line. "Don't you even want a family anymore? Don't you want Chloe to know who you are?"

"She's a baby. She doesn't care about anyone except you and Joe for now."

"But what are you going to do? How are you going to support yourself?"

"Believe it or not, there are jobs in Philadelphia. I'm sure I'll find something."

"Can't you at least come home so we can talk this out face-to-face? Come home. Come for a stay, a nice long stay. A few weeks, even. We can enjoy each other like we used to."

"I can't. My lease starts in two days. I'll come home soon. When it makes sense, I'll come visit."

"Why does a visit home have to make sense? Home is home, family is family—"

"And people are who they are. You know me, I need to keep moving. I'm not like you. I never stay in one place..."

Pam had known she wasn't getting the whole story. Callie could tell by her frustrated sigh, her resigned hum of acceptance. She could be annoying, Pam, but she was smart. Still, Callie couldn't bring herself to reveal the truth about why she needed to move out of New York City so fast. She was too ashamed. She didn't want to face Pam's judgment, her disappointment. Her renewed assessment that Callie was making a mess of her life.

"Fine," Pam had finally said, her voice clipped. "Go, do what you want."

"That's exactly what I'm trying to do," Callie had replied.

"But don't forget," Pam had added with a tinge of softness before Callie could hang up the phone. "You always can come home. This is still your home and always will be. Do you understand?"

Callie had nodded, hoping Pam would somehow feel the gesture through the phone line. Because she knew what her sister meant. She and Pam had inherited the house when their parents died, and Pam and Joe had been in the process of slowly buying Callie's half. Pam wanted Callie to still feel like it was hers. Callie had appreciated the sentiment so much that she felt tears form in her eyes, and she'd struggled to keep her voice steady as she said goodbye. She couldn't let Pam know how conflicted she was about leaving. She had to make this move to Philly work, and she had too much pride to reveal her true motives.

Callie had no idea what would happen with the house now. But that was a matter for another time.

Reaching the second floor, she approached the bedroom that had once belonged to her parents. It was Pam and Joe's now. They'd made some changes, painting the mauve walls white, putting in a pretty platform bed with a silky gray comforter and simple metal headboard, and replacing the old, dark furniture with modern, white wood. Callie crossed the threshold. The room smelled like Pam, that vanilla-scented body fragrance she liked so much, and Callie sat on the edge of the bed and inhaled the sweet, clean smell. For a moment, she felt at home. She realized this was exactly what she'd been hoping to feel ever since she'd set foot in the house. But then she glanced down at her black dress, and the feeling passed. Lifting her gaze, she spotted a framed photo of Pam and Joe on their wedding day, Pam looking so happy in her simple satin gown, her hair loose on her shoulders. Pam had grown up shy and fearful, unable to play sports or go to sleepovers or do so many things kids normally do because of a heart condition she'd been born with—hypertrophic cardiomyopathy, Callie had memorized the term long ago—that could make her feel weak and dizzy. She'd never even expected to get married.

But about two years ago, she'd run into Joe, a high school friend, at a singles night at the community center. Both nearly forty, they'd fallen for one another as though they were lovesick teenagers. Their at-home wedding, planned by Joe's mother, had been small and elegant. For Pam, it was all like a dream she'd never allowed herself to have.

Callie left the master bedroom and went further down the hall, stopping at the doorway to her old bedroom. Pam always called it Callie's room, even though Callie hadn't lived there since she'd left for college. Callie's childhood furniture was still in place, her wooden student desk and six-drawer dresser, and although Pam had replaced the bed linens, the new comforter was pale yellow, just as the old one had been. Callie never understood why Pam didn't make more changes, and she bristled at what she'd seen as subtle pressure to reign in her adventurous streak.

"It's ridiculous," she'd say when she visited during college breaks. "I don't live here anymore. Do something else with this room. Make it a game room or something!"

But Pam wouldn't hear of it. She liked it as it was.

With a sigh, Callie turned to the room next door, Pam's old bedroom. This was Chloe's room now, and it was charming, with a pretty white crib and dressing table and a big toy chest with "Chloe" stenciled on the front in pink balloon-type letters.

Pam had loved pink. "There'll be plenty of time for her to choose her own path," she'd said. "But as long as she's a baby, I want her life to be filled with pink and lace and frills." Pam's delight was palpable. She was just so happy being a mommy.

The one piece of furniture that Pam had kept here from the old days was her student desk and chair. The desk was just like Callie's, with one horizontal drawer and three larger drawers stacked down the side. Callie walked further into the room and slid her hand along the surface of the desk, then opened the horizontal drawer. Inside were all the things that Pam loved: Her colored pencils. Her sketchpad. Her embroidery. Her reading journal. Callie fingered the pencils, half expecting that they would dissolve like a sugar cube in a hot cup of tea. How could Pam's things still be here, if Pam was gone? How could they exist? How could *Callie* exist, if she was no longer the impulsive, misguided younger sister who so often drove Pam crazy?

"It was an accident," Joe had told her when he'd called. Evidently Carolyn Greenbaum, the retired school librarian who'd lived next door for as long as Callie could remember and helped out with the baby occasionally when Pam was at work, had gone over in the late afternoon to drop off some hand-me-down clothes that her niece's toddler had outgrown. When there was no answer, she'd tried the front door, and when she found it unlocked, she let herself in. She hadn't been surprised that the house appeared empty, as she'd assumed Pam was capitalizing on the unseasonably warm October weather to take Chloe on a stroll around the neighborhood. She'd decided to make a cup of tea and wait. But when she'd entered the kitchen, she'd found Pam on the floor, a trail of blood emerging from below her ear. The paramedics surmised that she'd become lightheaded, fallen, and struck her head on the countertop, while Chloe napped upstairs. Joe was still at the office.

Callie was surprised but not shocked by the explanation.

Pam's heart condition had been serious, and their parents and grandparents had always been anxious, believing that she was living on borrowed time. Still, she'd defied the odds for so long. She'd been advised that having a baby could put a strain on her heart, but she'd been extra careful during her pregnancy. She'd rested and eaten well. She thought she had this heart thing beat, and she'd convinced everyone around her of the same. Even Joe.

But they all should have been smarter, Callie thought as she sat down on Pam's old desk chair. The more you thought you had things under control, the more you were setting yourself up for a big fall. Once when she was in middle school, Callie had read a story about a couple that had a baby long after they'd thought they'd completed their family because they needed some genetic material to help save one of their older children's lives. After that, Callie had sometimes wondered if her parents had had her to save Pam. So there'd be one more body around to help rescue Pam in an emergency. Why else would her parents have had her so many years after her sister was born? Yes, she could have been merely a mistake. But what if she wasn't?

Callie shook her head to clear her mind. Looking at Chloe's crib, she remembered what Pam had said to her the day she'd brought Chloe home from the hospital, Joe and Callie trailing her with diapers, blankets, tubes of petroleum jelly, and all the other supplies the nurses had loaded them up with.

"I know this is going to sound insane," she began, as she put Chloe down in the bassinet she'd borrowed from a neighbor, which she'd positioned in the center of the living room, right in the spot that got the most sunlight. "But I feel like if I were to die tomorrow, it would be okay. I did what I wanted to do while I was here on this earth. I gave the world Chloe. My work is done here, and anything else is gravy."

Callie had rolled her eyes. "I think they gave you too many drugs," she joked.

"No, I mean it," Pam had insisted. "Remember what

Grandpa used to say, that Jewish thing he loved to repeat? 'He who saves one life saves the world entire.' I saved the world entire. With my beautiful, beautiful daughter."

"You gave birth to her. You didn't save her."

"Same thing. Or close enough. Who knows what wonderful things Chloe will do? Just by being born? Just by showing up?"

Callie had laughed and gone over to the bassinet to look at her niece. She was so taken at that moment with Pam's total rapture over her newborn daughter. And yet, now those words, their grandfather's favorite phrase, seemed ominous, almost accusatory. I could have been here to save Pam, she thought. It was true—she could have visited more, she could have called more. That would have been the right thing to do, especially after hearing Pam's voice, begging her to stop home for a nice, long visit before she made the big move to Philadelphia. Maybe without being totally aware of it, Pam sensed some change in her own health. And maybe if Callie had come home, she would have seen something in Pam's appearance, in her gait, in her speech—something that would have alerted her that Pam needed to go back to the doctor. Sisters saw things that others—even husbands—might not. But Callie had been determined to get herself to Philadelphia, protecting her ego as she tried to put her life back in order.

Callie turned back to Pam's old desk. The bottom drawer was the one where Pam had kept special projects she and Callie were working on. Like the photo album they'd created for their grandparents' anniversary one year. And the scripts they wrote for pretend movies, along with the VHS tapes on which they'd recorded themselves speaking lines from those scripts using Nonno's old camcorder. Of course, the tapes were now impossible to watch because nobody owned VHS players anymore. Had Pam kept them all these years? If so, Callie wanted to find them and take them before someone else went through this desk. No doubt Joe's mother would soon clean out everything, thinking she was being helpful. Callie couldn't let her take the only recordings she might have of Pam's high-pitched, melodic voice. She should retrieve them now, so she could find a place that could transfer them onto a thumb drive or something.

She opened the bottom drawer and looked around, but didn't see any old tapes. Mostly there were pens and pads and brochures from a local toddler program, presumably for Chloe. But beneath the brochures, she noticed a wooden jewelry box, about the size of the boxes that once held her grandfather's expensive cigars, with a tiny combination lock built into the front. Pam had loved locking special things in boxes like this. She would always use Callie's birthday as the code. May 29th: 0-5-2-9.

This box was locked, and Callie wondered what was inside.

She removed the box from the drawer and set it on top of the desk. Not really expecting it to work, she turned the wheels to her birthday. Surprisingly, the lock released.

She braced herself for what the box might be holding. Maybe some notes, or birthday cards, or a photo or drawing, or a few of those old recordings. No doubt whatever it was, it would make her cry, but she didn't care. She probably could use a good cry. She lifted the lid, only to find that none of those things she'd expected were there. Instead, she found a printout of what looked to be an Italian train schedule. It started at Roma Termini, which Callie assumed was the train station in Rome. And there was a circle halfway down the page, drawn with orange crayon, surrounding a town called Caccipulia.

Callie recognized the name—this was the town where her grandmother had been born, a town that had been destroyed by the Nazis soon after her grandparents fled from there. Nonna had never wanted to talk about her childhood or her life with Nonno before they came to America. Yet, sometimes little spurts of memories would show up, damaging spurts, like tiny leaks that appear when gaps in a roof are not adequately repaired. Once when she was nine and Pam was nineteen, their grandparents had taken them on a vacation to Yosemite National Park, way across the country in California. It was a rare thing, a vacation, since Nonno had worked as a pediatric surgeon and would rarely take time off. One day, they walked through a grove of giant sequoias, some thought to be more than two thousand years old. Nonno had explained that the trees had been there before almost anything else, and he'd mused about how much the trees had seen, how many secrets they had.

"If the trees could talk," Nonno had murmured, his thick mustache spreading. "Oh, the stories they'd tell."

Suddenly Nonna was crying. Her eyes were glassy, and she was wiping at tears with her fingertips. "Maybe it's better that they can't," she said. "Maybe that's why they stand so tall. Because they never have to admit mistakes, or..." She breathed in and looked at Nonno. "She haunts me still. Emilia. I dreamed about her last night."

Nonno took her hand. "I know," he said softly.

"Such a mistake—and everyone died."

"It wasn't your fault. I think of Caccipulia, too."

"Nonna, what's wrong?" Pam asked. "Who's Emilia?"

"It's nothing. She's fine," Nonno said and kissed Nonna's cheek. "It's only memories," he told her. "They can't hurt you. It's because of what I said about the trees, isn't it?"

"She saved us," Nonna whispered. "And I never got to thank her."

"Nonna, are you okay?" Callie asked. It was distressing to see her grandmother like that.

"She just needs a moment," Nonno said. "Girls, please. Let her be."

A few minutes later Nonna took a deep breath and said she was better, and Nonno asked who was ready for ice cream.

It was the first time Callie had ever thought about her grandparents' past. Licking her ice cream cone, she wondered what Nonna was talking about. She'd heard her grandmother mention the name Emilia before, but just assumed she was talking about an old friend. Now, it seemed, Emilia was much more than that. Who was she, and how had she saved Nonna and Nonno? And what had happened to her? Callie had felt unsettled for the rest of their vacation week. Maybe it was because she and Pam had already lived with tragedy, having lost their parents so young. And maybe it also had something to do with Pam's illness, which always lurked behind the scenes. Knowing how much went unsaid in their family felt like walking through that heavily wooded forest in Yosemite. You never knew when something would pop out.

The night they returned home, Callie had climbed into Pam's bed and buried her head under the covers. Pam knew right away what was wrong.

"It's what happened with Nonna, right?" she'd said. "Who's Emilia? It bothered me, too."

"And why can't they thank her?"

"Probably because she's dead. Nonna said everyone died."

"Then how did she save them? And what was the mistake Nonna made? If we ask her, you know she won't answer, and then Nonno will say we're upsetting her. But it's not fair to keep this from us."

"How about this?" Pam said. "One day, you and I will go to Italy. And we'll find our way to Caccipulia, or whatever is there now. And we'll learn what happened and even who Emilia was and how she saved them, and what big mistake they're hiding. So you don't need to feel bad, okay? We'll learn all about their lives, so there'll be no more secrets."

It sounded like a good plan. But Callie still felt a separation from her grandparents that never eased. Even after her grandparents died, she never forgot that name, Emilia. Who was she? A sister? A friend? A daughter, maybe? What was her role in their grandparents' lives? She and Pam occasionally talked about taking that trip to Caccipulia, but they had never gotten around to going. By the time Callie was in high school, she and Pam had started to drift apart. They never again were as close as they'd been that night after the trip to California.

Picking up the train schedule, Callie took a closer look. Along the side of the orange circle, in Pam's handwriting, were the words *Albergo Annagiule*, along with a street address—8 1 *Via Sopra il Mare*. She looked up the Italian word *albergo* on her phone and found that it meant hotel. The Hotel Annagiule.

Callie didn't know what to make of this. Could Pam have been planning a trip to Caccipulia? But why would she do that without speaking to Callie first? Callie had opened the drawer wanting to feel closer to her sister, but now she felt even further apart. Pam never traveled. She didn't like traveling, and she didn't have any desire to go anywhere. Last spring, a few of the teachers at Pam's school were planning a girls' weekend upstate over in July, and they'd wanted Pam to come. Joe had encouraged her to go, and had urged Callie to help convince her. He wanted to give her a break. He was willing to take the entire week off from work, and his parents had also volunteered to help with Chloe, who would be eleven months old by then, no longer an infant. And Mrs. Greenbaum was available to help, too. But Pam had said no. She didn't want to be away from home. She and Joe had barely even had a honeymoon, just a long beach weekend out on the east end of Long Island. Neither one of them felt a need to go any further.

Callie looked into the box again and spied her grandparents' wedding picture, the five-by-seven black-and-white photo that was normally on the mantel downstairs in a silver frame with the names *Corinne and Tom* printed along the bottom. They looked elegant and sophisticated, her grandmother in a slim, white suit with a veiled hat, her light hair parted on the side and flipping up just beneath her chin, a neat curl resting on one side of her forehead. Her grandfather was in a black suit, so dashing with his dark, wavy hair and curved mustache. Callie wondered why Pam had taken it from the living room. Why had she locked it away?

Beneath the wedding picture was a photo that seemed to have been copied from an old newspaper, maybe from the 1930s or 1940s. It showed three teenage girls in fancy gowns, looking as though they were going to some kind of party or ball. An arrow had been drawn pointing to the smallest girl, who was shorter than the others and looked younger, and was wearing a sparkling tiara. The arrow was in orange crayon, so Callie suspected that Pam had drawn it.

Looking further, Callie discovered a very old, black-and-white photo of a stone building, the entranceway rimmed with lush vines and topped with a sign that read *Ristorante* in elegant cursive. It looked like a very fancy restaurant, and while Callie assumed it had to have been located in Italy, there was no clue as to what city or town.

She put the photos aside, and next found a piece of five-by-seven cardstock, creased and yellowed. On it was some kind of list in red, handwritten in Italian: *pollo, pomodori, riso...* chicken, tomatoes, rice maybe? Above the list were the words *Caccipulia Club Della Cena*. She looked up the meaning on her phone. *Caccipulia Supper Club*, read the translation.

Then, on the back of the card, she saw some additional writing, which she also translated.

Devi restituirmi questo. Sarò in attesa per te.

You must return this to me. I will be waiting for you.

The name "Emilia" appeared beneath the words.

Callie studied the childlike handwriting. Could this be the Emilia that Nonna had mentioned on that trip to California—the girl who haunted her dreams?

Callie leaned back. Why had Pam gathered these things into this little box—a box with a lock that only Callie knew the code to? She put the card beside the train schedule. And that's when she noticed, at the very bottom of the box, the strangest thing of all: Two boarding passes for a flight to Rome. ITA Airways 603. They were dated for this afternoon.

One was in Pam's name.

And the other was in Callie's name. Attached with a paper clip to Callie's missing passport.

TWO

SEPTEMBER 1943

Emilia listened to the familiar tap of her footsteps on the cobblestone street in the town square. The soft breeze fluttered against her legs, bare from her knees to the top of her ankle-high socks, and the air was fragrant with the scent of violet-colored bougainvillea and wisteria overflowing in planters and window boxes. It was a new day, and she couldn't help but feel relieved to be here in her beautiful Caccipulia, the town that was home, the place where she'd spent all fifteen years of her life. Being back somehow helped ease the pain of the last twenty-four hours. It had been awful to return home yesterday morning, eager to see her papa, only to learn that he'd drawn his last breath the night before. It had been awful, too, to realize it would be her job to break the news to her two older sisters, who would be following her back soon.

But at least she was here, she thought—and with Signora Jorelini next to her through it all. A family friend since before Emilia was born, Signora Jorelini had spotted her on the street yesterday and brought her inside to fill her in about her papa. Emilia was so grateful for the way the woman had hugged her close as she spoke, her arms thick and solid. And for the cozy bed Signora Jorelini made up for her, the warm food she'd cooked, and her gentle touch as she sat next to Emilia last night and combed the knots out of her long, sienna-colored hair. Grateful, too, for Signora Jorelini's decision to take her into town today to replace her worn shoes and outgrown jacket. It felt like an unspoken but rock-solid promise that Emilia would never be alone.

Of course, Emilia was in no mood for shopping. But she'd held her tongue when Signora Jorelini brought it up during breakfast today. Partly because she didn't want to be rude in the face of such generosity, and partly because she knew her shoes and coat wouldn't last another season. But mostly, it was because the shops were not far away from her own house, which she hadn't set foot in since she and her sisters left town five weeks ago. As they walked through the town square and toward the approaching shopping district, Emilia looked up at Signora Jorelini, whose plump cheeks and clear blue eyes had always radiated kindness. She hoped the woman would let her stop inside her house. She was anxious to see what state her father had left it in when he became too ill to do the normal chores. She would see what she needed to do to fix it up. So it would look clean and well-kept when her sisters returned. She might even start to pack up their belongings. So they could leave for America as soon as possible.

Because she was determined to do these small things for her sisters. Although she was the youngest, she wanted to spare them as much sadness as she could. She was glad that unlike her, they wouldn't have to see Papa laid to rest alongside Mama and the family's youngest daughter, who died in infancy. At the cemetery, Emilia had been troubled that so few people showed up to pay their respects. Papa had been familiar with death. The local tailor, he'd often sewed burial clothes or mended and pressed somber suits and dresses for family members to wear when someone in town had died. No funeral in town had ever taken place without dozens of people offering hugs and sharing memories with those grieving. And dozens of people would visit the mourners afterward, bringing platters of hot food or baskets of homemade bread and pastries. "Funerals bring out the good in people," her father would often say.

But it hadn't brought out the good for Papa.

Emilia knew it would be hard to tell her sisters—eighteen-year-old Annalisa and seventeen-year-old Giulia—that Papa had died. They would be as shocked as she'd been, especially since they were coming home with medicine for Papa, thinking he was still alive. But before long, Emilia told herself, things would get better. Annalisa would take charge, as she always did. She had decided months ago that the family should relocate to New York, as it was becoming harder and harder for Jews to live comfortably, to work and go to school and be part of the community. Discrimination, which Annalisa said had been evident elsewhere in Italy, was spreading, even to beautiful little towns like their own Caccipulia. Emilia was sure that Annalisa would want to continue with the plans to leave Italy, even without Papa. And while Emilia waited, she would be strong and brave, as her father would want.

Emilia looked back from Signora Jorelini toward the street corner ahead—and then she froze. Even though she knew it was near, it was still a shock to see it. But there it was, up ahead: Home. Her home. The only house she'd ever known, the simple white stone building with the green door. She yearned to run to it, to rush right into it, to see if she could absorb some of what made it so special, even with her papa gone.

But her legs wouldn't move. And she knew it was because she sensed that something was off. Yes, the house was right there. And yet it had changed. Her father's old metal business sign mounted above the door—SANCINO TAILOR in fancy lettering—was missing. Now a smaller, wooden sign hung there, which simply read TAILOR. And while she would have expected the house to be dark and closed up, she saw the downstairs windows open and the overhead lights of Papa's shop switched on.

Then, through the window, she made out a figure inside the shop, sorting clothes on the long counter. It wasn't Natalia, the woman who sometimes helped out when Papa was very busy. No, it was a man, with short hair and a mustache. Emilia walked a few steps closer, hoping he'd begin to look familiar. But he was a stranger. She paused, watching as he seemed to call someone over, and a thin woman appeared, her blonde hair gathered in a ponytail that draped over her shoulder and reached below her elbow. They spoke to each other, and then the man squeezed her hand, and she nodded and left the room.

Emilia started to ask about the couple, but before she could get a question out, Signora Jorelini shook her head and quickened her pace, grasping Emilia's hand. Emilia let herself be pulled because she wasn't used to going against adults' wishes. Signora Jorelini clearly didn't want to stop and talk, much less let her get any closer to the house. Emilia felt a chill travel up her back. Who were those people who had tampered with her father's sign and were now inside the shop, acting as though it was theirs? Who were those people in her home?

Watching Signora Jorelini's impassive face, her eyes focused forward, Emilia wondered if she'd ever get a straight answer.

That evening, Signora Jorelini made a supper of fragrant vegetable soup, with a chunk of hearty bread on the side. Emilia didn't expect to be able to eat more than a spoonful or two. She was still puzzled by those two strangers in her house. But the soup was so tasty that she cleaned her bowl. There was something about Signora Jorelini's cooking that soothed a person's longings and eased their spirits, if only a little bit. She was a wonderful cook, and owned the best restaurant in town, which had been in her family for decades. Emilia always begged to go to Signora Jorelini's restaurant on her birthday and special occasions, and her sisters did, too. They all loved the pasta orecchiette with sausage and spices. Papa never refused—and always arranged beforehand for Signora Jorelini to bring a special dessert to their table. Emilia and her sisters would pretend to be surprised, although they knew he wouldn't celebrate their birthdays any other way.

After they'd finished the soup, Signora Jorelini led Emilia upstairs and into one of the three bedrooms on the second floor, the one that belonged to Signora Jorelini's adult daughter, Corinna. "You can continue to sleep here for now," she said. "You'll be comfortable. You like being in Corinna's room, don't you?"

Emilia nodded, trying to be agreeable, as her papa had always instructed her to be with adults. She wished she could ask questions about her house and her father's shop and those strange people inside. But Signora Jorelini had looked tense and distracted during dinner, and Emilia couldn't risk angering her. If Signora Jorelini got mad and told her to leave, where would she go?

And if she had to be here, she was glad to be staying in Corinna's bedroom. A few years older than Annalisa, Corinna had always been like a fourth sister. She was smart and fun and beautiful—not in a glamorous, movie star way, like Giulia, but in a simple, natural way, with her fair skin and pale eyes and fine, blonde hair. She wanted to be a teacher, so last spring she had moved to Rome to live with friends and pursue her studies. Although she hated to see Corinna go, Emilia knew she would make the most wonderful teacher. There'd often been times when Annalisa was at the library studying and Giulia was helping out at Papa's tailor shop, so Emilia would go to the Jorelini house and ask Corinna for help with her homework. Corinna had a knack for making even the most boring exercises and assignments enjoyable. Often she'd invent stories about magicians and wizards who had their own secret language and cast spells on evil people who lurked in the forest. Each time Emilia solved a math problem or spelled all the assigned words in her schoolbook correctly, Corinna would invent a new story, right there on the spot.

"Emilia, dear," Signora Jorelini was saying, and Emilia turned her attention away from those long-ago days. "I know your father would want you to be strong and try to settle in here. You'll find nightclothes in the dresser along with clothing that Corinna left behind, which you can make do with for now. And there are towels in the hallway closet. Feel free to use anything. This is your home now."

"Thank you, Signora Jorelini. And thank you for the new shoes. I love them," she said, trying to muster some enthusiasm. Because Signora Jorelini was being so generous, and Emilia was truly grateful. But she had so many questions. Why did she need Corinna's clothes? It was true that she didn't have much in the small suitcase she'd brought back with her when she left her sisters—but why couldn't she go back to her house and get her own things? She could tell that Signora Jorelini was anxious to leave the room, and she could wait for most of her questions to be answered, but she needed at this moment to ask about her family.

"Wait... Signora Jorelini... have you heard anything from my sisters?" she asked.

The woman hesitated, then shook her head, her hand on the doorknob. "I'm sure... that if they possibly can get here, they will."

Emilia studied Signora Jorelini's face. It was such a strange and disconcerting answer. A simple no would have been better. "But I don't understand," Emilia said. "What would stop them from coming?"

"Things are very confusing right now," Signora Jorelini said, looking down and patting her thick gray bun. "We'll talk more in the morning."

Emilia looked down, her arms by her sides. She wanted to press for more of an explanation. But Signora Jorelini clearly didn't want to discuss the matter any further, and Emilia knew her father would be appalled if she was rude. But maybe asking a different question would be okay. "Wait, Signora Jorelini?"

The woman turned back toward Emilia, her hand still on the doorknob. "Yes?"

"Can you tell me... I mean, why can't I go to my own house to get my own things... my nightdress and things?"

"Because you live here now," Signora Jorelini answered, her tone firm. "I took your father in to help him when he was sick, and I'm... well, you'd rather be here than in your empty house, wouldn't you?"

Emilia supposed she would. But the more she thought about it, the more it didn't make sense that her papa had been staying with Signora Jorelini before he died, that he'd taken his last breath here in the Jorelini home instead of his own. He'd never wanted to leave home, never wanted to sleep anywhere else than in the bed he'd shared with Emilia's mother. She supposed that when he got so gravely sick, he needed care, and perhaps Signora Jorelini had insisted that he take up here.

"Yes, of course," Emilia said. "But... my house isn't empty." She took a deep breath, summoning the courage to continue despite Signora Jorelini's eagerness to leave. "That man and woman I saw... why is someone else in our house, my father's shop, our—"

"Emilia, dear," Signora Jorelini said after letting out a sigh of impatience. "There's a lot that happened while you and your sisters were away this summer... a lot that we will discuss. But not tonight. We'll talk tomorrow about everything—"

"Signora Jorelini, one last thing?" Emilia pleaded, not wanting the woman to go until she received at least one complete answer. "If I write letters to my sisters, do you think they'll reach them on the island where we waited for the medicine? In case they're still there? In case they haven't left yet?"

"That's a fine idea," Signora Jorelini said. "Why don't you write them? I'll do my best to get your letters out to them, your sisters."

"Thank you, Signora Jorelini," Emilia said. The woman was gone and the door was closed even before Emilia had finished her sentence.

In the silence, Emilia turned herself around, taking in Corinna's bedroom. She'd been here many times before, but never all alone. The furnishings were exactly as she remembered—the twin bed against the wall, the bedcovering decorated with sunflower blossoms; the dark wooden student desk with a roll top; the pale-blue throw rug on the wooden floor; the wide wooden dresser by the window and the scallop-framed mirror hanging on the wall behind it. There was a bulletin board above the desk, now empty. Emilia remembered that it used to hold photographs of American movie stars torn out of magazines. Corinna had given all of them to Giulia, who loved looking at movie stars, just before she'd moved to Rome to study.

Yes, the room looked familiar, and it smelled familiar, too— the sweet scent of lavender perfume. Corinna had used it so often and so liberally, it had probably seeped into the furniture and bed linens. But there was also a fresh and disturbing sense of tension in the air. In this room, and in the whole house, actually. Emilia wondered if it was just her own sadness that was blanketing everything.

Or maybe it was Signora Jorelini's behavior, she thought as she walked to Corinna's bed and sat on the edge. She would have expected Signora Jorelini to stay with her longer. To envelop her again with her strong arms, as she'd done at the cemetery. Emilia would have liked that so much, to be hugged and held once more by someone loving and motherly. Maybe she would finally cry, good and hard, and then the awful heaviness she felt would ease. But somehow it seemed that perhaps hugs were no longer casually doled out. Something had changed in the five weeks that she and her sisters had been gone. There was no comfort in this town anymore. Signora Jorelini was trying, but Emilia could tell it was an effort. She'd handled the arrangements for Papa not with love but with efficiency.

Emilia wished so hard that she could go home. She yearned to see the beautiful fabrics Papa had worked with, the soft cottons and wools, the vibrantly colored threads, the old sewing machine he'd named Rosa. She wanted to smell his smell, earthy and warm and slightly tangy from perspiration. She wanted to make tea for him, or pour herself a glass of milk in her own kitchen. But Signora Jorelini had made it clear that Emilia was to stay here. And there was something in Signora Jorelini's manner that still made Emilia uneasy. Something in the way she'd kept her hand on the doorknob as Emilia asked her questions. The way she'd pressed her lips together, bracing herself for what Emilia would say next.

She seemed exhausted. Weary. But more than that, Emilia could sense... fear.

She didn't know what time it was, but she was tired and ready to close her eyes and drift away from this place, this moment. Leaving the bedroom, she went to the hallway and pulled a fresh towel from the closet. Downstairs, she could hear Signora Jorelini in the kitchen. She wondered why she hadn't needed to be at her restaurant today. Had she finally hired more employees to help out with the cooking and serving, as Corinna had always wanted her mother to do?

She changed into the simple white nightdress she found in Corinna's top drawer and went to hang up the dress she'd been wearing, one of the few she'd had in her suitcase. When she opened the closet door, her gaze landed on three large boxes on the floor, with her last name, Sancino, penned in black ink on the lid of the uppermost one.

She dropped the dress and opened the top box, pulling the tape up with her fingernail. Inside, wrapped in newspaper, was the framed photo of her mother that her father had always kept by his bed. Beside it was her father's wristwatch, the one he used to put on without fail every day, with its worn black leather band and large, rectangular face. Deeper in the box, she found her father's clunky shoes, the left with an extra thick sole, as he'd been born with one leg shorter than the other. She'd always been embarrassed by those shoes, wishing he'd wear normal ones like everyone else's father. But now she felt ashamed for wishing her father pain. She'd like nothing more than to see him in those shoes right now, fetching a customer's order from the back room, maybe a pair of hemmed trousers or a vest that had needed the seam opened up.

Turning away from the shoes, she moved the box to the side and pulled up the tape on the one beneath it. This one was full of her things and her sisters' things: her math notebook and Annalisa's science notebook, Giulia's clippings of movie stars—Jean something and Greta something—and a little ceramic box with Giulia's charm bracelet. Some sweaters, skirts, pants, and underwear from their dresser drawers, a hairbrush and a handful of barrettes, Giulia's favorite red lipstick. It was as though someone had hurriedly tried to gather random things from the bedroom she and her sisters had shared. Slipping as much of their lives as could fit into one box.

Who had done this? Papa? Had Papa decided he wanted to remove all signs of his daughters from the house? Had he given up on them, even though Annalisa had sent a note saying they'd be back with medicine? Did he hate them? Would he have turned his back if he'd been conscious when she'd arrived? No, she couldn't believe that. He loved her. She was his little girl, the daughter who looked most like Mama. He loved all three of them. So what had happened during these last five weeks?

She needed to find Signora Jorelini right now. She had to hear the words. She had to know her father still loved her, up until he no longer could love anyone. She pushed aside the second box and started for the door. But she paused before taking the doorknob. Signora Jorelini had said they would talk in the morning. She'd said that Emilia should try to sleep. Emilia never contradicted adults. Her father had taught her to respect grown-ups.

She turned and went to the desk by the window. Signora Jorelini had said it would be okay to write to her sisters. Hopefully tomorrow the letter would be posted to Parissi Castle. The important thing was to make contact with her sisters. If they knew what had happened and how she felt, they'd come back for her right away. She was sure of it. Yes, the three of them fought. Giulia was sometimes jealous of Annalisa for being so smart. And Emilia hated that the older two sometimes excluded her from their secrets and plans. But they still loved each other. The two of them loved her. And if they knew how much she needed them, they wouldn't ignore her.

She sat at the desk, where she found some paper and a pen, and started a letter.

Dear Annalisa and Giulia,

Papa was buried yesterday. Hardly anyone was there for him. There are strangers living in our house. We have to get them out. Signora Jorelini doesn't want to talk about it.

Please come back soon. I don't know what to do.

Your sister,

Emilia

Folding the letter, she put it in an envelope she found inside a drawer and placed it on the desk. As she did, she glanced out the window and saw a figure hurrying down the street. Emilia knew it was the woman who was living in her house, the woman she'd seen as she and Signora Jorelini were walking toward the shops. She had the same very long blonde ponytail streaming down the back of her coat, the same thin frame and long legs. She was carrying a large woven basket with a lid, the handle draped over her arm. And she was clearly in a rush.

Emilia watched her by the light of the streetlamps until she disappeared around a corner. She wished she could run downstairs and scream at the woman to get out of her house. And what was the woman carrying in that basket? Clothing she'd repaired, using Papa's threads and needles and sewing machine? No matter if she used Papa's supplies, she'd never be able to sew as well as Papa could. Nobody could.

Emilia rose and switched off the lamp on the bedside table. She sat on the bed and slipped her legs beneath Corinna's pretty yellow bedcovering. She slid herself down and lowered her head to the pillow.

We're going to get our house back, she promised herself. *I'm not going to give up until I do.*

THREE

OCTOBER 2019

Monday

The hum of movement and voices downstairs caught Callie's attention, as she sat at Pam's old desk, the wooden jewelry box still in front of her. It sounded like a lot of people were showing up. Callie couldn't even count how many times Pam had mentioned on the phone that she was going to deliver soup to a friend with the flu, or drive to the service station to pick up a neighbor whose car popped a tire. She was always the one to pick up medicine or groceries for an elderly neighbor who didn't drive, or a fellow teacher who was stuck at home with a sick child.

With a sigh, Callie looked down at her lap. She couldn't deny that Pam had always been generous with her time and her love. She was good to people, and that was why so many were here today. Callie pictured herself back in Philadelphia these last three weeks, alone in her apartment, with no job and no friends yet. She'd even begun to regret her impulsive decision to move, despite still believing that it was the right decision. Pam must have suspected this was the way Callie would feel, and she'd tried to open Callie's eyes during that last phone call before Callie left New York. But as usual, Pam had sounded so accusatory. Judgy and demanding. At least that's how it had always seemed to Callie, even from way back:

"Why do you need to go so far away to college? There are plenty of good ones close by."

"Why get a job in Manhattan? You can work and live right here in town."

And then, in one last-ditch effort before Callie said goodbye and continued to pack up her apartment:

"There's something going on that you're not telling me. You've never sounded so confused before. Don't move to Philadelphia. Whatever's wrong, we can work it out at home."

Callie had never wanted to listen to Pam's observations or face her disappointment in her decisions. She had hated that polite yet unending pressure Pam could apply, which made her feel like she was in a tiny room without windows. She'd convinced herself that Pam was too sheltered and unsophisticated to understand her. And she'd resisted allowing Pam's words to penetrate, because to do that, she'd have to deny her instincts and become someone else. A Pam clone. A mini Pam.

Callie turned back to the objects from the box. The news that Pam had been planning a trip to Italy for the two of them didn't make sense. If this trip had something to do with their family, their grandparents, whose wedding picture had been taken from the living room and inserted into the box with the menu card and train schedule, then surely Pam would have mentioned it to Callie. Surely she would have reached out long ago. Pam was so methodical. She never did anything on the spur of the moment. It was one of the aspects of her personality that drove Callie crazy.

So why had Pam done all this so secretively? Had she, too, felt the chasm growing between them? Did she think finding out the truth about what happened to their grandmother would bring them back together? When they were young, they had promised each other they'd get to the bottom of their grandparents' story. Not just that one night after they'd returned from California, but several times later as well. And the more time that passed, the more questions they had—questions whose answers seemed even more unattainable once their grandparents had died. How had their grandparents even met? What had happened to their families back in Italy? How had this Emilia person saved them? And most puzzling, what was the mistake that had reduced their grandmother to tears that day among the sequoias?

Callie hadn't thought about those questions for years. But now she remembered them. And her heart ached at the thought of what Pam had planned, the lengths she'd gone to, just to reunite with her younger sister and fulfill the promise they'd made to one another so long ago.

The voices downstairs were growing louder, the front door repeatedly opening and closing. Callie knew she should go downstairs to accept people's condolences and thank them for coming. It wasn't right to leave it all to Joe. She couldn't imagine how Joe must be feeling. He had lost the love of his life, and now he was going to be a single parent. If anyone had the right to be sitting upstairs alone feeling awful, it was him. Not her. Because she'd been such a bad sister for so long.

She closed the box and placed it back into the bottom drawer of the desk. She couldn't possibly catch the flight that Pam had booked—it was due to leave in a few minutes. So what would she do with all this information and these gathered items now?

She considered this question before shutting the drawer. Her thoughts of Pam had been so negative for so long—the nagging, the judgment, the slights. But the wooden box, and what it represented, now spurred her to recall the good moments. The loving memories.

Like the day the big snowstorm hit. She was six, and Pam sixteen, and their parents were an hour away at one of her father's business functions. That's when the unexpected storm blew in. Stuck home on that Saturday afternoon, she was thrilled when Pam suggested they walk through the snow to the Italian bakery in the shopping center, which made the most delicious cannolis and custard-filled donuts and pignoli cookies almost the size of a Frisbee. They'd had two of each boxed up, and then decided to stop next door to bring back a hot pizza, too. When they finally got home, they were soaked and cold, their fingers numb inside their mittens. They'd dried off and gotten into pajamas and had a delicious feast on the living room rug, watching Christmas movies on TV as they munched on reheated pizza and Italian desserts, and drank hot chocolate. Even now, she remembered how cozy she'd felt, wrapped up in blankets on the living room rug with her big sister. Back then, she loved when Pam spent time with her. It was fun to have a sister already in high school. There was nowhere else she'd rather have been.

Of course, the awful irony was that the same snowstorm that led to their memorable evening together also caused their parents to drive off the highway and be stranded in the freezing car until morning. Neither one of them had survived. Pam had kept her safe that day, and had tried to keep her safe in the years that followed, while their grandparents were alive and later, as Callie's legal guardian. "Don't worry," she'd told Callie who, at twelve years old, didn't understand how they could live together with no grown-ups, dismissing the fact that Pam was twenty-two. "We'll do fine. Sisters are the closest relative there is," she'd said.

Downstairs, Callie peeked into the dining room, which was filled with people piling sandwiches and treats from the buffet table onto their plates. They all seemed to know one another, even though she didn't recognize most of them. Who were they?

Neighbors who'd moved in after she'd moved away, friends from the mental health center where Pam volunteered one evening a week, teachers from the school where she taught? In the center of the table was a vase of pink and white carnations that someone must have brought over. Somebody—maybe everybody—knew that Pam loved carnations. The room was filled with the energy of a community coming together, an energy she wasn't a part of. She felt like an outsider. An outsider where she should have belonged.

She turned and made her way to the living room. Joe was sitting on the floral sofa, his hands clasped between his knees, his head down. Next to him was his mother, Rose, a young-looking woman with a slim build and auburn hair. Callie watched her pat her son's back with her hand, gentle and steady. Joe didn't acknowledge the gesture, but somehow Callie could tell by his body language, his motionlessness, that he was comforted by her touch. Chloe was sitting on the rug by Joe's feet, and Joe's father, Sam, sat cross-legged opposite her, hiding his eyes with his hands to play peek-a-boo. Chloe giggled one of those sweet toddler giggles, loud and joyful, the kind of giggle that makes everyone who hears it smile.

Leaning against the wall, Callie watched them. Joe lifted his head and leaned it onto the sofa back, covering his eyes with his hands. His mother stayed where she was, rubbing his shoulder now. And suddenly Callie knew Joe was going to be okay. And Chloe was, too. They may have lost the most important person in their lives, but they were not alone. They had family and friends to love them and hold them up during the long days ahead. Callie was moved by Joe's parents. She knew Pam had loved them and was grateful for them. Up until now, Callie felt so strongly that she'd made much better life choices than Pam had. But at this moment, she wasn't so sure.

"Why are you going to Philadelphia? Why are you leaving?" Callie couldn't shake those questions, Pam's last phone call,

from her mind. *I didn't have a choice*, she insisted inside her head, almost as if she were speaking both to herself and to Pam. *I needed to go. I had to get away. I was sure it would all make sense to you one day.* She'd been certain she was doing the right thing. She thought so still. And yet, she regretted so much not seeing her sister one last time. Not coming home before moving to Philly, as Pam had begged her to. She thought again, as she had earlier when she was upstairs, that maybe she could have made a difference. Maybe if she'd been here, if she'd delayed her move-in date and stayed for a long visit, she could have saved Pam. By helping her to a chair when she felt lightheaded. By steadying her and calling the doctor. By making sure Pam was getting enough sleep and eating good meals. Maybe just by being here, she could have changed the course of events. Maybe instead of mourning Pam, she could have been on the airplane with her right now, waiting to take off for Italy.

But she had made her own decisions for so long, her own stupid decisions that had led to her move. She thought about what Pam would likely tell her now, in her sweet, lyrical voice: *You'll be okay without me. You'll be fine.* She wondered how long it would take before she wasn't able to hear Pam's voice anymore. She couldn't even remember her parents' voices, and barely remembered her grandparents'. That was the last thing to go, she'd been told. And the thing that was most painful. Because it was so final.

Joe placed his head on his mother's shoulder. Callie wished she could help. She wanted to provide comfort, too. But she wasn't the person Joe needed now. She'd just never been around enough to be that close.

A moment later she felt an arm circle her waist. It was Mrs. Greenbaum, wearing a black dress with a single strand of pearls around her neck. She looked pale, her brown eyes sunk into her cheeks. But she still managed a smile.

"How are you doing, honey?" she said.

Callie shrugged. "I'll be okay."

Mrs. Greenbaum took her hand and led her to the small loveseat by the window. "I know how hard this must be for you," she said. "Pam was always talking about you, thinking about you. She missed you."

Callie looked at her hands on her lap. "I didn't mean to be away so long. I wanted to come back. I would have been back to see her... and the baby..." She paused, trying to hold back the tears. She felt guilty crying. As though she didn't have the right to, after staying apart with no clear explanation.

"Oh, honey," Mrs. Greenbaum said, taking a tissue from her pocket and handing it to Callie. "She never stopped loving you. She knew you'd come back when you were ready. She understood. And she knew you loved her."

Callie wiped her eyes. Mrs. Greenbaum could say what she wanted, but the truth was, Pam didn't understand. Not everything. There was so much Callie hadn't been able to bring herself to say. She took Mrs. Greenbaum's hand. "How are you doing?" she asked. "It has to be hard for you, too."

Mrs. Greenbaum took out another tissue and flicked it against her nose. "Such a shock, I mean, yes—we all knew about her health. But I still never expected this."

She looked over at Joe and shook her head. "Joe's going to have it hard, poor thing. I hear he's decided to take a little time off from work."

Callie nodded. Joe had told her last night in his parents' cottage, as Chloe fell asleep in his arms, that he was going to take two weeks off from the law firm and stay with Chloe and his parents at their country house in Michigan. Callie had promised that she'd be here when he came back, to help with the baby while he started to put his life back together. She'd kissed Chloe's head and stroked her little hand and gazed at her puckered lips, her dark eyelashes, long like Pam's, resting atop her round cheeks. She watched Chloe sleep, taking in her utter stillness, punctuated every so often by a tiny wriggle of her shoulders or a soft sucking motion of her little mouth. No wonder Pam had thought she'd given the world the most precious gift possible when Chloe was born. She only wished Chloe could feel this kind of peace forever.

"Oh, my heart breaks," Mrs. Greenbaum continued. "They were so in love, the two of them. Pam never wanted to be anywhere else but here at home with Joe and Chloe. When she had the baby—it was as though she'd never want another thing in her life. She was an open book, wasn't she? A beautiful open book. And she was so happy that she'd found a way past the loss of your parents and grandparents. By making her life an extension of theirs."

Callie nodded. Yes, and that was what separated them as they dealt with their multiple losses. Pam had moved forward by digging down and Callie had moved forward by heading for the hills.

She pressed her lips together. The mention of her grandparents made her think of the box with that old wedding picture and all the other items. She wished she had more clarity on what Pam was thinking when she'd pulled together all those things.

"Mrs. Greenbaum..." she began.

The woman looked at her.

"Was it possible... I mean, did Pam ever talk to you about going on a trip? With me, maybe?"

"A trip?"

"Like... to Europe? Did she ever tell you about that?"

The woman chuckled and shook her head. "You know your sister. She never wanted to go anywhere. She never wanted to be anywhere but home."

"I know... but could she have been planning something? Maybe some adventure?"

"Honey, you were the adventurer. Not her."

Callie nodded and looked down. She was on the brink of telling Mrs. Greenbaum about the box. Why not?

But then she heard Pam's voice in her head: *Sisters are the closest relative there is.* And that's when it all started to make sense to her: that Pam had put the train itinerary and the supper club card and the old photos and the boarding passes into the drawer where she kept the special things she and Callie had shared. Things that were only meant for the two of them. She'd locked the box using a code that only Callie knew.

Pam had put all those things there so that if anything happened to her, Callie would be the first one, maybe the only one, to go through that desk. To find the box. To know the combination that would open the lock.

"What is it, honey?" Mrs. Greenbaum said. "Your whole face just turned white."

Callie didn't answer. All she could think was that Pam had wanted her to find these things. Pam had left them for her and her alone. And she knew what she had to do.

FOUR

OCTOBER 2019

Tuesday

The next morning was sunny and warm, and after having breakfast with Joe and his parents, Callie took Chloe to the neighborhood playground. As she pushed Chloe on the baby swing, she watched her fine brown hair blow in the breeze, and listened to her giggle, and felt so sorry that Pam wasn't there to enjoy her sweet little girl. From the time she was young, Pam had loved being home with family. She'd adored their grandparents and was so considerate of them, even though Callie often found their tastes old-fashioned and their rules unreasonably strict. Like Pam, Nonna and Nonno lacked spontaneity—and spontaneity was what Callie always craved. Still, they were good people, Callie reminded herself now. Loving and nurturing. And utterly devoted to their granddaughters.

Thinking about them, Callie couldn't help but wish her grandmother was here right now to hug her and make her some hot soup and soft biscuits, the food she always used to serve when Callie wasn't feeling well. And she wasn't feeling well now. She was grieving—not in the same way Joe was, but grieving still. And unlike Joe, she had no one to comfort her. She had no parents, no grandparents, no husband, no children. Pam had been her family. And now she had no one.

Pulling herself together, she brought Chloe back to the guest house and got ready to leave. She had been strong and independent before now, she told herself, and she could be that way again. Pam's death was a nightmare, and she was going to be sad for a while, but she would get through it. As Joe went to start the car to drive her to the train station, Callie said goodbye to his parents and hugged Chloe. It should have felt normal, rote, she thought, to say goodbye to Little Bridge, her hometown. Leaving home after short visits was something she'd been doing since she'd started college. Still, this time it seemed strange to be leaving so soon. She'd expected to stay for a while to help Joe with Chloe, not realizing they would be taking off right away for Michigan. But it made sense. There was something so right about Joe being in a place he'd known since he was a child, surrounded by his parents' love. It would be good for Chloe as well, to see her dad finding comfort.

As she said goodbye to Joe at the station, she promised again that she'd be here in two weeks, when he returned from Michigan. And she'd stay as long as he needed her to. Then, climbing out of the car and going around to open the trunk, she pulled out her rolling suitcase and hoisted the tote bag up over her shoulder. The bag felt surprisingly heavy, and she wondered why she hadn't noticed that when she came here. And then she remembered.

It was heavier now because it held her sister's locked wooden box. She was leaving for Italy tonight. And she was taking it with her.

She'd had to bring it with her, she thought as she found a seat on the train and pushed her suitcase onto the overhead rack. And she had to keep it a secret. She assumed that Joe would have mentioned the Italy trip to her this morning if Pam

had told him about it. She figured that Pam had decided it
would be fine to leave Joe and Chloe for a few days to take this
special trip with her sister, knowing that Joe's parents would be
available to help out. So Callie had decided to keep the tickets
from him. She didn't want to put any news or questions onto his
plate, when he was already dealing with so much pain and so
much concern about his baby daughter. She'd tell him about the
trip later, after it was over.

She'd snuck back to the house late last night to get the box,
after all the guests had left and she'd returned with Joe and
Chloe to the guest house, loaded down with leftover containers
of hot food, cheeses, cut-up fruit, and fresh rolls and muffins. It
had moved Callie almost to tears last night as she helped wrap
up the food, the way so many people had offered to go grocery
shopping or prepare food or watch Chloe or do whatever Joe
would need in the difficult weeks and months ahead. Joe and
Pam had such a strong and loving community. As the train
lurched forward to pull out of the station, Callie grimaced,
thinking that there was no one for her to call and talk to about
Pam. She'd only been in Philadelphia for three weeks, and
hadn't yet made any friends. No one knew her except her land-
lords—the couple who lived upstairs from her in the duplex.
And she didn't have any close friends from her previous job in
New York. She had had a boyfriend, for a time. But he wasn't
someone she would call now. Or ever again, for that matter.

She thought back to how she'd returned to the house and
retrieved the box. It was still her house, of course, but she'd
nevertheless felt as though she were trespassing. She was glad
she still carried the key on her keyring. Using the flashlight on
her phone, she'd unlocked the front door and made her way
upstairs to Pam's old room. She hadn't wanted to turn on any
lights. She was scared that Mrs. Greenbaum or Joe or his
parents or another neighbor might see a lamp switch on and
come over to investigate—or even call the police, fearing a break-

in. It was that type of neighborhood, where everyone looked out for one another. And she didn't want to have to invent an explanation for why she was there.

Upstairs, she'd instinctively avoided the long-standing creaky floorboard that Joe intended to fix, made her way into Pam's room, and gently slid the bottom desk drawer open. She knew that nobody would have heard her even if she'd dropped the box and it crashed onto the wooden floor; but still, what she was doing felt illicit, and seemed to require silence. As she reached for the box, it struck her that secrecy was familiar to her, a place where she knew the layout of the rooms, the quickest path from one floor to the next, and the areas where the sun never reached, allowing her to sense when she could temporarily let her guard down. She wasn't proud that keeping mum and avoiding certain topics had become her superpower.

But with any luck, she'd thought as she placed the box beneath her jacket, feeling the sharp edges through her dress as she stole back outside into the night, this would be her last secret. Maybe this trip her sister intended would help her find her way.

The train picked up speed and made its way toward Manhattan, where Callie would transfer to the train to JFK Airport. Calling the airline last night, she'd been able to switch her own ticket to this evening. She figured she'd deal with getting a refund for Pam's ticket another time, since she didn't have the strength to cope with explaining about Pam's death so soon. It was lucky, she thought, that she'd filled a large suitcase when she'd left Philly, figuring she'd be staying on a while to help Joe. It meant that she didn't have to waste a day traveling to Philly to pack before leaving for Rome. After giving the matter some thought, she'd decided to keep the return ticket for next Sunday that Pam had purchased. She knew that would only give her four full days in Italy, but she wanted to be back in Little Bridge early, in case Joe chose for some reason to come home sooner than planned. Caccipulia seemed a tiny town, and she hoped she could track down her grandmother's story quickly. She knew she could always rebook her return if she found that she needed more time. But the priority was to make sure she was available to help Joe with Chloe as she'd promised. She wanted to be responsible, to conform to a schedule for a change. She wasn't going to let Joe down.

She wasn't going to let Pam down.

Sitting back for the one-hour trip to New York, she leaned her head on the headrest and closed her eyes. The last time she'd been to JFK was last winter, about eight months ago, when she'd traveled to New Orleans on a company retreat. The night that had started her longest—and her last, as it would turn out—rift with Pam. Over *him*. The night she would head down a road she should have been smart enough to avoid. *"Stay out with me tonight,"* he'd said that night in New Orleans, when they were both so far from home. *"Stay out and let's forget everything else we think we know."* It had felt deliciously dangerous to say yes. The tingle she'd felt down her back had overshadowed the warnings sounding in her head. She could handle it, she'd thought. She could handle *him*. His encouraging, sexy tone gave her confidence. His clear attraction to her made her feel strong and talented and smart. And beautiful.

Callie shivered and opened her eyes, not wanting to relive that moment any longer. She breathed in and looked around, hoping for a distraction. Across the aisle was a mother and daughter. The little girl was around seven and wearing some kind of homemade bunny costume, a pink jumpsuit with a white felt patch on her belly, pink cardboard ears pinned to her head, and a pink pom-pom on her nose. On her feet were white ankle-high boots with green construction-paper circles glued on. Callie assumed the costume was connected to Halloween, which was... what, about a week away? She couldn't help but think about Chloe as a seven-year-old, and all the Halloweens she'd never share with Pam. Would she be sad when all the other kids in the neighborhood had moms to help choose their costumes and take them to parties? All the Halloweens Chloe had ahead, all the holidays and birthdays, and Pam would miss them all. Callie knew Pam would have loved thinking up Halloween costumes with Chloe and making them from scratch.

The little girl noticed Callie's gaze and turned her body sideways, pulling down on her shirt with her hands to give Callie a full view of her white bunny belly.

"Is that your Halloween costume?" Callie asked.

The little girl nodded. "Do you know who I am?" she asked.

"A bunny rabbit?"

The little girl sighed heavily and turned to her mom. "See?" she said. Then she turned back to Callie. "I'm Wally the Rabbit," she told her firmly, as though explaining a math concept to a younger sibling. "He's from my book, and when he does something nice, his boots sparkle with bright-green dots. Like this." She kicked her legs out toward the aisle so Callie could see her boots.

"What a great costume," Callie said.

The girl shook her head. "It's a very bad costume," she said. "I went to one school party and two friend parties, and none of the grown-ups knew who I was. I had to explain over and over and over. If I knew nobody knew about the book, I would never be this costume at all." She turned back to her mother. "Mom, isn't there time to change to a princess or a witch?"

Her mother smiled at Callie and raised her palms as if looking for commiseration on how hard parenting can be. Then she kissed her daughter's head. "I'm sorry this is such a disappointment," she said. "But isn't it nice to be something special and unique?"

The little girl shook her head. "Not when nobody recognizes you. You might as well be nobody if nobody knows who you are."

Callie suddenly had the feeling she was going to cry.

Pulling a tissue out of her tote bag, she turned toward the window to wipe her eyes, not wanting the mother and little girl to see her tearing up. She knew it was her own fault that people back home didn't know her anymore. She had chosen to separate herself from Pam and from home starting long ago. But now she felt like she was the one wearing the Wally Rabbit costume.

The thought confirmed her decision to go to Italy tonight, to the little town where her grandmother had grown up. She didn't know what she would find in Caccipulia. She was surprised it even existed, as her grandparents had led her to believe that the Nazis had totally destroyed it. But going there to find whatever was left seemed the only way she might feel part of something again. Maybe she would feel a new connection with her family, and not feel so very alone. Maybe she would get some relief from the grief of losing her sister. She hoped she would learn what their grandparents had never wanted to speak about, what had happened to make Nonna feel so haunted by the past, so guilty about this Emilia person. And hopefully when she came back, she would feel at home with herself. She would be a person she liked. A person her sister would have been proud of. She had to give it a try.

Because she couldn't go on like this. She couldn't go on feeling awful about how bad things had been with Pam. And she had no other ideas.

FIVE

SEPTEMBER 1943

Emilia spent a fitful night, waking often and finding it nearly impossible to fall back asleep. The mattress was soft but not too soft, the pillows were plump, and the covers were the perfect weight for mid-September. But this wasn't home.

Still, when morning finally broke, she was reluctant to rise. There were answers out there, answers from Signora Jorelini about all that had changed since she and her sisters had left town, and overnight she'd grown scared to hear what they might be. She remembered how her town had started changing, subtly but unmistakably, way before she and her sisters snuck off on that warm summer night in search of medicine for their father. Some longtime customers had stopped coming to her father's shop—not many, but enough to notice. Although no one had said it to her directly, she'd sensed that they no longer wanted to support a Jewish business.

That was why Annalisa had decided they would move to America. Things would get worse, she'd told them, although she hadn't wanted to be any more specific. She'd said Emilia was too young to know more. Always so organized, Annalisa had repeated her plan to Giulia and Emilia as they quietly packed clothes and then tiptoed downstairs: they'd go to Parissi Castle, a beautiful Gothic structure off the Mediterranean Coast, where they'd heard that scientists were working on a host of inventive discoveries; they'd get their hands on a new medicine to bring home to Papa; and then they'd travel down the coast to Naples to board a ship to New York. They wouldn't give up the house or sell it, Annalisa had assured them. They'd keep it, so it would be there for them when things finally returned to normal.

Emilia had found the plan to move to America thrilling, the way she'd felt when she was little and would imagine that she was the heroine in the fantasy stories Papa would read her at bedtime. It seemed so exotic, spending days upon days on a huge ship crossing the ocean. She had no idea what New York would be like. Her only hints were the occasional photographs she'd seen in Giulia's magazines, with fancy restaurants and Broadway theaters and skyscrapers like the Empire State Building dotting the background of a crowded spot called Times Square.

But all that was in the past, a fantasy like Papa's stories. She was alone, Papa was dead, and there'd be no possibility of feeling at home again until her sisters came back to get her. She closed her eyes, wishing that when she opened them again, she'd be back in Parissi Castle, back in the beautiful bedroom she'd been given, with a huge, canopied bed and a view of the turquoise sea out of the arched windows. Or if not that, then back in her childhood bedroom in her own home down the street, in her cozy bed from where she could see Annalisa at the desk reading a library book on molecules or rock formations or some other topic that only Annalisa could understand. Where she could hear Giulia, who loved to sleep late, softly snoring in her bed by the window.

Emilia looked ahead at the closed bedroom door across the

room. Papa wouldn't want her to cower beneath the covers like this, she told herself. He would urge her to face whatever was on the other side of that door. To be bold. They'd had a system for sharing messages, something just between the two of them. Papa had been a cartoonist among his many talents, and from the time she was young, he'd put small scraps of paper decorated with his cartoons in her lunch box. If she was scared about an upcoming spelling or math test at school, or had been assigned to speak before the class, he'd draw a small lion with the word "courage" hidden in its mane. Or else he'd draw an arm with a bulging muscle, penning the word "strong" in tiny letters near the elbow. A kitten with the words "forgive" hiding along the fur was what he'd leave for her on days when she and Giulia had quarreled. And a picture of a short, stout candle with a vibrant orange flame—that was the picture that showed up each year on April 6th, on the anniversary of her mother and baby sister's passing, the word "remember" hidden in the blaze.

Emilia had loved having a secret language with her father. A code that no one else would crack because no one knew to look for those hidden words. Finding the drawing when she sat with her friends at the long lunch table at school, she'd felt so loved. She was special, the youngest daughter, the baby who'd survived.

Courage, she whispered to herself, picturing her father's penned lion. *Courage, courage.* Say it three times, her father would sometimes tell her. Three is a good number.

She rose from the bed and carefully made it, smoothing out the bedcovering and plumping the pillows. Then she put on a skirt and blouse from the box of her things in the closet. She laced up her new shoes and slipped the letter she had written to her sisters last night into her pocket. Then she left the bedroom.

The sun was streaming through the windows, bathing the small rooms and the hallway with golden light. The other two rooms on the second floor were empty, the beds neatly made. She paused for a moment, wondering which one her father had been in when he'd taken his last breath. Fall had always been Papa's favorite time of the year. He loved when neighbors brought in clothes to be lengthened or let out to accommodate growing bodies. He took pride in knowing that his creations, his craft, were part of the foundation of this small community. He loved playing a part in the way families grew and changed, remaking clothes to be handed down to a new baby, a grandchild, a niece or a nephew. He loved when people told him the reworked garment was more beautiful than it had been when it was new.

Grasping the letter in her pocket, she went to the staircase and down the steep, narrow steps. As she approached the kitchen she could see sunlight filling the room, the white poplin curtains on the window parted. A lone onion sat in a ceramic bowl painted with vines of green ivy on the countertop. She remembered sitting in this kitchen with Corinna, doing her homework. That same ceramic bowl had always been filled with gorgeous fruit—cherries and plums and bright-yellow lemons.

Then she heard Signora Jorelini's voice coming from the other side of the room, where the table was.

"*Dio mio*," she was saying, evidently talking to someone else at the table. "I never thought I'd close the restaurant. But there's nobody to serve. And ingredients, even basics—so hard to find."

Emilia held her breath, waiting to hear more. She hadn't known Signora Jorelini's restaurant was closed. They'd been planning to go there for Giulia's eighteenth birthday, which was just a few weeks away.

"Some people can get word from family about how the war is going. But nobody really knows much these days," Signora Jorelini continued. "Newspapers rarely showing up, and the

radio reports unreliable. We do get some news from our meetings at the Possano house. But that's about the new people... on
their way... where they need to go next..."

Again, Emilia was surprised at what Signora Jorelini was
saying. She hadn't realized news was hard to come by. She
remembered the Possano family. They lived a few houses away
from here. But the other thing Signora Jorelini had said, about
the new people—what did that mean?

"It's very bad in Rome," a younger voice responded. "The
streets are so dangerous. They are arresting people all over the
city. They are beating people in the streets..."

Suddenly Emilia recognized the voice. Corinna, Signora
Jorelini's daughter! She must have come back from Rome late
last night or early this morning. Emilia longed to run into the
kitchen and wrap her arms around Corinna's waist. If she
couldn't have her sisters here right now, then Corinna was the
next best thing. But she stifled that impulse. The women
sounded serious, and she suspected they were talking about
things Signora Jorelini had refused to talk about last night.
Pressing herself against the wall, she strained to hear more of
their conversation.

"I had to come back, Mama," Corinna said. "I was so scared.
I couldn't concentrate on school or anything. There are German
soldiers on the streets."

"You were right to come home," Signora Jorelini said.
"Now's the time for families to be together."

"How's Signor Sancino? Is he feeling better?"

"He died three nights ago, *cara mia*."

"Oh, no." There was silence for a moment, and Emilia knew
Corinna was sad. Corinna's own father had died when she was
young, so Papa had tried to help look out for her.

"And the sisters, do they know?" Corinna asked. "Any word
from them?"

"I haven't had a chance to tell you—Emilia has returned. I put her in your room. I didn't have the heart to make her sleep where her poor papa died. She's been through so much."

"And what of Annalisa and Giulia?"

There was silence.

"Does she know about what happened?" Corinna asked.

"You mean her father's shop? No, I don't think so. But she's seen the De Luca family in her house."

"And she didn't ask about them?"

"She did. It was late last night. I told her we'd talk in the morning."

"Poor Emilia," Corinna said. "What a world. Her father forced from his house and her sisters missing..."

Still pressed against the wall, Emilia felt her limbs start to tremble. She was freezing, her toes almost numb. Who was the De Luca family? She knew she shouldn't be eavesdropping. She'd been taught not to. But how could she turn away? What did that mean, her father forced from their house?

"Emilia? Is that you?" Signora Jorelini called.

Emilia took a deep breath and walked into the kitchen, thinking of her father's lion cartoon. *Courage.*

"Oh, you're awake!" Signora Jorelini said, her upbeat tone sounding forced. She rose and put an arm around Emilia. "Look who came home this morning. How's this for a surprise?" She pointed across the room to Corinna, who was sitting at the table.

Emilia couldn't help but smile. It was so good to see beautiful Corinna. She was pretty as always, with her light-blonde hair gathered at the nape of her neck. Her eyes were a pale blue that reminded Emilia of the waves that would crash against the shore of Parissi Island, a sight she loved to see from her bedroom in the castle. Corinna's time in Rome had changed her. She looked older than her twenty-one years, in her brown suit and matching hat. There was rouge on her cheeks and red lipstick on her lips, and her eyelashes were long and curled.

"Emilia!" Corinna stood, her arms outstretched, and Emilia wrapped her arms around her waist. Without warning, tears started spilling down her cheeks.

"I'm so sorry about your papa," Corinna said, lifting Emilia's chin with her slim fingers. She reached for a hand-kerchief in her handbag and gently wiped the tears. "I know how you're feeling. I lost my papa, too, when I was young. You probably don't even remember my papa, do you? I know how hard it is to lose a parent. Your papa was a wonderful father. He loved you and your sisters so much."

Emilia nodded.

"He was so very sick," Signora Jorelini said. "There's nothing anyone could have done. He knew you and your sisters were coming back with medicine. He just couldn't make it any longer.

"He knew you all loved him," she added. "And he loved being your papa."

"Don't worry about a thing," Corinna said. "We will take care of you, as he would have wanted us to."

Emilia looked up at her. The words were jarring because they sounded so permanent. "That's okay. Thank you, I mean— but my sisters are on their way back for me. And then we will go to America, like we planned. They're still going to want to do that. Papa would be glad about that. And Annalisa is very determined."

She'd tried to make her voice sound firm, but she saw the two women exchange glances. What were they thinking—that Annalisa and Giulia weren't coming back? That they'd aban-doned her? Or forgotten about her?

"They *are* coming back," Emilia repeated. "Somebody had to go back to take care of Papa, so they sent me on ahead. But they're coming, too. As soon as the medicine was ready, they said. They promised."

"Of course," Corinna said. "You will only need to be here for as long as you like."

"I have a letter for them." Emilia patted her pocket. "To tell them about Papa and let them know where to find me. Signora Jorelini," she added. "You said letters can be sent, remember? So they would reach my sisters, if they haven't left Parissi Island yet? They need to know about Papa. That there's no reason..." She looked down. "... To wait for the medicine now."

There were a few silent moments.

"Yes, I remember," Signora Jorelini finally said. "Corinna will post your letter, won't you, Corinna?"

"Certainly," Corinna said. "I'll send it this morning. And I'll send any others as soon as you've written them."

"And they'll receive them, right?" Emilia asked.

Signora Jorelini licked her lips. "We'll do our best. Now, who's hungry? I made some bread—with barley since it's so hard to get wheat, but there's a little jam, or you can soak it in milk. And I have some cheese, some figs. Some coffee, although as I'm sure you both know, it's not like the coffee we once used to have..."

Emilia looked at the two women, who were now setting the table. She didn't quite trust what they were saying. It was as though they were speaking in a code that only they understood, a code as secretive as her father's hidden words in her lunchtime cartoons.

"What does that mean, your best?" she asked. She knew she was being rude, but she couldn't help it. "What does any of this mean? Why are there strangers in my house? Why are my clothes and my family's things in boxes? You have to tell me. I'm not a baby," she added, even though at the moment she felt very, very young.

Signora Jorelini paused, forks and spoons in her hands. "Of course you're not," she said. "But Emilia, do you not know what has been happening? Did you not hear anything of the war when you were there on the island? Were there no news reports at all?"

Emilia knew Signora Jorelini was asking out of concern, but it sounded as though she was being accused of something. Maybe she and her sisters should have been more aware of what was happening. But did that mean she should feel ashamed?

"Sit, Emilia," Signora Jorelini said. "We will tell you."

SIX

SEPTEMBER 1943

Emilia walked further into the kitchen and sat at the table. Corinna offered her the basket with bread, but she shook her head. She didn't feel like having anything. Her heart raced so fast that her arms tingled with fear.

Signora Jorelini sat beside her. "You knew... before you left, you knew what was happening to Jews like your father, didn't you?"

Emilia nodded, thinking of the customers who'd stopped coming to her father's shop, and the way Annalisa had insisted they needed to leave Italy very soon.

"It became worse while you were away," Signora Jorelini continued. "There were laws about Jewish people. They'd been around for years, although nobody paid mind to them here, so they didn't affect your father much while you and your sisters were still home. But then they started enforcing these laws, even in small towns like ours, even here. Jews are no longer allowed to own businesses. So your father had to sell his shop, which meant he had to sell your house as well."

"He sold the house?" Emilia said, incredulous. "No! He would never have done that."

"He had no choice," Signora Jorelini said. "It's the law. And they are good people, the De Lucas. They made an arrangement. They bought the business and the house for a few lire, and plan to sell it back to your family after all this madness is over. Lots of people are complying with the law that way for now. Your family will own the business again one day. Just not today. But hopefully soon."

Emilia stared at her. "But he loved his shop," she said. "Sewing, making clothes and things for people's homes..." She shook her head. Her poor father, to first lose his daughters and then lose his work. Her chest ached, as she thought about how much he probably had wanted his daughters with him when all this was unfolding. To warn them, to protect them, to soften the blow of learning all about this. But he'd had no way to reach them. They had intentionally not told him where they were.

"He must have been so sad," she added softly, dropping her chin.

Signora Jorelini stroked Emilia's hand. "I think he was. But nobody thought it would come to this. And most people, many of his customers, they wouldn't turn their backs on him. Only the scared people. The cowards."

Emilia remembered the lion cartoons. "Papa always wanted me to be brave," she murmured.

"He was a good man, and he was brave, and he wanted his girls to be brave, too," Signora Jorelini agreed.

"Can I go there?" Emilia asked. "Will they let me inside? To see the house, to even get some of our things—"

Signora Jorelini shook her head. "It's not a good idea. Let's not stir things up—"

"But it's my house—"

"But it's not. Not now," Signora Jorelini said.

Corinna reached out and touched her hand. "Maybe another time," she said. "We'll let you know. There'll come a better time when we can ask, okay?"

Emilia looked at both women, one and then the other. What kind of answers were they giving her? What did any of this mean—stir things up, a better time to ask? She pressed her lips together, thinking again that it was too much for her to be going through this on her own, with no family, no older sisters, to help her figure out what to do. "I have to find my sisters," she told them. "I can't wait for my letters to reach them. I have to go back to Parissi Island. If you tell me the train to take, I can get there on my own."

Signora Jorelini shook her head. "My darling, you can't. It's too dangerous. Italy is at war with Germany now. The Nazis have overtaken Rome, and they are heading this way. The only thing we can do is hope the Allied forces reach us before the Nazis arrive. It is not safe to travel. You must stay put."

"But Corinna traveled. She came back from Rome."

"But you're a child. And the daughter of a Jew."

She sighed, and Corinna continued. "Emilia, there are rumors that Nazis will start rounding up Jews and sending them to Poland. As they've done in other countries."

"But I'm not Jewish. I'm only half Jewish."

Signora Jorelini was quiet. She didn't seem to think that that little fact would keep Emilia safe. Exempt from the worst of what the Nazis were capable of.

"So... what will I do while I wait for my sisters?" Emilia asked.

"You will stay with us," Corinna said. "And we will all wait together."

"You mean just go to school and try to be normal?"

Again the women exchanged looks. "You can't go back to school," Signora Jorelini said. said. "Jews are not allowed in school anymore."

"I have to go to school," Emilia said. "I have to see my friends. I have to get my assignments. Papa never let us miss school."

"I know," Corinna said. "Again, it's just temporary. And it will be okay. I will teach you for now, until things go back to the way they were. It will be just like having a private tutor. That will be fine, right? Your papa would approve, I know."

Emilia looked from one woman to the other again. She'd barely heard what Corinna said. She wasn't allowed to go to school? How could that be?

"It's a lot of change, terrible change, *piccolina*," Signora Jorelini said. "But I promised your father before he died that I would watch out for you and your sisters when you came back, and I will. This is not the way any of us want it to be. Neighbors against neighbors, towns torn apart. But we will stick together for now, the three of us. Okay?"

Emilia felt her breath catch in her chest. This wasn't okay. She couldn't help but think how different everything would be if her sisters were with her. Annalisa would have a plan, she'd get the three of them out of this town, where so much had changed, and they'd find their way to America. But instead, Emilia was bearing the brunt of all these changes on her own. And her sisters... they were likely still at the castle, enjoying themselves, totally unaware of what she was going through. They had betrayed her, sacrificed her, she thought, her anger rising. They'd always been closer to one another, those two, and she'd been the outsider, the baby. They had sent her back here by herself maybe even knowing what might be happening. They had sent her back here so they didn't have to leave Parissi Island.

She got up and went to leave the kitchen. "Emilia, wait," Signora Jorelini said. She rose and opened a cabinet, then reached inside and pulled out a small stack of scrap paper bound by a string. "I found these when I was packing up your things for you from your house," she said. "I wanted to give them to you myself." She handed her the stack. "It's from your papa."

"Thank you," Emilia murmured and went upstairs to Corinna's room, where she'd slept last night. She wondered where she'd sleep tonight now that Corinna was home. She knew she should be grateful. What would happen to her if Signora Jorelini weren't here? She'd have no bed at all, no house, no food. *Neighbors against neighbors*, Signora Jorelini had said. People who used to care about her and her sisters now wanted nothing to do with her. They hadn't even come to Papa's funeral. How had things gone so wrong? How could people's feelings change like that? For no good reason. She hadn't changed, her father hadn't changed. But the person he'd been all his life—and who she was, as his daughter—now meant something very different.

She wished she could go back in time. She wished she and her sisters had never left. She wished the last five weeks had just been a dream.

Sitting on the bed, her legs crossed in front of her, she untied the string on the paper scraps Signora Jorelini had given her. They all held drawings her father had made, pictures of a night sky with crescent moons and white stars. Along the side of each moon he'd written, "Go forth."

His message was for her eyes only. She supposed he'd drawn this when he knew he'd soon be gone. She knew he'd want to remind her about a story he used to tell her. A story, he said, that he'd learned from his childhood, a Jewish story with a strange Hebrew title, *Lech L'cha*. It was about a man named Abraham who was called upon to leave his home. His reward, her father had said, would be all the future generations of his family. His descendants would be as numerous as the stars in the sky.

She sighed and, pushing the scraps away, she went to the window to look outside. This was her town, her beautiful town, the place where she'd never had any fear at all. Down below were all the places she'd loved, the places that she'd grown up around, the places that felt like hers. To her left a block away was the food market and the stationery store with the notebooks Annalisa loved to buy for her studies, and the pretty colored pencils Papa would buy them on the first day of school, and the movie magazines Giulia could afford by saving the coins Papa gave her for helping out at the store. And further down was Signora Jorelini's restaurant, and the library where Annalisa spent many of her afternoons, and the theater where they sometimes saw children's shows on Saturdays. And the school where they'd all gone, the school she could no longer attend.

To the right, she could see the archway and stone stairs that led up to her street, where their home had been, with Papa's shop on the ground floor, next to the *pasticceria* where she and her friends liked to get pastries and sweet treats. Her home, and all the places that surrounded her home and felt like home, too. She thought of those words, *Go forth*, that her father had written and illustrated. What could he have been thinking? Where did he want her to go? Did he mean to go here, the Jorelini house? To leave home and come here, as he'd done when he was dying? Or was there more to it, the story and the words? What more could he have meant?

In the days that followed, Signora Jorelini went about settling Emilia into the house. While she wanted to be in her own home, she knew she wasn't old enough to live there alone, so she was glad that at least she'd be close by. She had to keep an eye on all that was happening at her father's shop. Corinna and Signora Jorelini moved an extra mattress into Corinna's room, so Corinna and Emilia could share the bedroom. They seemed to have sensed that Emilia would be more comfortable that way, as she'd grown up sharing a bedroom with her sisters.

Emilia was grateful to have these two strong women taking care of her. But at the same time, their generosity made her anxious. It was such a stark contrast to the mood in town, the forces that had driven her father out of his house and forbidden her to attend school. What shoe would fall next? How much more would Signora Jorelini have to do for her—and would there ever be a time when she simply wasn't allowed to help Emilia? If her sisters continued to be delayed, what new rules would appear here in town? What would be required of her or taken from her in the days or weeks to come? Where would she rest her head next?

Sometimes in bed, Emilia would listen to Corinna sleep. Her breath was steady and rhythmic, almost melodic, and for those few moments before she finally drifted off, Emilia felt peaceful. If she tried hard, she could almost believe she was back in her own bed, with her sisters nearby and her papa across the hall getting a good night's sleep so he could be up at dawn to start his sewing.

One night Emilia heard her father desperately shouting, *Emilia! La mia bambina!* She tore out of bed and ran down an unfamiliar hallway trying to find him. When she couldn't locate him in any room, she found a doorway and, still in her night-dress, she ran out into the dark courtyard. "Papa!" she cried, as his voice became weaker and more distant. She could see his tortured face in her mind, his glassy, sunken eyes and thin, pale lips, and the deep lines around his jaw. She could picture him moving, his stooped shoulders, his labored walk, his limp.

"Papa!" she cried again. "Papa!" And suddenly she was awake, in her bed in Corinna's bedroom, hearing the sound of her own screams. When she realized that she'd screamed aloud, she was embarrassed. Only babies cried out in their sleep. She turned toward the wall, pressing her knees to her chin, hoping no one had heard her. A moment later, though, Corinna was at her bedside. Emilia felt her sit down next to her, and then she felt Corinna's fingertips stroking her shoulder. She felt her body relax, but her mind kept racing: How could things have changed so terribly for her papa? How could this new family have taken her papa's shop? Emilia knew that this was one thing her father wanted to give them, the one thing he said would secure their future.

"This will be the place that will always be yours, the place to come back to," he'd said to her one night last spring as she went into his workroom to kiss him goodnight. "You know that, don't you?"

"Of course," she'd said back then, confused by the question. She wondered now if he'd sensed what was happening. If he suspected that one day, she'd have to fight for her home. "Why are you asking me that?" she'd said.

"Because my girls are full of dreams and ambitions. Annalisa wants to make discoveries, Giulia wants to be in the movies. How about you, my little one? Have you decided yet?"

"I want only to be here," she'd said. "At home with my family."

"You are like me," he'd told her. "So don't you worry. You will have this place. This will be your ground, your home, your rock. Remember what I once told you, about placing rocks on a gravestone? Rocks are forever. Your home is forever. Even if you have to leave for a time, you must never forget to return. I will leave this house for you. You will never be lost while it's in our family."

Corinna went back to her bed and soon was asleep, breathing steadily. But Emilia stayed awake, thinking about her dream and the conversation she'd just remembered. It was her responsibility to keep her papa's shop and the whole house safe for them, she realized. To never lose it, even if they had to leave for America. She wondered again about the couple she had seen through the window. Were they eating dinner in the kitchen where Papa used to call them, serving up the delicious foods that neighbors routinely dropped off, eager to help the mother-less family? Had they already begun to make changes?

Discarded their books, their dishes, their furniture? Or were they using everything Papa and Mama—the mother she had never known—had chosen so lovingly for their daughters?

She had to watch over the house. She had to make sure everything stayed the same. Her sisters would expect that of her. She would watch the couple who lived there now. She would watch what they took out of the shop and what they brought in. She would keep track of their comings and goings, the work brought in, the customers they had and the ones they lost. She would count all the stones in the patio, all the panes in the windows, all the scratches in the door to make sure they didn't harm even a tiny portion. She would keep the shop safe, as Papa would have wanted.

She thought of the Abraham story, and the reward of a future full of new generations. And of the way their family's future now rested on her shoulders. She had to leave it for now, as her papa had somehow predicted. But it was still theirs. She would watch over it, so she could one day reclaim it for sure. For her family and their future.

SEVEN

OCTOBER 2019

Tuesday

That evening at the airport, Callie checked her suitcase and proceeded through security to her gate. With an hour to go before boarding, she found a seat and reached into her tote bag for Pam's wooden box. Slowly, she lifted the lid, thinking how Pam had closed and locked it maybe as recently as a few days ago. She studied the expired boarding passes and the menu card with its note on the back, and her grandparents' wedding photograph. The collection of items made her feel more distant from Pam than ever.

How she wished she were going on this trip with Pam! Or even better, that she was already in Italy, that she and Pam had used the tickets Pam had bought. But most of all, she wished she could have been with Pam when she fell. If only she hadn't been so stubborn, too proud to come home. Maybe then, Pam would be alive now. Maybe they'd have already started to repair their relationship. To be as close as they were on that snowy day they bought the sweets from the Italian bakery and feasted on them in front of the TV.

Still, it had been so hard to bear Pam's judgments lately, her harsh reactions to practically everything Callie did.

"I thought you liked what I am," Callie remembered saying during their last phone call three weeks ago. "Always running around on new adventures and such. You used to tell me that."

"Because it's what you wanted to hear. And because you were young. But you're older now. And the truth is, you're not running around. It's more like you're always running away."

"That's ridiculous. What would I be running away from?"

"I don't know, Callie. Is it me? Or something else?"

Callie sighed, the imagined conversation echoing in her ears. She'd always tried to tell herself that Pam had supported her choices, even though they weren't the ones she'd choose for herself. That she just wanted to be sure Callie was safe and happy. But Pam had clearly recognized something troubling deep inside of Callie—a need to always be somewhere she couldn't stay for too long. Had Callie stumbled on the truth just now, in her imagination? Had she actually been running away from Pam?

No, Callie thought. Of course not. She loved Pam. And she loved home. She simply didn't want to live the kind of life Pam did. It was too quiet, too small. She'd alternated between rejecting it completely and thinking there was something appealing about it that she just didn't get. Sometimes she'd even felt a tinge of jealousy, wishing she didn't always have a sense that if she didn't keep moving, she'd be missing out.

And yet, Pam had decided to step out of her comfort zone when she organized this mysterious trip for the two of them. What did that mean? Were she and her sister more alike than Callie ever thought? Or alike in some way she didn't understand?

Suddenly Callie felt bad for being critical of Pam's life. In so many ways, Pam had been the best sister. Callie had relied on her when she was young. Nonna, who'd run the household almost single-handedly since Nonno worked so many hours at the hospital, had found Callie to be a handful. She couldn't keep up with Callie's constant activity. For her part, Callie never understood why her grandmother found her so hard to deal with. At eight years old, she didn't recognize that Nonna didn't have the stamina of her friends' mothers, who were far younger than she was. Callie didn't see why what she was doing, or wanted to do, was always such an ordeal. Just wanting to go out to a movie with her friends? Just wanting to try a dance class, a guitar class, a gymnastics workshop, just wanting to enter a bike race or join a softball team with games all over the state?

Pam, who was a freshman at the local community college when Callie was eight, would often step in to drive her to wherever she wanted to be. "It's not you," she'd say as she went to get the car keys from the hook in the kitchen. "It's just the situation." And that always made her feel better.

Callie turned back to the box and pulled out the train schedule with the town of Caccipulia circled, and the name of the hotel: Albergo Annagiule. She took out her tablet and searched for the place, but the only website that came up was for something called the "*Annagiule Scuola di Cucina,*" which she discovered translated as "cooking school." She wondered if Pam had googled this as well, if Pam had intentionally chosen to stay somewhere connected to cooking, and what she should make of that. Because there was also that photo of a restaurant in the box, she remembered. She dug further and pulled it out. Studying the proud sign over the front door, she wondered if this cooking school had anything to do with the restaurant. It was hard to say, as she had no idea what the word "Annagiule" referred to or how it could possibly be connected to Nonna.

What she did know was that Nonna had been an amazing cook. She never owned a cookbook or referred to recipes yet somehow she knew how to combine ingredients in ways nobody would ever think of.

"That's what you learn in war," she'd told them as she served bizarre-sounding but utterly delicious dishes, like lamb filled with almond paste or eggplant coated with lemon and tiny bits of chocolate. "You learn how not to search for what you want, but to create with what you have." Cooking always made Nonna smile. And she looked beautiful when she smiled, Callie remembered, her teeth so even and white, and her blue eyes shining beneath feathered gray bangs. The only other thing sure to make her smile was Nonno. Theirs was a love so strong, a love that seemed unique compared to how she'd seen her friends' parents or grandparents look at one another.

The gate agent announced that the flight would begin boarding in thirty minutes, and Callie went back to her tablet. She was intrigued by the cooking school she'd found, and wondered if she could learn more about the town where her grandparents had come from, the town they never wanted to return to. Since she hadn't found any information about the hotel, she decided to see if searching for Caccipulia would yield more. All she knew was what she had gleaned from the train schedule in Pam's box—that it was south and slightly west of Rome, an hour away by train. She typed "Caccipulia" into her browser, and was pleased when a list of websites popped up. The first listing was a link to an excerpt from a book titled *Italy Over the Decades: The Ten Most Historic Small Towns on Italy's Mediterranean Coast.*

She clicked on the link and read:

> In its heyday during the 1930s, the picturesque town of Caccipulia was a small but bustling center of culture and commerce, the main boulevard filled with shops, restaurants, cafés, and other thriving businesses. Located south of Rome and nestled between the Mediterranean Sea and the foothills of the

Apennine Mountains, it was removed from the effects of Mussolini's Fascist policies, Hitler's rise to power, and the growing unrest in Europe. Despite the alliance between Italy and Germany, signed in 1936, and the racial laws that put harsh restrictions on the ability of Italian Jews to work, own property, and go to school, the enclave's small community of Jews was deeply integrated into the fabric of everyday life, and the laws initially had little effect on the lives of its Jewish inhabitants.

But things changed in the early 1940s, and again, more dramatically, in September of 1943, when Italy surrendered to the Allies in Sicily, and the Nazis responded by invading the country from the north. Almost instantaneously, Germany occupied Rome and the northern part of the country. Food became scarce, and residents in the central part of the country could only hope that the Allies from the south would reach them before the Nazis streamed down from the north. By October of that year, the roundups of Rome's Jews for transport to Nazi concentration camps, principally Auschwitz, began.

In late October, 1943, the Nazis reached Caccipulia and the surrounding small towns, and began going door to door in search of Jews. While some Jews had left the town, taking their chances by trying to escape to Switzerland or travel south to where the Allies were in control, many had gone into hiding. Nevertheless, those who'd remained were rooted out, in some cases with the help of Italians who would reveal Jewish hiding places to the Nazis in exchange for money or food.

In the end, the Jews of Caccipulia were either killed outright or sent off to Poland where they died in concentration camps. Also killed were non-Jews who were known anti-Fascists or who had hidden or helped Jews escape detection, as an example to others.

Callie felt herself recoil at this news. The history of this little town that Pam had intended to visit was nightmarish. She wondered if its fate was somehow tied to her grandmother's decision to never return. She knew that *she'd* never have wanted to return, if this had happened in the town where she was raised. And what about that woman, Emilia, she thought— the one who Nonna said had saved her and Nonno? Did the destruction of Caccipulia figure into that relationship?

Callie read on, wondering how the town had rebuilt itself, how people could possibly settle there, given its horrific past.

But Caccipulia stands out for a reason other than the brutality of the Nazis, because of its connection to one of the most storied and wealthy families Italy ever produced. Not too far south of this town is the Mediterranean island of Parissi, home to Parissi Castle. Patricio Parissi, the last patriarch of the family, was an inventor and patron of the arts, and in the early- to mid-twentieth century, he opened his castle to the most promising of artists, sculptors, writers, philosophers and more of his day. At one point, residents also included his three nieces, who were born and raised in Caccipulia. They were the daughters of Patricio's sister, Olivia.

Sadly, Parissi Island was stormed by the Nazis during the war and most of the residents—including Patricio—were slaughtered. While their remains were never found, it's believed that his two older nieces were among the dead. The youngest sister returned to Caccipulia before the Nazis arrived on the island. While her half-Jewish parentage put her at risk, she was hidden by neighbors and survived the war. It's unclear where she spent the three decades after the war; but in her fifties she returned to Caccipulia, where she single-handedly funded a major rebuilding of the town, later opening a hotel, a cooking school and a bakery known as the Pasticceria Sancino.

Below the text was a picture of the bakery's glass door. The image made Callie feel a new pang of grief. She'd always loved Italian bakeries, as had Pam. They'd both enjoyed their treats at the Italian bakery back home, especially the ones they'd brought home on the day of the big snowstorm. She remembered how delicious they'd tasted, how much fun it was to be with her big sister safe at home that day, with treats to share. With no knowledge that by the next morning, their parents would be dead.

Callie lowered her tablet and sighed. This was such a sad story, and one she wasn't sure she was glad to know. It felt a little too close to home, a younger sister who became the family's sole survivor. How sad this girl must have been, to have had her two older sisters murdered. How brave, too, to move back to her childhood town decades later to pick up the pieces. And to start three new businesses—a hotel, a cooking school, and a bakery. Callie couldn't help but wonder how this woman had gone on, having lived through so much. Where did that kind of strength come from? What drove her to return to her childhood hometown?

Still curious, Callie searched for the Pasticceria Sancino in Caccipulia. Again, there was no website, but she did find an entry about the bakery in an online travel guide. The article had been translated into several languages, including English. Callie was enchanted by what she read:

A trip to Caccipulia is not complete without a stop at the little bakery known as Pasticceria Sancino. It is here that you will taste the most delightful treats imaginable. Sponge cakes that melt in your mouth, chocolate smooth as silk, and spun-sugar tarts with fruits that add a luscious tang. Though the owner, Emilia Sancino, stays isolated most days, she does occasionally deign to give cooking lessons to willing students who will tolerate her harsh tone and impatience. Don't miss a stop here.

Callie gasped so loudly that the woman next to her startled.

She put her hand to her mouth, even though it was too late to stifle the sound. *Emilia.* That was the name of the person who'd haunted Nonna's dreams. And just below the paragraph that mentioned Emilia was an old photo with three teenage girls in long ball gowns. There was no mistaking the picture—it was the same one inside Pam's wooden box, the same one on which Pam had drawn an orange arrow toward the smallest one with the tiara. Below the picture was a caption:

> *Emilia Sancino, right, the youngest Sancino sister, pictured here in 1943 with her two older sisters. Now ninety-one, she owns the Pasticceria Sancino as well as a hotel, the Albergo Annagiule, and a cooking school.*

Callie read the caption again. There seemed to be no other conclusion. The woman in these articles, Emilia Sancino, had to be Nonna's friend Emilia, the one who had saved Nonna and Nonno, the one whose memory made Nonna cry that day among the sequoias. This is what Pam had evidently discovered, why she'd put the picture of the three sisters in the wooden box and drawn the arrow.

But it didn't make sense, she thought. Nonna had said that everyone she knew in Caccipulia had died. That was why she couldn't go back to thank Emilia. She had made some mistake, and she couldn't forgive herself.

So how could Emilia still be alive?

Callie paused, realizing that she was in a better position to get answers than she ever could have hoped for. Because the hotel Pam had booked them in, the hotel where Callie was staying, was the Albergo Annagiule. Emilia's hotel. She would be meeting Emilia in person in just a few hours.

When the announcement came that her flight was boarding, Callie hurried to the gate. She could hardly wait to reach Italy.

EIGHT

OCTOBER 2019

Wednesday

When the plane landed in Rome, Callie made her way through the airport. Despite having slept very little on the flight, she felt alert and ready to get on with her trip, eager for what she might discover. Although she'd been questioning her life's decisions ever since she'd arrived back home for Pam's funeral, at this moment she appreciated her independence and ability to navigate unfamiliar places. She took an Uber to the city's main train station, found a seat at a sandwich bar for a panini and a coffee, and then proceeded to her track for the 1:30 p.m. train to Caccipulia. Sitting beside the window as the train sped southward, she felt a spark of delight at the sight of the shimmering Mediterranean Sea. It felt cleansing. She was tired of thinking of herself and how she'd failed Pam. She was glad to be looking forward. It would be good to be someplace where nobody knew her or any part of her story.

Because it was a story she hadn't yet come to terms with; she hadn't yet been able to get past her shame. And it had

started, too, on a trip to somewhere new. Having hopped
around from job to job for years—gravitating to positions
involving travel, as she was desperate for a glamorous, sophisticated life that would once and for all free her from Pam's inter-
ference—she'd finally landed a marketing position in the
Manhattan office of a global consulting firm. It was a job with
lots of potential, and she was certain that over time, she could
make good money and meet lots of smart, worldly people. Her
first week, she was sent to New Orleans, where her firm was
holding a training session for new marketing managers from
across the country.

And that's when she'd met the man who'd shown her
around the Big Easy.

He was a vice president with one of her firm's top clients,
and he'd come to the conference to give a presentation on client
needs. Watching him on stage speaking before a crowded ball-
room filled with ambitious interns and junior-level employees,
she'd been smitten. He was so charismatic, so put-together in his
appearance, and so good-looking, with his artfully tousled dark
hair combed away from his forehead, his short, neatly trimmed
beard, and his strong, square jaw. She knew he was older than
her, maybe in his early forties, but she liked that. She'd never
felt strongly about any of the men her age whom she'd dated in
the past.

The meeting ended with a dinner for all attendees, and he'd
approached her afterward as she was heading to the elevator
and asked if she'd like to take a walk that evening. He said he'd
noticed her across the room, and loved how serious and atten-
tive she'd been. How mesmerizing her dark eyes. How lovely
the color of her hair. "Like butterscotch," he'd said, pushing a
strand away from her face.

Of course, she'd agreed to the walk, and—thankful for the
mild temperatures that week—met up with him after changing

from her business suit into her favorite sundress, a white, tiered style with spaghetti straps and decorative buttons down the front. He showed up wearing jeans and an ocean-blue shirt that matched the color of his eyes.

It was her first time in New Orleans, and she found the city sexy and exciting that night, especially since she was with such a handsome and successful man. They'd walked along Bourbon Street, listening to the sounds of jazz quartets coming through the wide, open doors of the bars and clubs. It was February, shortly before Mardi Gras, and he'd ordered a king cake at a small eatery for them to share. It was so sugary that it made her eyes tear, and they'd laughed and laughed at the bizarre treat. They'd bought colorful masks at one of the shops along the way, black with gold rims and purple feathers, with long sticks attached for holding them over their faces.

Back in New York, she'd imagined where their relationship could go. She envisioned hosting big dinners for important people, living in a huge house, going to galas and benefits, wearing fancy gowns. She imagined how lucky everyone would think she was, and how lucky people would think him, too. Because she was young and pretty, and he was so in love with her.

One day, on a lark, she bought an evening gown, an elegant, black strapless number with beading around the bodice. His firm sponsored a charity benefit at Lincoln Center each spring, and she hoped to appear in public on his arm. But he'd never invited her, and she hadn't asked about it. She'd given the dress away the week she'd moved to Philly, shoving it into the clothing donation bin outside of Stan's Sundries on Broad Street. She hoped someone would get a beautiful surprise when they found it, tag still on, never worn. She didn't deserve anything so beautiful, but maybe someone else did.

Now, as she sat on the train eyeing the gorgeous blue sea in the distance, she thought back on that evening in New Orleans. There were times she'd wished she could relive it, over and over again, that exciting evening when wonderful things seemed to lie before her. She wondered if Pam had ever felt that way, ever had a moment so wonderful, she didn't want to leave it behind. Maybe her wedding day? Or the day Chloe was born? But no, Pam would never have wanted that. Those days were wonderful for Pam not just in and of themselves, but because of what they would lead to. All that was ahead. Part of living the most wonderful day of your life was knowing that tomorrow, there was more wonderful to come. Which was why that evening in New Orleans was not so wonderful at all.

The train arrived in Caccipulia, and Callie followed the other passengers through the station. Outside on the raised entrance-way, she looked around, thinking that it seemed she'd traveled not just across the ocean but back in time as well. Caccipulia was a quaint, picturesque town. The buildings were mostly stone, the colors white and pale orange and a muted, tea-stained brown. The cobblestone streets were winding and narrow, and there were no cars or buses at all. She'd expected this wasn't a touristy place—but now the thought scared her. At least if she were somewhere popular with tourists, there'd be people to help her find her way. It bothered her, that despite her efforts to come across as so tough and independent, deep inside she could be so timid. She told herself to muscle up, that she was here now and had a job to do.

After consulting her phone for directions to the Albergo Annagiule, she started down what seemed to be the main commercial block, wheeling her suitcase alongside her. There were pink frangipani and other flowers in bloom that evidently didn't realize it was fall. The street was largely empty, and many stores were closed, as she remembered was common in

Italy at this time of day. It was hard to follow the directions from her phone, as there weren't many street signs. And when she went to check the map on her phone again, she saw that she had no service.

Ahead of her was what appeared to be a coffee bar, the lights on and a green sign with the word "*Aperto*" taped to the window. She assumed that *aperto* meant the place was open—the only open place as far as she could tell. She decided to go inside and see if she could get some help finding her hotel.

The shop was small and dark, with a long wooden bar and several round bistro tables. A server was sitting behind the bar, reading a newspaper. He looked her way when she entered.

"Signorina?" he asked. "*Posso aiutarla?*"

She assumed he was asking her what she wanted, and she hesitated, feeling bad that she didn't know more than a few words of Italian. "Um... *buon giorno...*" she started. "I am... *sono...* trying to get to this hotel... *albergo...*"

"You're American!" the man exclaimed, sounding as though he could have been a neighbor back home. She was taken aback and laughed, happy for the familiar cadence and pronunciation.

"Have a seat, let me get you coffee," he said. "What a surprise—we rarely see Americans. Where are you from?"

Though he seemed to be about her age, he reminded her of a puppy, with his mop of curly, dark hair, his long limbs, and his effusive personality. And he had a warm, wide smile. She was charmed by his friendliness. She liked him immediately.

Letting go of the handle to her suitcase, she sat down on a stool at the bar, glad for this unexpected welcome. "New York," she said. "Well, New York until recently, now Philadelphia."

"No kidding. I'm from Boston myself. I know, far from home to be working in a coffee bar, right? In real life, I'm a high school teacher. Physics and chemistry."

"Oh?" she said. "How did you wind up here?" She knew it

was a forward question, but she had the feeling he wanted to chat.

"I'm on sabbatical," he said. "And possibly making a career change. I'm thinking of investing in an Italian restaurant with some buddies back home. And if you're looking to open an Italian restaurant, this is the place to learn about Italian cooking."

"It is?"

"Absolutely. This town has quite a culinary history. And an amazing cooking school."

"Oh, yes," she said, nodding. "I saw that online."

"Hey, how about an espresso?" he asked. "Make yourself at home, I'll bring it right over."

She watched him turn to the big espresso machine behind him and expertly move his hands along the pipes and knobs. The spigot belched steam and then released the rich, dark liquid into a small cup he'd placed underneath.

He brought it to her. It was strong and smooth, and felt good going down.

"So are you staying in town?" he asked.

"That's my problem, I don't quite know." She showed him the name of the hotel on her phone. "I have a reservation here. Albergo Annagiule. Do you know it?"

"Oh, Emilia's place!" he said. "Sure. The white building at the end of the road. At the top of the steps."

"Yes, Emilia's place," she said. She wasn't sure whether to be surprised that he knew Emilia or not. After all, it was a small town, and she was a bit of a celebrity.

He nodded. "I'm surprised you got a reservation. She doesn't take in a lot of guests these days, and—hey, wait a sec! Are you the American woman she's been waiting for? Pam Something, the one from Connecticut with the baby daughter? The one who wanted to learn to cook? She wasn't going to accept the reservation at all, but she liked the letter you wrote. That's why she said yes."

Callie looked at him, stunned. Pam had wanted cooking lessons? Callie didn't know how to respond. She didn't want to explain to this stranger that Pam had died. And she also didn't know what to make of his statement that Emilia had accepted Pam's reservation only because of this nice note she'd evidently written. Would Emilia turn her away if she admitted she was Pam's sister, and not the woman who'd written the letter? Then what would she do?

"Yes, that's me," she said. "Pam. Pamela Crain."

"I'm Oliver Verga," he said, reaching over the bar to shake her hand. "Nice to meet you, Pamela Crain. You probably should get up there. She closes up in the afternoon. If you don't check in soon, you won't get your room."

"She closes up?"

"She takes a nap sometimes. She gets tired. I mean, she is ninety-one."

"And she has no one to help her?"

"There's a woman who helps in the mornings with breakfast. But that's it. And by the way, when you get there, don't let her intimidate you. She's quirky and kind of cranky, although I think you need to give someone that age some slack, huh? But she's really interesting. And so talented. She's a world-class cook, you know. I've attended some of her classes. Amazing. So you're here for a class, huh? I didn't think she was well-known back in the States. How did you even hear about her?"

"Well, I'm not only here for the cooking," she said. "You see, I'm actually here for some information. There seems to be some connection between her and my family. My grandparents left Italy for America sometime in the 1940s," she added, thinking of the wedding photo Pam had put into the box. "I think she and my grandmother knew each other. I'm hoping to learn more about her."

He put the rag he was holding down. "Wait. You're here to talk to her about what happened back then?"

She nodded.

"Nooo," he said, shaking his head. "I wouldn't do that."

"Why not?"

"She doesn't talk about any of that. You'll be out of that hotel before you can say spaghetti Bolognese."

"What do you mean?"

"She went through a lot during the war. She lost family to the Nazis. This town was totally destroyed. They killed all the Jews and they killed the people who helped them, and she saw everything. She came back here with money, lots of it, and she rebuilt the town from the ground up. Shops, restaurants, and her cooking school—it's all thanks to her that this little town is thriving again.

"But the thing is, she was betrayed by a very good friend of hers when she was young," he added, his voice lowered, as if he were telling a deep secret. "When the Nazis were coming to town, that's when it happened. She never got over it. It messed her up for years. Don't make her relive all that."

Callie paused. *Betrayed by a very good friend?* She wondered for a moment if that friend could be her grandmother. After all, her grandmother had spoken on that trip to California, and afterward, too, of a big mistake she'd made, a mistake that she felt guilty about. A mistake that seemed to involve her friend Emilia, who had somehow saved her life, and Nonno's life, too. A mistake that made Nonna cry when she thought of it.

But no, Callie thought. A lot of betrayals had no doubt gone on during the war. She'd read about it while she was waiting to board the plane last night, how people had turned in Jewish neighbors or Jews in hiding to the Nazis for food or money. Her grandmother was a good person. She may have made a mistake or been unable to keep a promise, but nothing on the scale she'd read about online. And this sounded like a huge betrayal, according to this guy, Oliver. A betrayal that Emilia had never gotten over. That didn't sound like anything her grandmother was capable of. And it certainly shouldn't stop her from asking Emilia for information about Nonna.

"I wouldn't make her relive it," Callie said. "I'm not here to talk about whatever this betrayal was. But I do need to talk to her about my family. You're telling me not to ask her any of the questions I came here to ask?"

"I'm urging you not to. We don't want to see Emilia hurt. She's an institution here."

"But I came all the way here for information. And I don't have that much time," she added. Her flight back was on Sunday. And even if she were to extend it, it couldn't be for long. She had promised to be home when Joe arrived back with Chloe.

"Sorry to hear that. But the situation is what it is. You can't go there and harangue her—"

"I wouldn't harangue her—"

"That's what it would feel like to her. Just another annoying dilettante invading her privacy. This is why she doesn't take many people at her hotel. She only offered you a room because of that letter you wrote. You should have told her the whole truth, what you really came for. She would have saved you the time and expense of coming here."

Callie shook her head, wondering what Pam had said in the letter and what had been in her mind when she wrote it. "Wait a minute," she said. "You're telling me I shouldn't ask her a couple of simple questions? I don't even know you."

"They're not simple questions. And that's exactly what I'm telling you... asking you... well, telling you. The townspeople are all very protective of her. We're like family. And she'll kick you out. I'm telling you, she won't let you check in. And if you check in first, she'll ask you to leave.

"Look, she's been through enough, okay? Get your information some other way. Do a DNA test or something to learn your family story."

Callie held her breath, annoyed at this guy's nerve, thinking he could control what she did. A DNA test wouldn't help. It wouldn't tell her why Pam had wanted the two of them to take this trip. It wouldn't explain what had happened to her grandmother, why her grandmother had never wanted to face this town again.

He glanced past her shoulder, and when she turned around, she saw that a couple had sat down and were looking at him a bit impatiently.

"What do I owe you?" she asked.

He held up a palm. "No need. You didn't order it, I offered it to you."

"Oh, but you don't have to... I'm happy to pay."

"No, no need," he said. "It's on the house. I own the place."

"You... you what?" she said. "I don't understand. Didn't you say you're a teacher from Boston?"

"It's a long story." He picked up the rag and wiped his hands, then came around the bar and headed toward the seated couple. "Come back after you get settled. I'll tell you all about it."

"You think giving me free coffee is going to make me avoid asking Emilia my questions?" she said.

"I'm hoping," he said, looking over her shoulder as he crossed the shop. "Do the right thing, Pam Crain," he added.

She grabbed the handle of her suitcase and left, annoyed that she'd stopped in. She didn't even know this guy, and he'd put such an unfair burden on her. She didn't want to hurt this woman, of course, but she'd come here for answers and she had only a few days to get them. Why all this secrecy about this woman's past? She heard Oliver's explanation in her head, and to an extent, it made sense. It was sweet, that he and others in town, apparently, wanted to protect Emilia. But Callie wasn't about to let this opportunity go, not after traveling all the way here. Pam had hidden her plans in a box only Callie could open. She had an obligation to learn what Pam had in mind.

She didn't like making enemies. But she'd come here with a mission, and she was going to fulfill it.

She only hoped that Oliver had exaggerated. And that Emilia wouldn't kick her out for asking a few questions.

NINE

SEPTEMBER 1943

Emilia resolved to settle in at the Jorelini house while she waited for her sisters, and before she knew it, more than a week had passed. She did the schoolwork Corinna assigned her, helped Signora Jorelini clean and fix meals, and wrote to her sisters nearly every night, leaving the envelopes on the bedroom desk for Corinna to take the next morning to the post office. As often as she could, she walked down the street to check on her family's house. Although the strange couple who'd bought it—the De Lucas—were still there, Emilia was relieved that they seemed to have made no changes other than the tailor sign they'd installed to replace her father's.

All in all, she felt comfortable and safe. But then everything changed.

It started one night when the sound of the front door opening woke her with a start. The house was dark, and she had no idea who would be entering at this hour. She shot up in bed and held her breath, thinking of the couple that was occupying her own home. Was somebody now trying to take over the Jorelini house, too—because she was living there, the daughter of a Jew? If Signora Jorelini's house was seized, where would she go?

And what hope did she have of keeping her own house safe, if she could no longer live here, just down the street, to keep an eye on things?

Frantic with fright, she tiptoed past the bed where Corinna slept, and peeked out the window. With dawn approaching, she could see down to the front step. She was relieved to see that no stranger was breaking in. No, it was Signora Jorelini who had opened the door, and was now hurrying down the walk, dressed in trousers and a thick jacket, her shawl covering her head against the wind.

Draped over her elbow was the handle of a large, covered basket—the same type she'd seen Signora De Luca carrying that first night she'd spent in the Jorelini house. Emilia wondered where she was going so early in the morning. It was way too early to shop for food, if anything worthwhile was available. Or for anything else. The shops in town wouldn't be open for hours.

She had just finished washing her face and getting dressed when she heard activity in the kitchen. She tiptoed downstairs and peeked around the corner, and saw Signora Jorelini by the table, emptying her basket, now overflowing with tomatoes, carrots, potatoes, eggplants, some greens and bunches of herb, and a packet wrapped in paper that could have been meat or fish. And there was a green-tinted glass jar with what looked like oil and several small cloth bags filled with sugar or flour or rice, maybe. These were the ingredients that were always on the counter when Emilia came downstairs.

Emilia had known all her life that Signora Jorelini was a wonderful cook. Her restaurant in town had been a small, sun-filled place that served the most savory meats, flavorful soups, and rich, buttery cakes. Now that the restaurant was closed, Emilia was able to see close up how Signora Jorelini worked her magic, as her kitchen became her substitute. Emilia appreciated so much how her dishes were steeped in Caccipulia tradition, flavored with olives and fennel and fresh, local tomatoes. Thick, red sauces bubbled in deep iron pots starting early in the afternoon. Good food was almost magical, Emilia would think as she sat down at the table each evening with Signora Jorelini and Corinna for dinner. It made the bad thoughts go away, if only for a while. She looked forward to lunch from the moment she finished breakfast, and to dinner soon after finishing lunch. She craved mealtimes, and the transforming effects they had.

Still, the availability of all these ingredients was puzzling. Signora Jorelini had told Corinna that with the war raging on, food was becoming scarce. As she'd hidden behind the kitchen wall, Emilia had heard her utter those very words. So how was Signora Jorelini able to keep her refrigerator and pantry stocked? There were always fresh vegetables and grains and eggs and cheese. And often there was chicken or duck, simmered to perfection so the meat slid right off the bone. Now Emilia understood that it was no accident or stroke of luck that Signora Jorelini was able to get her hands on all this food. No—Signora Jorelini was actively going out to fetch it. Early in the morning, when no one was watching. Who was supplying her with this bounty?

Still curious, Emilia tiptoed back to the bedroom. Corinna was awake, sitting up in bed. She yawned and rubbed her eyes.

"Why are you up so early?" she said. "Where did you go?"

"Nothing, nothing," Emilia said. She didn't want to reveal what she'd seen, because she didn't want to admit that she'd been spying. Still, she couldn't help wondering where all that food had come from. And why Signora Jorelini had had to go out before dawn to get it.

That afternoon, Emilia went to help Signora Jorelini cook dinner. It was her favorite part of the day. She loved watching Signora Jorelini study her ingredients, like an artist surveying her tools before getting started on her newest masterpiece. The woman never measured the flour or scraped the rim of the cup to make sure the sugar was level. No, she tossed and sprinkled and let ingredients rain down from her fingertips into ceramic mixing bowls. She adjusted and readjusted the flames under the pots and pans, making the tiniest of changes every few minutes, and she dipped her wooden spoon into her sauces and soups repeatedly for a taste. She frequently incorporated unexpected ingredients into her recipes when the more traditional options were unavailable—rice instead of flour in desserts, polenta instead of meat covered in tomato sauce. And through it all, she made cooking look easy. She never looked surprised at how good her dishes tasted; she seemed to expect nothing less.

When all the work in the kitchen was done, and the ingredients had been left to simmer, Emilia went upstairs to compose a letter to her sisters. She still didn't know what was taking them so long to find her. They'd promised they'd leave for home shortly after she did, and yet here it was, nearly two weeks since she'd arrived back in town. She decided that today she'd write about Signora Jorelini's meals. She hoped they would be a further incentive for her sisters to hurry up and return:

Each meal starts off with an aroma, often both sweet and tangy, that tickles your nose and gets your stomach rumbling. I watch Signora Jorelini so closely, trying to figure it all out, narrating the steps in my head so I will be able to recreate it for you when you finally come home. But it's hard to make sense of. Now she's adding something brown from a small glass cylinder, now something from the garden I don't even recognize. She worries about shortages of eggs, butter, meat, and flour, but somehow she always has what she needs.

And then it arrives at the table—what joy for all your senses! Your eyes drink in the colors, your ears hear the meats sizzle, your tongue savors the taste so much that you hate to let yourself swallow. But then you do, and your stomach gets its chance to be delighted.

When you get here, you are in for a treat! Giulia, don't worry about your waistline! You can slim down after we leave for America. Corinna had some friends in Rome who were leaving Italy, and they said that the food on the ships going across the ocean is terrible. We will have to fill up with all this good food before we make that journey together.

I'm waiting for you to arrive every single day. What is holding you back? Please be safe, but please come as soon as you can. There's too much going on here, and I can't stay much longer by myself. I need you. I need my family.

Your sister,

Emilia

She hoped this note would do the trick. She didn't want to say much else. She knew it would be better to tell them more about Papa once they returned home, so Signora Jorelini and Corinna could help comfort them. She also didn't want to include anything additional about the De Lucas living in their house or the way Papa had been forced to sell it. But she never stopped thinking about it all. Never stopped hoping she could go inside her own home and see what changes had been made, what condition it was in. She had no idea of how the De Lucas were treating all their possessions, and she wanted them to be in good shape for her sisters, once they returned. She desperately wanted to begin packing up the clothes and keepsakes she and her sisters would want to bring to America with them. Her sisters would be happy if she got that task started. And her papa would be proud. Go forth, he'd said, imploring her to be brave and resolute like Abraham in his story. She wanted to live up to those words.

She was putting the letter into an envelope for Corinna to post the next morning when a figure outside the window caught her eye. Standing up to get a closer look as the evening darkness began to take hold, she realized that it was Corinna walking briskly down the street. The sight wouldn't have been unusual, except that Corinna was carrying a large, covered basket with a long handle, the same kind of basket Signora De Luca had been carrying, the same kind Signora Jorelini had used when she'd snuck out of the house and come back with all the food and ingredients. Now Emilia was determined to learn what was going on. Did it involve her father's shop? Did the baskets have some meaning that she should know about?

She hurried downstairs to the kitchen, where Signora Jorelini was checking the flame under a steaming pot. She noticed that there now seemed to be only enough food for the three of them. Where were all the vegetables and ingredients that had covered the counters this morning when Signora Jorelini returned home?

"Something wrong?" Signora Jorelini asked.

Emilia ignored the question. "Where did Corinna go?" she asked.

"To the school. She has taken on some students to tutor."

Emilia shook her head. The school building was in the opposite direction. "She didn't go back to school," she said.

Signora Jorelini kept her gaze fixed on the flame beneath the pot. "It's no matter to you where she went," she said. "She'll be back soon. Now if you've finished the reading Corinna assigned, you can set the table for dinner."

Emilia did as she was told. But she knew there was something the two were keeping from her. Something important. Something involving Signora De Luca as well.

What was going on?

TEN

SEPTEMBER 1943

As the days went by Emilia noticed that the mysterious comings and goings continued. Every other morning, Signora Jorelini, or sometimes Corinna, would leave the house before dawn with a basket, only to return with that same basket overflowing with food. And every evening, she'd spy Corinna hurrying down the street with that basket. Sometimes she would see Signora De Luca, too, or one of a few other women who lived nearby, always holding a covered basket.

The longer it went on, the more curious she became. One night just before dawn, she pretended to be asleep as Corinna left the bedroom. Through the window, she watched Corinna head down the street. She stole downstairs and was waiting in the kitchen when Corinna returned.

Corinna gasped when she saw her. "What are you doing up? Go back upstairs!"

"No," Emilia told her. "I want to know what you're doing. Where are you getting all that food? And where does it go? Where do you and the other women take it, so there's only a little left for us for dinner?"

Corinna paused, then put the basket down on the countertop and motioned to Emilia to follow her upstairs. There, she closed the bedroom door firmly, and the two sat on the edge of Corinna's bed.

"I shouldn't be telling you this," Corinna said. "It's dangerous to know too much. And my mother would hate for you to feel sorry for her. The ration cards don't allow us very much food at all. But there are ways to get more if you have money. Mama has some saved up from the restaurant, but it's not enough. So there's a box in the kitchen of valuables—just small things, some old jewelry, some trinkets, some silver pieces handed down from her parents. The brooch that my father gave her long ago. My things too, birthday gifts—my pearl earrings and my silver hand mirror. Mama or I go out in the mornings and sell what we have to for vegetables and grains and meat, and then Mama trades what she won't use for other ingredients she needs."

Emilia looked at her. "She sells her jewelry? And yours, too?"

"It's not just us," Corinna said. "Others in town are doing it, too. The nice ones."

"There are people who'll buy your beautiful things?"

"There are always people willing to take valuables from others. We sell to them, and they sell to others. *Alla borsa nera.* It's illegal, but it goes on."

Emilia thought of her sister Giulia, who hated even lending out her hair combs or barrettes. "She's selling something almost every day?" she asked. "And you too? How can you all give up the things that you love?"

"We do what we have to," Corinna said. "I know this doesn't make sense to you now. But you will understand one day. All we have, all we own... surely you've seen these last few weeks that it's not as permanent as we let ourselves believe."

Emilia considered this. "But... but you bring back so much

food in the mornings. And by the evening there's only enough for our dinner. Where does it all go?"

Corinna pursed her lips, as if deciding how to explain a complicated math problem in Emilia's workbook. "My mother has been involved in something very important with a few of the neighbors," she said. "So we're not helpless, so we can make things better. As better as we can.

"There are Jewish people in town trying to get out of Italy now that the Nazis are in power," she said. "And there's a group guiding them to safer places. Part of a whole network seeking to undermine the Nazis. The Resistance. Some of our neighbors have opened their houses, so the Jewish people have somewhere to stay until they are told where they can safely travel next. And my mother is cooking for them. Mama knows how to make meals out of few ingredients, or ingredients that normally wouldn't go together. The people coming through town would have nothing to eat without her.

"You've seen the baskets we carry?" she added. "They're just regular baskets, nothing suspicious. That's how we carry the food to the houses where Jews are staying. I made a name for what we do. I call it the Caccipulia Supper Club." She smiled.

Emilia was taken aback. She had never suspected anything like this. She had never even heard of anything like this. "But how do you know where they are?" she said.

"Mama goes to the Possano house for meetings," Corinna said. "She finds out where the Jewish people are staying and for how long. Usually it's a couple of days, maybe three. Then they get instructions on where to go next."

"And this is all secret? That's why you go out in the mornings so early?"

"And why we deliver the food when the sun has started to set," Corinna said. "There are people in town who wouldn't like what we're doing. They're scared of what the Nazis would do if they found out. Mama tells people that the meetings at the Possano house are for the women to exchange recipes or share any extra food they have. We try not to attract attention."

"So... is it dangerous?" Emilia couldn't help but ask. "Could you get in trouble?"

Corinna shrugged. "We don't think about that," she said. "Because we couldn't *not* do it. What kind of people would we be if we were okay letting others starve? The war will be over one day, Emilia, and we will all have to account for ourselves. We can never let the Nazis take away our humanity. What matters is what you can do for someone else, without worrying about the risks or sacrifices. If we can feed people for a day or two before they travel on... I mean, Emilia—just think. If you and your sisters were trying to leave, wouldn't we hope there'd be people to help you, as we are helping Jewish people now?

"What I'm trying to say is that we must build a world that we will want to live in, when this war is finally over," she said.

Emilia let the words echo in her mind. She hadn't even considered what would happen to her and her sisters as they set out for America. And of course, yes—they would need help, food, as the Jewish people here in Caccipulia did. But suddenly Emilia didn't want to think about herself anymore. Corinna was right—what mattered was not what you had to risk, but what you could do for others. She was safe now, and warm, and well-fed. But there were others—Jews like her father, Jews like her, too—who were not. There was loss in what Signora Jorelini and Corinna were doing, selling their possessions. And there was danger. But there was also peace. And grace. And humanity.

Which meant there was only one question left for her to ask. She could no longer think only of herself, her sisters and the shop.

"Will your mother let me help?"

Corinna nodded. "I'm sure she will."

ELEVEN

OCTOBER 2019

Wednesday

Callie started for the hotel in the direction Oliver had indicated. Although her suitcase had wheels, it was still heavy and took effort to drag along the street. It also made quite a racket as the wheels bumped and banged against the cobblestones underfoot, making a sound like a truck on a pothole-riddled highway. She smiled apologetically at the growing number of people she saw, who were now starting to emerge from their homes as the afternoon wore on.

At the end of the street, she looked up. Ahead was the narrow stone stairway Oliver had mentioned. There were at least thirty steps. Callie took a deep breath, wishing to spot a ramp or elevator. She wasn't going to be able to drag her suitcase up the uneven stairs, so would have to lift it and carry it. But that's okay, she told herself. She was strong and she could make it up to the top. She reminded herself that she was here on a mission—to find out the connection between this place, this woman Emilia, and her grandmother. So she would have the answers Pam had always wanted. And she would accomplish it, no matter what it took.

She began her climb, leaning her suitcase against her hip. As she set one foot after the other on the steps, it occurred to her that she knew so little about what she would find when she reached the top. She had arranged this trip so quickly, and at a time when she was not at all at her best—shocked by Pam's death, saddened by the loss, and still reeling from the sudden upending of her life and her move to Philly. Now that she was thinking more clearly, it felt kind of foolhardy, trying to recreate Pam's trip when she knew so little about what Pam had intended. What was she doing here?

What am I doing here? It was a question she asked herself often. She'd asked it that night in New Orleans, when she'd found herself at a bar on Bourbon Street drinking Sazerac—a blend of whiskey, bitters and sugar, and a specialty of New Orleans, she'd learned. It tasted like nothing she'd ever tried before, sweet and sour and deliciously intense. She wanted to believe she was being wonderfully spontaneous, heading out into the night with a very important executive. She wanted so much to live that way. It seemed such a stark and important contrast to the life Pam was always pushing her toward. Saying yes on a dime, switching direction without warning—it gave her a sense of power. She knew she wasn't in danger that night. She knew she'd arrive back safe and sound at her hotel that evening —which she did. She'd consider the evening a success, and she'd be excited to see her new friend again, when the conference attendees convened for breakfast. And yet, she'd also had the strange sense she was being impulsive and adventurous to make a point. And every so often, that night and afterward, she couldn't escape the question—what point was she making? Who was she trying to impress?

Pausing on the first landing of this steep stairway, she

started to ask herself the same questions now, questions that never seemed to have a good answer. But now, she sensed an answer at the ready. She was here for Pam, she was here for Chloe, she was here for Joe. She was here for her family, those who came before and those who would come after. She was here to finally unpack her grandparents' legacy, which had been shrouded in grief and guilt for too many years. She was about to pour sunlight on that forest of sequoias where her grandmother had cried.

Despite how sweaty she was, she felt a new energy and sense of conviction. She took a firmer grasp of the suitcase handle and heaved the bag higher, then continued on to the second landing. And finally the steps were all behind her.

She continued walking until she came to a white stone building with a cast-iron sign hanging from a scroll bracket that read *Albergo Annagiule*. She knocked on the door, and when no one answered, she turned the doorknob and stepped inside and into a small, square reception area. The floor was a gleaming mid-tone wood covered in the center with an ivory rug. The wood-framed sofa was covered in a gold-and-white damask fabric, and sat in between two slim end tables. Two armchairs faced the sofa, sporting the same fabric. The place was modern and elegant, and very European in feel, Callie thought. Straight ahead was a staircase that went up three steps, reached a small landing, and then continued to the left. The landing had a tall window covered in sheer white curtain panels, which were pulled back by gold tassels. The air smelled fragrant, slightly orange with a floral tinge.

To the right was a long, wooden reception desk next to an arch that led to the rest of the first floor. She could hear the sound of a cello playing over a sound system. The melody was haunting and beautiful.

"Hello?" she called. "I... um... *buon giorno? Buona sera?*"

Once again she regretted that she knew so little Italian, but there was nothing she could do about it now. As she waited for someone to show up, her gaze shifted to a small glass door across from the reception desk. *Pasticceria Sancino*, it said in ornate cursive letters. She breathed in, realizing that this was the famed bakery she'd read about online. Her curiosity piqued, she had to take a look. She walked over, and when she found the door unlocked, she pulled it open and stepped inside. The first thing she noticed was the glorious scent—fresh-baked bread combined with vanilla, toasted caramel, lemon zest, and something a little more sophisticated. Amaretto, maybe.

There was no one in the room, which was about the size of a large closet and had wide glass cases filled with the most luscious-looking sweets she'd ever seen. Tiny sponge cakes smothered in white cream; dense bars the color of honey dotted with slivered almonds; cannolis covered in chocolate and powdered sugar; glass dessert cups filled with custard and drizzled with chocolate. To her right was a case of pignoli cookies, just like the ones she and Pam had bought at the Italian bakery during the snowstorm all those years ago, although smaller and thicker. She remembered how she and Pam would marvel at how many pignoli nuts were at the bottom of the bag when they arrived home—and still, the cookies were studded with them. What fun they'd had, licking their fingers and reaching inside the bag to make sure they gathered up all that had spilled.

She was still lost in that long-ago moment when she heard shuffling behind her. She turned to see a woman in the doorway —a woman who looked older than anyone Callie had ever met before. She was short and thin, with tiny, sunken eyes, the brown bags beneath them deep and mottled. There were wrinkles beneath her chin and two short, deep lines between her eyebrows. Her wispy white hair was brushed back from her face, her hairline beginning well past her forehead. Still, there was something incredibly regal about her. Maybe it was her long neck, or her firm shoulders, her posture straight despite her years. She wore a floral wraparound dress, the skirt flowy as it draped to just below her knees. Her calves were slim, her low-heeled tan shoes practical yet stylish. Callie was sure this had to be the famous Emilia. She looked as though she owned not only the hotel and bakery, but the whole town.

"*Si?*" the woman asked.

"*Sono...* I mean... hello, do you speak English?" Callie asked.

The woman looked at her disapprovingly. "Of course."

"I'm sorry, I didn't mean to insult..."

"The store is not open." Her English was clear, her accent sounding more British to Callie's ears than Italian.

"I didn't know. It smells so good, and everything looks so..." Callie couldn't believe how intimidated this woman made her feel. "I'm here to check in," she added.

"Oh? Oh, you are the American, yes? Pamela Crain? I am Emilia Sancino. Come." She waited for Callie to leave the little shop, then locked the door and went behind the reception desk in the hotel's lobby.

Callie followed, feeling a little breathless. The mention of her sister's name, the knowledge that Pam had made this reservation sometime earlier, having no idea she'd never live to make the trip—it was all jarring. Callie didn't want to continue to pretend she was Pam, as she'd done with Oliver. But she also couldn't bring herself to tell this stranger that her sister had died or try to explain how she'd found the name of the hotel and decided to come in Pam's place. She didn't know what Pam had written in the letter to Emilia, didn't know if Pam had revealed that Emilia may have known her grandmother, didn't know if, after accepting Pam's reservation, Emilia might not be inclined to host anyone else. Oliver's warnings made Callie nervous. The woman didn't seem particularly happy to see her, and she was scared that admitting she wasn't Pam might encourage her to turn Callie away. She hoped this woman wouldn't ask for her passport, as many hotels in Europe did.

"That's right," she said. "Pamela Crain."

"Si, si," she said. "Signora Crain. You were meant to arrive yesterday. I thought maybe you'd changed your mind."

"Oh, well, yes, about that..." Callie stammered. "There was a problem getting here. Delays. I got a flight as soon as I could—"

"And you are still interested in... cooking? That's why you're here, right?"

"Yes... I mean, well, yes," she said. "That's why I came. That's what I said in my letter, right?"

"The problem is, as you know, that the cooking session is only two days. And because you are late, you have missed much."

"Oh," Callie said. "I see..."

"But you have already paid for your stay. So I will do a quick lesson after the others leave. Tomorrow, maybe."

"Oh... thank you," Callie said. It was all so strange. Why had Pam given this woman the impression that she wanted to learn to cook? Was it only a pretense so she could ask questions —the same questions that Oliver had warned Callie not to ask? Was Pam that devious?

"Is this your first time in Italy?" the woman asked.

Callie nodded. "It's very pretty, this town."

"Yes. It's much busier in the summer. It gets quieter at this time of year. So, I see you are all paid up. Have a seat, let me get you the key to your room."

Relieved that there had been no passport request, Callie watched the woman come out from behind the reception desk and walk through what appeared to be a dining room, with a large wood table and a huge chandelier. She sat down to wait on one of the armchairs in the center of the lobby. It was a very pretty little hotel, she thought as she looked around. In a very pretty little neighborhood. She usually didn't like small towns. That was what had driven her to leave her home for New York City long ago. She'd always felt so antsy, wondering what else was out there in the larger world, what she was missing, who else she could be meeting.

It used to infuriate Pam sometimes, that need of hers to look beyond whatever four walls were surrounding her. "You're not even listening!" she'd say when Callie's eyes would drift to the window. "I'm trying to tell you something." Callie would feel bad, having no idea what Pam had been saying. But she couldn't help it. Her mind was always busy.

And as she'd grown up, she'd found that she loved being seen that way. It made her seem exciting, romantic. Unpredictable. When she went home for a visit, she always wanted to have something new to share, some wild recent encounter to describe. She liked being a woman who was ready for the next challenge, the next goal, the next adventure. The one who was always full of surprises.

But it was exhausting, too, she'd come to realize. Exhausting trying to be the person she wanted Pam to think she was.

Waiting for Emilia to return, she started to wonder if it was ridiculous to carry on this charade. She didn't want a cooking lesson. All she wanted were answers about what her grandmother had done to make Emilia as angry as Oliver had described, if her grandmother indeed was the one who'd betrayed her. Callie had already annoyed Oliver at the coffee bar by telling him what she intended to do. And she seemed to have annoyed Emilia, too. So why even check in? Why stay any longer than the few minutes it would take to ask her questions and hopefully get a meaningful response? That's all she needed to do—nicely ask her questions, show the menu card and the note scribbled on the back, and leave. She could go back home and spend the time getting the house clean and the pantry stocked in preparation for Joe and Chloe's return. She usually didn't like such tasks, but she felt it was the least she could do for them.

And if Emilia was still nursing some hurt from decades ago, something she hadn't ever forgiven Nonna for, some mistake Nonna had made... well, that wasn't her fault. Callie was confused, too, and sorry that Nonna hadn't shared more. That Nonna had left this mystery in her wake. They'd both get over it. It would be a relief to put this cat-and-mouse game behind her.

Emilia returned to her spot behind the reception desk, and Callie could see her making notes in a binder. She got up and moved to the reception desk. There was actually no reason to even lie anymore. She took her passport out of her bag, so she could set the record straight on who she was and why she was there. As she looked up, her gaze landed on some small, framed black-and-white photos on the edge of the desk. The closest one was familiar, with three teenage girls in ornate gowns, the smallest one with a sparkling tiara. Callie realized this was the same photo now in the locked box in her tote bag. The photo on which Pam had drawn an arrow in orange crayon, pointing to the smallest girl.

Callie blinked and then looked closer. The dark eyes, high forehead, and delicately pointed chin of the smallest girl were unmistakable. She was very, very young, but she was definitely Emilia.

"Oh," Callie said, charmed by the sweet picture, this reflection of the girl this austere, elderly woman had once been. "The youngest one... is that you?"

Emilia shrugged and continued with her notes.

"It is you, isn't it?" Callie said. "Where was this? And who are the others?"

"My sisters," Emilia said, her voice a growl.

"What a wonderful picture," Callie said. She was struck

now by how connected the sisters seemed, their arms around each other. The middle sister held Emilia's shoulder so tightly. It seemed such a heartfelt expression of love and concern. Callie didn't think she'd ever taken such a picture with Pam. At least not since she was very young.

"You're all beautiful," Callie said. "You all look so happy here. You—"

"Signora Crain," Emilia said harshly. "Please give me a moment to finish!"

"Of course. I'm sorry. I'm just taken with this picture. You see, I have a sister, too—"

"That picture means nothing," Emilia said. "I keep it there because guests seem to like it. It adds to the..." She waved her hand, grasping for the word. "The... *atmosfera*. Now, did you need a map of the town or a list of places to eat?"

"Well... sure. Yes, thank you." Callie paused. There was something in Emilia's voice that touched her. Something she hadn't heard earlier. Passion. Pain, even. Maybe it was because she'd so recently lost Pam and was feeling guilty about her behavior. But hearing this woman, who also was a little sister, denigrate her older sisters... it felt too mean, too harsh. Too unfair. And she couldn't let the conversation go.

"I just... it seems to mean something, the way you're all hugging here. My sister and I, we were on our own from the time we were young. She always said... says, that sisters are the closest relative there is—"

"No, it is a mistake to think that way," Emilia said. "Sisters are not always the protectors you expect them to be. Sisters who have secrets, they are not to be trusted. Secrets destroy a family..."

The word "secret" stung. And suddenly Callie felt as though Emilia were attacking not only her own sisters, but her, too. And Pam as well. She and Pam had kept secrets from each other, too. "Maybe they had their reasons..." she murmured.

Emilia sighed with exasperation, and Callie took the key and the map that Emilia placed on the desk. She reached for the handle of her suitcase, her hands trembling. Emilia's harsh words echoed in her mind: *Sisters who have secrets, they are not to be trusted...*

Yes, Callie thought. Sisters shouldn't have secrets. But did that make them untrustworthy? Couldn't there be an understandable reason that a sister would keep something to herself? Maybe not forever, but for a period of time? Emilia's words made her wonder. She'd given Pam the benefit of the doubt up until now, thinking there had to be some good reason why Pam never told her about this trip. But now she wondered if she was giving Pam too much credit. Could Emilia be right about her sisters, and could Pam have secrets, too?

As she maneuvered the suitcase, her hip bumped into the desk, and the framed photos started to topple. Emilia reached out to steady them, then lifted one that had fallen face down.

"Ah, and that one," she muttered, pointing to the photo in her hand. "She was like a sister, too. I trusted her. A lot of good it did me."

Callie looked at the photo. The picture was of the young Emilia and another girl, a few years older, their arms wrapped around each other's waist. Emilia was in trousers and this other girl was in a belted dress with buttons down the front and a white collar. She had thick, wavy hair, light in color—maybe honey-blonde or champagne-blonde, it was hard to tell in the black-and-white photo. Still, Callie was sure she'd seen that other girl before...

And then she caught her breath. The girl was Nonna. There was no mistaking that round face, that wavy hair, those long limbs. It was her grandmother, whose wedding photo Pam had placed in the locked box.

Her grandmother had been like a sister to Emilia. And had apparently done something to make Emilia hate her.

At that moment, Callie knew she wasn't leaving. She was going to stay and continue to pretend to be Pam. It wasn't worth risking Emilia kicking her out. She wasn't going to fail before she'd even started. The only issue was whether she could win Emilia over. And get her to talk.

She only had four full days to make that happen.

TWELVE

OCTOBER 2019

Wednesday

A short time later, Callie was upstairs in her third-floor guest room. It was small but quite pretty. There was a full-size bed neatly made with cool white linens and an array of pillows in crisp, scalloped pillowcases. An antique wooden dresser with a honey-gold finish was positioned against the wall, alongside a slim writing desk with a gleaming wood surface. A small, uphol-stered loveseat in a gold brocade fabric was adjacent to a round, glass-topped coffee table on a black iron base. An arched glass door opened up on to a narrow balcony with a filigree iron railing.

Pushing aside her suitcase, Callie unlatched the balcony door and stepped outside. The air was cool but not too bad for late October, and the view from this height was lovely. Below she could see the street she'd walked along earlier, the brown and orange buildings aglow from the slanted rays of the late afternoon autumn sun. A sweet scent—partly citrus, partly floral—flowed up from the bushes and plants on a low stone wall by the cobblestone road. Beyond the streets she could see the pitched roof of the train station, and in the distance, the turquoise waters of the Tyrrhenian Sea. According to the map Emilia had given her, those waters flowed south into the Mediterranean, which was dotted with small islands, including Parissi Island—the island Callie had read about, the island where Emilia had spent those five heavenly weeks with her sisters and her uncle before returning to face the horrors of the Nazi invasion.

Callie came back inside, leaving the door open so she could continue to breathe in the pleasing scent of the air. She supposed she should start to unpack. Because in the moments after Emilia had commented on those old photos, Callie had grown increasingly sure that she wanted to stay. It wasn't so much about Emilia's puzzling resentment toward Callie's grandmother and her own sisters. It would have been easy for Callie to say that the girl in the picture was her grandmother. She could have shown her grandparents' wedding photo as proof. Maybe Emilia would have revealed something, maybe not. Either way, Callie could have left Caccipulia with as much information as Emilia was willing to share. She could have rebooked her flight home for tomorrow, scolding herself for traveling so far when she might have saved herself a lot of cost and time by writing emails or calling the hotel and asking to speak to Emilia.

But then she'd watched Emilia turn back to her binder. And she noticed what Oliver had been trying to tell her. He was right—she came across as tough, but there was so much pain underneath. Callie had watched the elderly woman shuffle behind the desk, her lips pursing as though each step took an effort she didn't want to acknowledge. She'd watched as Emilia donned a pair of wire-rimmed glasses, her fingers trembling, and tipped her head to the right while squinting to study her handwriting on the pages. The inside corners of Emilia's eyes were bloodshot, and the skin at the base of her chin was inflamed and peeling.

Thinking about that moment, Callie felt her eyes well up. How did she ever think she could go into this place, guns blazing, and demand information? How could she insinuate herself into this woman's deep, troubled feelings, introducing information about her grandmother without even knowing if it would be welcome or not? People were often not nearly as strong as they made themselves out to be. Especially when it came to family. And sisters. Sisters could hurt one another even in the most veiled of ways. Even when it seemed they were in the right.

It had happened so often that way between her and Pam.

She remembered the weekend she'd come home for a visit when Pam was six months pregnant. That's when Pam had told her that Joe's parents were coming to live in the guest cottage in the back of the yard. It had been a shock, the way Pam said it, tossing it out in an offhand way. A done deal.

"Joe's parents are moving into the cottage," she'd said as they prepared dinner, Pam marinating the chicken breasts for the grill and Callie cutting up vegetables for a salad. It was as though she was simply updating Callie about something routine, the way a person might mention that they'd stopped for a dozen eggs, so no need to add that to the weekly shopping list.

"Sure... isn't that where they always stay?" Callie had asked, thinking Pam was planning their visit for when the baby was born. They'd moved to Arizona years before, when Joe's father had retired. What had Pam thought she expected—that they'd stay in a hotel?

"No... I mean for good," Pam said. "I need the help, and they don't need a big place. It makes a lot of sense. It's empty now, and it doesn't need much, just maybe an upgrade to the heating system. I wanted to tell you, because it belongs to both of us, you and I, at least for now. Until Joe and I finish buying you out."

"They're staying there long-term?" Callie had asked. "Like... forever?"

"What do you mean, forever?"

"That this will be their home? Permanently?"

"It's hard, having a baby," Pam had said. "And you don't intend to be around much. That's fine, of course. You deserve to live your life. But don't you see that I'm going to need help?"

"What? Well, sure."

"Good. I knew you'd understand."

They'd continued with the preparations, and by the time they brought the chicken and veggies out to Joe to grill, the conversation had moved on. Pam seemed very solicitous, asking her about her job, her travel, her friends, her new assignments, living in the big city, and so on. She told stories about work and her apartment, and Pam and Joe laughed where appropriate, and cheered her, and acted like she was the most interesting person they'd ever met. She'd felt the attention was patronizing. They were trying to butter her up.

Later that night she'd stopped Pam in the kitchen. Pam was having trouble sleeping and often roamed around downstairs at night. Callie wanted to continue their talk. It felt so wrong, so insulting. She couldn't really explain why. Pam and Joe were in the process of buying the whole property. That's what they all had agreed. And Pam had a right to make the best decisions for herself and her child. But still, Callie had the sense that she was losing out. And she knew Pam understood this, which was why she'd so craftily brought up the topic, her tone artificially casual. She'd apparently known Callie would have a problem with this decision, even if Callie couldn't articulate what the problem was.

"So... they're moving into the cottage?" she said as she sat at the table in her pajamas, and Pam brought over a quart of milk and two glasses. Callie waved her off, and Pam shrugged and filled her own glass.

"Yes." She took a sip.

"And then what?"

"Then they'll help with the baby. I have to go back to work. I get three months off and that's it."

"What about the furniture that's there?"

"They'll use that. It's nicely furnished."

"What about their own furniture?"

"They'll sell it. Or put it in storage. Or keep it and rent their place. I don't know."

"So they may be here for a long time? Like, just living there?"

"I suppose at some point they may offer to buy it."

"They'd buy it?" Callie asked.

Pam put her glass down and rolled her eyes. "What are you going on about? It's just sitting there."

"But it's ours."

"But nobody's there. What... you're going to come home to live there?"

"I don't know... maybe..."

"Please. You know you're not coming back to this town."

"I might."

"And live in the cottage?"

"Maybe. I like to know it's there. Just in case."

"And you'd rather have it sit empty, just in case, than have family there to help me?"

"I can help you out."

Pam laughed and shook her head. "Yeah. Right. You're going to give up your career to watch my baby while I go back to work."

Callie bristled at Pam's sarcasm. It was mean and unjustified. "So they're just going to stay there rent-free?" she asked.

"Do you want me to charge them rent?"

"I don't know... *we* could rent it out, you know."

"You never said that before."

"We could make some money."

"I need their help more than I need money. Without them, I'd have to get a sitter or put the baby in day care. Which would be fine, but expensive, and since they're available, I'd rather have her grandparents take care of her. At least while she's an infant."

"I thought Mrs. Greenbaum was going to help you."

"Well, sure, she'll help. But she can't watch the baby every day."

Callie pressed her lips together and nodded slightly. "So you just decided all this on your own? You and Joe?"

"And I'm telling you about it."

"Long after I could do anything about it."

"What would you want to do about it?"

Callie stood. "If you don't know why this is so upsetting... then fine. Forget I said anything. I'm going to sleep."

She'd gone upstairs but hadn't fallen asleep for hours. She didn't know what had gotten into her. She knew she was wrong. And it was cruel for her to torture Pam like this. Pam was right about everything: yes, she needed help; yes, the cottage was empty; yes, this was a great solution that would save Pam and Joe money and allow the baby to be cared for by her grandparents. And no, Callie had no intention of coming home.

Still, there'd been something about the news that had gotten under her skin. She felt betrayed. Overlooked. Like a rug had been pulled out from under her feet. Like she no longer had much of a voice around here. The request for her buy-in had been perfunctory. Pam had never treated her that way before—as a "less than." But she'd done that now.

Callie had sensed that same feeling in the lobby when Emilia had accused her sisters of abandoning her. And betraying her.

Emilia was ninety-one, according to Oliver, and Italian, and Callie was American and sixty years younger. But once again, as had happened when she'd read about Emilia online, she couldn't shake the feeling that they were alike. *Sisters are the closest relative there is,* Pam had liked to say. Which meant, Callie now saw, that they could hurt you in a way no one else could. And the hurt didn't go away, no matter how many years or decades passed.

Callie scowled as she contemplated her situation now. It felt as though Emilia's anger had brought her own to the fore. She was mad at Pam for leaving this family mystery for her to solve and for never telling her about it. She was mad that Pam had planned to trick her into taking this trip, to shove an airline ticket into her hand, assuming she was scattered enough, had few enough responsibilities, and could just take off. Maybe it was true, maybe she was pretty much free right now, with no job or other obligation there in Philadelphia; but still, she didn't like being judged that way. She didn't like that Pam thought she had Callie's life pegged.

The whole situation wasn't fair. It bothered her that she couldn't ever know what had been in Pam's mind when she gathered those items and put them in the box, locking it with Callie's birthday as the code. It infuriated her that Pam may actually have known a lot about what went on between their grandmother and Emilia, and that she couldn't ask Pam about it. And the memory of that argument about Joe's parents only reinforced how very divided she and Pam had been.

She wished so much that she could speak to Pam just one more time. One last conversation. To tie up all the still-loose threads.

But since she couldn't, it seemed the only way to move forward was to get to know Emilia. To develop a bond. She wanted to know how Emilia came to hate her sisters as well as Callie's grandmother, and why that feeling was still so ripe even after so many years. And she wanted to know what role her grandmother played in the story of Emilia's family.

Now she understood what Oliver had been trying to tell her. She wasn't going to get answers by demanding them. Just from the few minutes she'd spent with Emilia, she knew Emilia wouldn't respond well to that. No, she would get answers by being patient. By waiting until Emilia trusted her. And believed she could be a friend. Even though she had less than a week to do it.

She opened her suitcase and took out the wooden box. She slipped it inside one of the dresser drawers.

She didn't need it now. She would retrieve it when the time was right.

THIRTEEN

SEPTEMBER, 1943

That evening after sunset, Emilia found herself hurrying down the main road of town, following closely behind Corinna, her tense fingers grasping the handle of a basket. She watched how Corinna tried to keep close to the buildings, staying in the shadows formed by the flickering streetlamps and the tall umbrella pines and narrow cypress trees along the way. Emilia didn't know what to think. This was her town, after all. It was familiar. She'd traveled these streets for her whole life.

And yet, she could tell from Corinna's behavior, her bowed head and hurried steps, that there was danger in what they were doing. Even though there were no German soldiers here in town—at least not yet, as Corinna had emphasized—there were neighbors to be wary of. People in town who would disapprove of feeding Jewish refugees. Especially foreign-born Jews, who were not even allowed to be in Italy anymore, Emilia had learned. Corinna hadn't been specific about what might happen to them if their activities were discovered by the wrong people. Emilia didn't know what the consequences might be. Prison? Something worse? She didn't want to imagine.

She followed Corinna along a bend and onto a connecting

street, and then up to the front door of a narrow, tan house. Corinna knocked and a moment later a young woman with a toddler on her hip opened the door.

"Signorina Jorelini," the woman said. "How nice of you to come."

"We heard your husband wasn't feeling well," Corinna said. "My mother thought it might be hard for you to take care of him and the children. She made you a dinner to help you out." She offered the basket.

"My, how kind," the woman said as she took it. Emilia was shocked at how easily the lie had flowed off of Corinna's lips. She remembered now how Signora Jorelini had insisted there was always the danger of being overheard. It was hard to know who to trust these days, she'd said, so there could be no mention whatsoever of the true purpose of the delivery unless it was behind closed doors.

"We hope he feels better," Corinna said. "We will come again tomorrow, and however long he's feeling ill."

The woman thanked her and started to close the door, but not before Emilia caught sight of two teenage boys she didn't recognize peeking out from an inner room. Corinna pulled the door shut and gave Emilia a quick nod. "Now your basket," she murmured.

She followed Corinna back toward the center of town. This area was busier than the other neighborhood had been, with people walking from or toward the train station.

"Corinna!" someone called, and Emilia saw Corinna stiffen as she turned. Emilia turned, too. She didn't recognize the man who was waving and crossing the street to approach them. And he didn't seem to know her either.

"Good evening, Signor Kapuletti," Corinna said. "How are you? Sofia," she said, looking at Emilia. "This is the father of one of my old classmates from school, Marco. Signor Kapuletti, this is my cousin visiting from Trento, Sofia."

"We thought you were studying in Rome," the man said.

"I had been, but I came back to be with my mother," Corinna answered.

"And what are you two doing out on such a brisk night?" he asked.

"Taking some food to the Hinna house." Corinna pointed to the basket on Emilia's arm. "They have many mouths to feed."

"Your mother has so much extra food?" the man said, prolonging the syllables, as though he didn't believe her. It was clear to Emilia that he was one of the bad ones, the people who would disapprove of the supper club if he knew about it. Think it was too risky. Try to stop it.

"Well, we do what we can. For people we care about. You know..." Corinna said, and Emilia was again impressed with how sly Corinna could be. "Excuse us, Signor Kapuletti. It is kind of chilly tonight. I don't want to keep my cousin out late. Please say hello to Marco for me."

The man nodded and continued on his way. Emilia looked up at Corinna, her breath jagged. Suddenly she felt danger in a way she never had before.

"It's okay," Corinna said. "He's a troublemaker, but he trusts me. Come on, let's finish up."

Before too long, they had made the second delivery and were back home. Emilia was glad to see that the other baskets she'd noticed before they left were gone, evidently picked up by other neighborhood women doing what she and Corinna had done. She was relieved that they didn't have to go out again tonight. As she washed her hands for dinner, she heard Corinna tell her mother about their evening. Signora Jorelini was less concerned about Signor Kapuletti—she knew Corinna had handled the situation well—than she was about the teenage boys who had been visible from the doorway of the first house.

"They mustn't do that," she said. "We'll have to make sure someone tells them so."

Corinna nodded as she set the table for the three of them. "Did you speak to Signora Possano?" she asked. "Any new arrivals?"

"Three more families are showing up later this week. And we're supposed to start using codes to tell people where to go next for travel documents and directions. A color system—red for the train station, green for the woods, brown for the church. It's become too risky to have these conversations aloud. Too many ears listening, too many chances for mistakes. Now I just have to figure out how to include the codes in our deliveries..."

She sighed, putting the matter aside, and then walked to the sink and put her arms around Emilia. "I'm proud of you," she said. "Your father would be, too."

Emilia smiled and sat down at the table. It was perilous, what she'd just done. And it was scary, listening to Signora Jorelini talk about codes and instructions that could be overheard. Her hands were trembling. But she felt something else, too. Something positive. She knew Signora Jorelini was right, that her papa would be proud of her. She thought of the paper with the stars and the Abraham story. Tonight she'd been brave. Tonight she'd gone forth.

Then she thought of her sisters who might still be far away. She could only hope that if they were in some strange town, there would be people with baskets, too.

From then on, Emilia looked at Signora Jorelini and Corinna in a new way. She'd already been more grateful than she could express, that Signora Jorelini had cared for her sick father and then taken her in when she had no home. When Emilia now watched Signora Jorelini bending over a pot on the stove, the steam causing her cheeks to perspire and the gray hairs around her forehead to form into tight, tense curls, she thought about what Corinna had said, how it was important to build the kind of world you wanted to live in once the war was over. The sadness and the fear and the deprivation that had bypassed her little town for so long had now overtaken it, as it had overtaken all of Italy. What couldn't be lost, Corinna had said, was people's humanity. And there was no better sign of humanity than nourishing those in need.

And no better feeling than having good, warm food to fill your belly. Emilia knew all about that. It was Signora Jorelini's cooking that had helped her adjust to life these last few weeks without her family. Good food made a person feel safe. It made you feel you were home. And here was Signora Jorelini, making delicious meals out of ingredients she was able to cobble together each morning. It was more than an art. It was almost as though by doing good, she was able to make a kind of miracle occur.

"How did you learn to cook like this, Signora Jorelini?" Emilia asked one afternoon as she rinsed eggplants and tomatoes, and Corinna sliced them up.

"From my mother," Signora Jorelini said. "I used to help her in the restaurant when I was a little girl."

"Do you miss your restaurant?"

The woman sighed and shook her head, resting a hand on her hip. "I miss it very much. The way ingredients were so plentiful and fresh, and the dishes were truly something to be proud of. How beautiful it all looked on the plates—the colors, the way the sauces looked as we brought the food out from the kitchen. Oh, how I loved it. Everything about it. Even setting the tables. Choosing the table linens. Selecting wines. I used to love watching from the kitchen as people ate. But, oh..."

She laughed softly and lowered her gaze. "Oh, maybe this will sound silly to you. It sounds silly to my own ears. But one of the best parts was the menus. I loved crafting beautiful descriptions of our dishes, seeing how they looked printed out on the page."

"She loved putting those menus into each person's hands," Corinna added.

Emilia continued to rinse the vegetables as she listened to Signora Jorelini reminisce. The last time she'd been at Signora Jorelini's restaurant was in the spring, to celebrate Annalisa's graduation. Annalisa had planned to continue her studies and become a botanist. Or was it a biologist? Emilia didn't remember. All she remembered was how proud Papa looked of his eldest daughter. And how much fun they'd all had, eating Signora Jorelini's specialty, *cacio e pepe*, with its creamy cheese-and-pepper sauce over spaghetti.

Emilia was sorry the restaurant had closed. It was so sad that this kind woman—who'd lost her husband when Emilia was young and had lost her parents long before that—had had to close the one thing she loved after Corinna. Such a beautiful restaurant. And yet, Emilia realized, the supper club was helping to bring the restaurant back to life. Her dishes wouldn't be forgotten. They were now going to people who desperately needed the comfort of good, warm food.

Then, as she watched Signora Jorelini start to boil potatoes for *gnocchi*, she had an idea. Something she thought would give them a smile. She took a card and a fine-tipped pen from one of the cabinets in the kitchen. These were the cards Signora Jorelini had used to list the daily specials, back when her restaurant was still open. Sitting at the table, Emilia began to play around with creating a menu for today's meal, using words she remembered from the castle's menus. She worked slowly, hoping to make her handwriting look as close to calligraphy as possible:

The Caccipulia Supper Club
This Evening's Menu
Hearty meatballs made with eggplant and cheese
Savory gnocchi with tomato topping
Wilted greens

Fresh-baked bread

When she was finished, she held the card up. Corinna smiled and Signora Jorelini looked like she was about to cry.

"Oh, Emilia," she said. "Oh, how lovely. Of course, I think this is a bit too fancy. Savory? Hearty? It's more accurate to say it's cooked and be done."

"I wanted to make something nice for you," Emilia said. "Something for you to hang up. Or keep. Or just look at."

Signora Jorelini shook her head. "Oh, *piccolina*, this is so sweet. And you take me back. How I miss the way things used to be. Today we are worried about hiding and codes and being overheard... I still don't know how to write the codes..."

"Wait! Codes!" Emilia exclaimed. "You mean the colors that tell the people where to go next? Red, yellow, brown—"

Signora Jorelini nodded.

"What if we add it to the menu?" she said. "Like my father used to do for me, with the code words he put into his drawings. What if I use colored pencils for the menu—and change the color depending on where the people are supposed to go?"

"So you'd write it in red if they're to go to the train station, green for the woods, brown for the church...?"

"And regular black ink if they are just to stay put," Corinna said. "That's... that's brilliant."

"We have six families sheltering people now," Signora Jorelini said. "Can you make six supper club cards? Black for tonight."

"Of course," Emilia said. "And whatever color you need tomorrow."

"That's fine," Corinna said. "We can include one in each basket of food."

"Oh, Emilia," Signora Jorelini said. "I know how much you miss your sisters. And I know you want to leave with them. But if you can't be with them, I'm glad you're here to help us."

That night after the deliveries were made and Corinna was asleep, Emilia wrote another letter to her sisters, using the full moon for light. She knew she couldn't tell them everything. But she wanted them to know she was okay.

Dear Annalisa and Giulia,

I know it must be hard for you to travel, with the war getting worse and the Nazis now in Italy. Please be careful, be safe. You don't need to worry about me. I am doing well here. This is a good place for me to be for now. I look for you out of my window every day.

Your sister,

Emilia

She sealed the letter in an envelope, addressed it to the castle, and left it on Corinna's desk, where she had left the others she'd written. She was always relieved to find them gone in the mornings.

Corinna began working more often as a tutor after school to try to earn extra money, so sometimes Emilia made deliveries alone. She usually could carry only two baskets at a time, but there were always neighborhood women who came for the other baskets. Signora Jorelini would stop by the Possano house each afternoon and come back with the color code for the day, and Emilia would prepare the menu cards accordingly and tuck one into each basket. The routine had started to give her confidence, so that after a week, she was not nearly as anxious going out each evening as she had been that first night with Corinna when they'd run into Signor Kapuletti.

Still, Emilia could tell from Signora Jorelini's increasingly tense manner as she cooked that the Nazi threat was growing.

One afternoon, Signora Jorelini came back from the Possano house looking distressed. Corinna took her coat and Emilia brought over a cup of tea.

"What is it, Mama?" Corinna said.

Signora Jorelini took a sip. "It seems the Possanos have taken in another Jew."

"So?" Corinna said. "They have done so before."

"Yes, but this young man has been very active in the Resistance. He was helping to transfer grenades and weapons. His family was arrested, and the Nazis were waiting for him at his home. Some in his group got wind of this and sent him here."

"And that's very different?" Emilia asked.

"He's the first person in town who is wanted for Resistance activities," Signora Jorelini said. "He has a target on his back. Some worry this will make the Nazis become aware of our little town. That they'll come here in search of him and others."

"So what's there to do?" Emilia said. She felt more curious than scared. To her, the Nazis still felt unreal. She'd gotten used to not going to school, and while she still hated seeing others running her father's shop, it helped to know that Signora De Luca was involved in the supper club. The actual war still seemed far away. "Will he leave with the others?"

"No, he's a special case," Signora Jorelini said. "He may be here for a bit. At some point the Resistance group in Milan will send word for him to make his way into the woods, where there will be people who can keep him safe and help him travel to Switzerland. For now, we will feed him and make sure no one knows he's here. You two will be the only ones bringing food to him. No one else. Yes?"

"Of course, Signora Jorelini," Emilia said. She was humbled to be included in this secret. And she felt very strongly her responsibility to secrecy. She wanted to help this young Jewish man. She hoped that there would be people who would protect her sisters if they were in any danger as they made their way back to town.

"Corinna? Do you understand?" Signora Jorelini was asking.

Emilia looked at Corinna. She looked ill. The color had drained from her face. Her hands were trembling, and Emilia saw her clasp them together, as if trying to make them still. She hadn't said a word since Signora Jorelini had started her story.

"Is he okay, this boy?" Corinna asked. "He's not hurt, is he?"

"No, not at all. But the Nazis are looking for him. So upsetting, he's quite a sweet young man. I met him just now. Very handsome, very tall. Dark hair and eyes."

"What's his name?" Corinna said, her voice soft and hesitant.

"Tomas Sachsel." Signora Jorelini got up from her chair. "Okay, girls, we need to put the food into bowls. We must feed this boy especially well to help him build up his strength. He will need it. Emilia, please get the supper cards ready. Brown tonight."

"Right away," Emilia said and went to the table to get to work. Corinna was standing in the doorway to the kitchen, still clasping her hands. Emilia looked at her questioningly, but Corinna shook her head and waved her off. Emilia didn't understand. What had Signora Jorelini said that bothered her so? Was she worried about the danger this Jewish boy would bring to the neighborhood? She hoped not. If Corinna and Signora Jorelini started to worry about hosting Jewish people, what would that mean for her? What if they wanted her to leave? Where would she go, if her sisters were still not back?

Emilia finished with the cards and placed them in the baskets, as Signora Jorelini prepared the bowls for transport. "Okay, now, Corinna, why don't you help..." She looked around. "Corinna? Where did she go?"

Emilia looked at the hallway. It was empty. She hadn't seen Corinna go upstairs. She hadn't seen her go anywhere.

"Well, let's get started, you and I," Signora Jorelini said. "Here, you can take this basket, and I'll fix the others, and hopefully Corinna will come back down so she can help deliver the rest. Why don't you go to the Possano house first? I put a little extra into his bowl and added some more bread, too. And use the back door. With Tomas there, the family doesn't want to attract any attention. It's best if there's not a lot of activity in front of the house right now."

Emilia nodded, put on her jacket, looped her arm under the handle of the basket, and headed out. She hoped this boy, Tomas, would be comforted by Signora Jorelini's food. They had something in common, she and Tomas. They were both Jews living in a changed world. She thought she might like to talk to him. With her sisters still gone, it would be nice to talk to someone who knew what it was like to be Jewish now. But she knew that would be impossible. She hadn't been allowed past the threshold of any of the homes they delivered to so far. And Signora Jorelini had specifically said to leave the food by the Possanos' back door and not to linger.

Emilia walked around the path to the back of the Possano house. Starting up the stone stairway to the door, she paused when she heard sounds coming from the thicket behind the yard. Small moans, whimpers. She looked over, and thought she could see movement. She wondered if the family's poor little kitten had gotten tangled in some vines, as she had last week. Silly kitten, to go back to where she'd gotten stuck and hurt before.

She put the basket on the ground and walked toward the thicket, then crouched down and crawled underneath. But she didn't spy the kitten. She crawled back out and took a few steps away to brush off her skirt. And that was when she noticed the source of the noise and the movement.

Beyond the thicket and beneath the branches of a maple tree, its leaves gold and orange, was a tall young man with deep-black curls. This, she knew, had to be Tomas. And he was embracing a young woman, with golden hair flowing free behind her neck. They moved, swayed, and now she could see that their lips were pressed together, that her hands were stroking the back of his neck, as he moved his hands to her jaw, his fingers weaving through her hair.

It took her just a second to realize it. The girl in Tomas's arms was Corinna.

FOURTEEN
OCTOBER 2019

Wednesday

With the box tucked safely away in her hotel room dresser, Callie looked outside at the sea in the distance. She was exhausted from traveling, but she wasn't ready to go to sleep. To her surprise, she realized that what she most wanted to do was go back to the coffee bar to see Oliver. She hated how she'd come across to him—heartless, capable of confronting an old woman and demanding information. Not that Emilia needed protecting. She had a tough exterior, and despite that touch of frailty and vulnerability Callie had noticed, it was clear that if she didn't want to talk about something, she wouldn't. Still, Callie didn't want Oliver to think she was a horrible person. He'd been so friendly and warm, and she wanted to redeem herself in his eyes. Not to mention that she'd been accused of being mean before. And she'd hated it.

"You're so defensive," Pam had said on the phone last spring. "You always think I'm out to get you, so you lash out."

"But you are out to get me. You're out to change me."

"I am not."

"No? Then why are you always trying to fix me up with one of Joe's friends? I don't need your help with dates. I don't need your input on who would make a good boyfriend. I can use my own judgment. I can!"

But she'd known back then that she wasn't using the best judgment. Not by a long shot. It was months into her relationship with Mr. New Orleans, and she'd known the end was inevitable. Nothing big had happened, no knock-down, drag-out fights. Just small, continuous digs, back and forth. They'd gotten into a big argument on Saturday afternoon, as he'd dropped her off at her apartment. They'd spent the day at a food fair in Brooklyn. It had been such fun—they'd tasted all kinds of foods, Latin and Greek, Korean and Indian and African. She'd enjoyed sharing exotic sandwiches and warm bowls, walking arm in arm, trying something at nearly every booth they'd passed. She'd wished life could always be this good.

She didn't know when things went off the rails. Probably it happened as the afternoon had waned, and the lights and carnival atmosphere had started to diminish. Vendors broke down booths while she was still eager for more. Suddenly she was aware of how temporary the day's festivities had been, and it upset her. By evening, there'd be no sign that the event had even taken place.

"You knew this about me," he said as he left her on the front step of her apartment building. "I thought you understood who I am."

"I did. And I thought I was okay with it—"

"So if you're not, you're not. Be like your sister. Maybe that's what you really want. Go back home and be just like her."

"You know that's not what I want," she'd said.

"Then what do you want?"

"I want..." She'd hesitated. She couldn't say it outright.

"You don't even know," he'd said. "Where is this getting us?

Who knows if you even want what you think you want? Why can't we just *be*?"

He'd started down the street. As if she was the one making unfair demands.

That was the last fight. But it wasn't the last time she'd seen him.

She took a shower, changed into a fresh pair of jeans and a pullover sweater, and threw on her jacket. Leaving her room, she paused on the bottom stair. It was just about seven, and the sky was dark through the windows. The lobby looked almost haunted, the lamps on the end tables switched on, the glow making the glass teardrops hanging from thick gold tassels on the drapes sparkle.

She peeked past the double doors behind the reception desk and saw a long dining room table set for dinner for eight people, with china and crystal and floral napkins and a beautiful damask tablecloth. Emilia seemed to be hosting a dinner party of some kind. Which seemed strange, as she didn't seem the dinner party type. But this was clearly set to be a lovely event. There were lilies surrounded by greenery in tall vases and a set of crystal candlesticks with tall tapers waiting to be lit.

Curious, Callie looked deeper inside the room. A dark-brown breakfront was on the opposite wall, sporting stacks of formal dessert plates and shallow bowls and linen napkins edged in lace, all waiting to be used. Suddenly a swinging door opened from what appeared to be the kitchen, and Emilia emerged carrying a thick iron pot, which she set on a trivet in the middle of the dining room table. The steam rose, and even from here, Callie thought it smelled heavenly, rich with seasonings like rosemary, garlic, and basil.

Stepping back, she pressed her shoulder against the wall so Emilia wouldn't see her, and glimpsed around the corner. A group of people followed Emilia out, one carrying a platter of steaming vegetables, and another a basket of bread. They all found a seat, and Emilia took the bowls from atop the break-front and brought them to the table. Using a silver ladle, she started to serve from the pot. It looked like a pasta dish, the food rich and red as she spooned it out. She scooped a generous portion for each person, added on vegetables, and then sent around the bread. The talk was a mix of English and Italian, but mostly Italian. One of the guests uncorked a bottle of red wine and poured. When everyone was served, they all raised their glasses and sang out, "*Salute!*"

Callie kept her gaze on Emilia, who was smiling and nodding as the others spoke. She wore a pretty patterned dress and her hair was pulled back into an elegant bun at the nape of her neck. She had not seemed nearly so warm when Callie had checked in this afternoon. The sounds in the room became muted as everyone began to eat. A kind of spiritual air took over the room, as the food and wine worked their magic. Callie supposed that was what a lovely dinner prepared in someone's home could do. She couldn't even remember the last time she'd been invited to a meal at someone's home. She always thought she preferred going out, the newer and trendier the place, the better.

But not now, as she peeked out at this joyful group. She yearned to be seated at the table, too. Even if she couldn't understand what they were saying, she thought she'd still feel at home. She wondered who these people were and how they came to be there. She wanted to know their secret. How they came to be so happy. How they came to share such love. Of food. Of wine. Of each other's company.

With a sigh, she crossed the lobby toward the front door. Nobody noticed her.

Outside, she made her way back down the steep staircase and onto the main street. It was busy now, the lights on in all the shops and eateries. Oliver's shop was packed, with people claiming tables and walking up to the bar to order coffee from one of the three servers behind it. Oliver was there, his dark curls hanging over his forehead, working the espresso machine: cleaning the pipes and twisting the knobs and gracefully placing the short cups under the spigot and then onto the saucer when they were filled. She stood by the bar and watched him. It was almost as though she were watching a delightfully choreographed dance.

She saw him catch sight of her. She waved, and he held up a pointer finger to indicate he'd be right there, then picked up a tray with four cups and brought it to a foursome at a small round table. He threw his towel over his shoulder and went back to talk to one of the servers, a young girl with blue hair and a line of studs along the rim of her ear. Then he threw the towel onto the counter by the espresso machine and came over to her.

"Hey," he said. She thought he looked happy to see her, and yet she sensed a bit of aloofness, too. "Did you meet Emilia? Did you find out what you wanted to know?"

"Well... no. Not really," she said with resignation.

"Why? She kicked you out?"

She scowled. "No, she didn't kick me out. But you were right. I didn't want to be rude. My needs aren't hers. She owes me no explanation."

"So you didn't ask anything?"

"I couldn't. She mentioned her sisters and..." She paused. She didn't know if now was the right time to bring up her grandmother's picture. She didn't know this guy at all, and it seemed too personal a revelation for this crowded space. "And she seemed so hurt by them. I didn't have the heart to ask her to relive anything painful. I found myself... I don't know. I can see why you want to protect her."

He nodded. "She's like that, isn't she? She seems the kind of person who never gets along with anyone. And yet everyone falls in love with her. I don't get it either." He raised his eyebrows. "So what will you do now?"

She thought about that. "I don't know. I don't want to leave just yet."

"No?"

"I want to hear her story. I want to share mine with her. I want to see where they intersect—because I know she does have this connection with my..." She hesitated, not wanting to reveal that Nonna was likely the person he'd spoken about earlier, the person he believed had somehow betrayed Emilia. She'd tell him later. Maybe.

"With this connection with my family," she continued. "But I don't want to bulldoze her. I want her to tell me because she wants to connect with me, too. I saw her with all these people, having dinner in her dining room and it—" She shrugged. "It had an impact on me."

He eyed the clock above the bar. "Are you hungry? Did you eat?"

She glanced down at her stomach, as if she'd find the answer there. "I don't know. I'm all messed up with the time. It's the middle of the afternoon for me. But sure... now that I think of it, I am pretty hungry."

"Look, I haven't had dinner yet, and I'm starving," he said. "I can probably cut out of here in about half an hour. How about we get something to eat? Sound good?"

She hesitated. She wasn't sure it was smart to make a friend here. She was leaving in less than a week. Still, she didn't want to say no to Oliver. He seemed very nice. And his concern for Emilia was sweet. She didn't want to spend the rest of her life second-guessing her instincts when someone kind came along.

"Sounds good," she agreed.

"Great. I want to know more about you. Here's what we'll do. Go past the train station, you remember where it is, right? Then through the arch across the street and up the stairs. That's Memorial Square. There's lots of great restaurants and a pretty view of the water in the distance with lights sparkling from the trees."

She nodded as he went back to the espresso machine. She liked what he said. That he wanted to know more about her.

She couldn't remember the last time someone had told her that.

She left the coffee bar and started back in the direction of the train station, enjoying how there were no cars around, just lots of people. She strolled down the winding cobblestone street, taking in alleys and archways that seemed to appear everywhere, with stone steps apparently leading up to whole other neighborhoods. It was a strange mix of scary and quite beautiful, this town, with vines hanging from flower boxes casting snakelike shadows on the street. She thought about what she'd read online, the destruction that had taken place here. Amazing, she thought, how strong and vibrant it now was. Many of the buildings looked quite old. It was sobering to think these buildings had been here, witnesses to the many people who'd been killed.

It made her think of that California vacation her grandparents had taken her and Pam on long ago. The way her grandfather had mused about how much the trees had seen and how many secrets they had, which had brought her grandmother to tears.

Callie continued to the train station, then through the arch across the street, as Oliver had instructed, and up a staircase that led to a square courtyard. There were glass-encased gas streetlamps resting atop wrought-iron fixtures attached to stone walls, and planters filled with greenery and flowers in bloom, purple and fuchsia and red. Most of the buildings were white, but some were pink or orange, a mix of pastels. The courtyard and streets were filling with people—elderly people walking hand in hand, young couples with strollers feeding ice cream to their children, lovers strolling with their arms encircling one another's waist. All around her was life and vivacity and vibrancy. But there was something more. There was an energy, a drive. It infused how people walked, how they conversed, how they ate their ice cream cones or other handheld treats, with joy and gusto. She passed bars and restaurants where people were singing, music was playing. Through another archway, she spotted a stone wall decorated with colorful posters of movies and celebrity appearances and museum exhibits in Rome, Venice, Florence.

It was mesmerizing, the energy, the laughter, the loudness. And this wasn't even tourist season, according to Emilia. These people were locals. But still, the town was crowded and exciting. And she somehow couldn't shake the feeling that she was in a place where people were trying to catch up. Mostly everyone here would have been born after the war, but perhaps they were still affected by it—the hunger, the deprivation, the fear, the occupation of their home by outsiders. The killing that had gone on in this very town. Perhaps it was in their DNA. There seemed to be an effort to live grandly and boldly and loudly, to live twice as loud to make up for those years of quiet and fear. She admired these people. She admired their drive to live well.

She walked back to the center of the courtyard, and then noticed a sign on a nearby wall adjacent to a set of stairs. The sign had an arrow pointing upward and the words *Piazza della Memoria*. She figured that was Memorial Square, where Oliver had suggested they meet.

She climbed up the staircase, which led to another cobblestone street, this one with restaurants and cafés on her right, all sporting gaslit streetlamps. To her left was a waist-high stone wall, beyond which was the sea. She walked over to look. She hadn't realized how high she'd climbed. But she was glad she had, because this was truly one of the most breathtaking views she'd ever seen. The sky was huge and vast and inky blue. The water formed a kind of cove, and she could see the white foam of soft waves.

It was amazing to be up this high, looking out on to this beautiful night. She felt as though she were seeing the whole universe from up here. No wonder people danced and sang and laughed all around here. There was so much to fall in love with.

She turned and saw some kind of memorial set into a wall, which no doubt was how the square had gotten its name. She walked closer. Lit by a single light underneath was a bronze etching of two women, one older and one younger. The older woman was holding a cauldron and the younger one had a large basket in each hand, her hair cascading in thick waves to her shoulders. Their skirts seemed to be blowing in the wind.

Callie looked down at the dedication, which also was lit from underneath.

Philippa Jorelini, 1888–1943
Corinna Jorelini, 1922–1943
Caccipulia Club Della Cena

She blinked in surprise as she recognized those Italian words. The Caccipulia Supper Club. The same words that were on the menu card she'd brought with her from home. The dates and last name seemed to suggest that the women were related, maybe mother and daughter. But it was the first name, Corinna, that most caught her attention. It was so close to Corinne, her grandmother's name. Could this statue be dedicated to her grandmother and her great-grandmother? The grandmother who was in a photo in the hotel lobby, embracing Emilia? It couldn't be, though. It had to be a coincidence. After all, her grandmother hadn't died in 1943.

No, she'd died almost six decades after that. Callie thought about her grandmother now. So tall and so beautiful, with her chin-length bob that had turned from blonde to gray over the years. And so kind and engaging, when she wasn't in one of her gloomy moods, as Nonno would call those times that she brought up Emilia's name. She'd been a teacher, like Pam. She'd loved it, and she'd been good at it, also like Pam. Callie remembered how parents of her grandmother's students would stop them in the supermarket or at the library, their smiles always proving how much they loved Nonna, how happy they were that she was their kids' teacher.

And she was the most remarkable cook. Even now, Callie remembered how delicious her grandmother's pasta would taste, how rich the sauce, sweet but not too sweet. Nonna hadn't had the patience to read or knit, and she hadn't particularly liked watching television. She was never as happy, never as at home, as when she was teaching a classroom of children or cooking in her kitchen.

Callie remembered sometimes sneaking down the hallway at school to peek into Nonna's kindergarten classroom, the one with the red cardboard heart with Nonna's name, Mrs. Sackes, affixed to the door. She always marveled at how mesmerized the children looked when Nonna was speaking. One time while Nonna was sitting in the front of the room reading from a picture book, a little boy started coughing. The kids were finishing their snack, and something had gone down the wrong pipe, as Nonno used to say. Nonna paused from her reading and caught the boy's eye. She looked at him with such encouragement and care that Callie could have sworn it was her expression that helped him catch his breath and clear his throat.

"Are you okay?" Nonna had asked gently, smiling and wrinkling her nose.

He nodded.

"Good," she said with a giggle and returned to the story. The other students all looked at her with such devotion. Callie was sure they would each happily swallow something down the wrong pipe if it would get them the attention she'd given to their classmate.

When Callie was twelve, her grandparents both died within a few months of each other. Nonno went first. A stroke. A few months later, Nonna was diagnosed with cancer, which progressed very quickly. She'd passed less than a year after Nonno. Pam had said that she died of a broken heart. That she couldn't bear to live in this world after her one true love was gone. He'd just—

"Pam? Pam!"

Callie looked up to see Oliver waving at her. She suddenly was jerked back to the present day, as she remembered that she'd introduced herself to him as Pam.

She was glad to see him. And yet, she couldn't help but think that lying wasn't the best way to begin a friendship.

FIFTEEN

OCTOBER 2019

Wednesday

"Yes, hi!" Callie waved and Oliver jogged over to her. They stood opposite one another awkwardly. The moment seemed to require some sort of physical encounter, but none seemed appropriate. A handshake was too businesslike, and yet a hug felt too personal. They barely knew each other.

Oliver recovered first. "Sorry I was a little late," he said. "The place was super busy because it's such a nice night. So warm for October. Everyone's grateful when the weather throws us a gift like this. It'll be cold before we know it."

"That's true," Callie said. "I've been enjoying walking around. I've never been anyplace like this before. I feel like I've gone back in time."

"I know, right? I love it here, too. And if you like this town, you're going to love where I'm taking you. This great place just down the street has some amazing local dishes."

He led her along the winding road, the stone wall on their left and more trees and shrubs appearing on their right. With fewer shops and cafés, the night felt darker now, lit only by strings of tiny glittering bulbs woven through olive trees along the way. There were fewer people here, as most of the activity was back at Memorial Square.

They stopped for a moment near the wall, the sea now a vast area of darkness dotted with glistening lights from islands in the distance. "I don't know how I'm going to get myself to leave when my sabbatical ends in December," Oliver said, his voice soft. "There's something so special about being here."

The breeze kicked up, and Callie gathered the collar of her jacket around her neck, imagining how wonderful it would be to stay here forever. At this moment, she didn't feel burdened by thoughts of Pam or her life or all her mistakes. "I would stay here longer if I could," she said. "It's like a hideaway. Removed from the world.

"Although I guess that's too simple, isn't it?" she admitted. "It's not removed from the world at all. I read about what happened during the war."

He nodded. "They rounded up all the Jews. And they killed those who helped hide them. To serve as a lesson to other towns."

"So hard to believe all that happened here," Callie said. "I mean, when you're standing right here, it doesn't seem possible."

"They killed or arrested the people, and damaged much of the town, too," Oliver said, leaning his forearms against the wall and looking out toward the sea. "But all that was damaged has been rebuilt. It's a very young town now. Which isn't a bad thing. I think that those who suffered would be happy to see so much life here again, as it was before. At least, I hope that's what they'd feel."

She looked at him. "Do you think Emilia feels that way? She seems pretty angry." She paused, thinking for a moment about the dinner party she'd witnessed, how warm and sociable Emilia had seemed among her guests.

"Well, I guess she's not angry all the time," she added. "Although she sounded pretty angry when she was talking to me. When I noticed that picture of her sisters in the lobby." She didn't mention the other photo she'd seen with her grandmother as a young woman. She wasn't yet ready to reveal to him that her grandmother and Emilia had apparently been close at one point. Close enough to embrace each other and pose for the camera. Before whatever happened to drive a wedge between them.

"As I told you, Emilia's had a hard life," he said.

She nodded. "I read a little about her. How she and her sisters spent the summer of 1943 with their uncle in some lavish castle. How her neighbors hid her when the Nazis were approaching, because she was half-Jewish."

"She left the neighbors' house before the Nazis arrived," Oliver said. "No one really knows how. Or where she went. But she came back about... maybe thirty years ago? And with a boat-load of money. She rebuilt this whole town, repaired the damage that remained, and paid for it herself. She turned her childhood home into the hotel you're staying at. The little bakery in the lobby—that's where her father ran a tailor busi-ness. The thing is, she never wanted to change the town in any way or take down any of the old buildings. All the stairways and arches—this is exactly how the town looked when the Nazis arrived. That's why you get this sense of going back in time."

"She wanted to recreate the town as she remembered it as a child," Callie said, thinking again of the restaurant.

"Seems that way," Oliver agreed. "But it's hard to know exactly what was in her mind. She never talks about the war or that time she spent in hiding."

Callie turned to look at the town, her back pressed against the stone wall. "I guess that's not unusual. My grandparents were Italian. My grandfather was Jewish, and somehow he and my grandmother were able to get to New York soon after the

Nazis invaded Rome. But they never talked about it. My grand-mother would get teary when there was even any mention of the past. The sense of secrecy they had—it was pretty intense, I remember. When we were young, my sister and I decided we'd come here one day and find out everything they were keeping from us."

"Your sister? Is she here, too?"

Callie caught her breath, remembering that she was supposed to be Pam. "No... um... she couldn't get away. I told her I'd find out everything, and... tell her when I got back."

"And they were from this town, your grandparents?"

Callie pressed her lips together. She didn't want to reveal that her grandmother was likely the person who had betrayed Emilia. "Well, we think they spent time here in Caccipulia. But I'm still trying to figure that out. Anyway, enough about me. How did you end up here? Do you have a family connection?"

He nodded, seeming perfectly happy to change the subject. He didn't appear to suspect any ulterior motives on her part at all. She admired how open he was, how trusting, and how easy to have a conversation with.

"My grandfather lived in this area when he was young," he said. "And boy, do I know a thing or two about secrets. Pop wasn't Jewish, but he lived on Parissi Island for a time—in that beautiful castle you read about, where Emilia and her sisters spent one summer. He was a musician and a fierce anti-Fascist. The Nazis would have killed him for sure if they'd found him.

"Come on," he said, pointing. "It's not too much further to the place I want to take you."

He led her beneath another archway, which opened up on to a wide restaurant patio. It sat in the middle of a square formed by several stone buildings, white and pink and sun-washed yellow. There were strings of twinkling lights overhead, and balconies along the sides of the buildings, many of which had ivy and orange frangipani blooms trailing from them. The tables were covered in floral tablecloths, and the wicker chairs had orange cushions that matched the flowers overhead. There were potted trees with tiny twinkling lights and tall, gaslit lanterns. Outdoor heaters were set among the tables, the flames dancing inside long glass tubes, and soft, jazzy music played in the background.

"Do you mind eating outdoors?" he said. "Maybe it's unusual for you, to eat outdoors this late in the fall. But here we eat out as often as we can."

"No, I love it," she said. She felt her cheeks glow from the warmth of the nearby flames.

A host approached them, and he and Oliver spoke to each other in Italian, which gave Callie a moment to look more closely at her new friend. She found him quite good-looking, with his large, dark eyes and those thick, dark curls. And that wide smile, that made his cheekbones rise and his eyes light up. There was a sweet, delicate quality about him, thanks to his thin lips, slender nose, pointed chin, and long eyelashes. But he looked solid, too. He was wearing tan pants and a vivid blue button-down shirt, and he had a firm physique, strong shoulders.

Still, it was the smile that really got to her, she thought as she watched him converse with the host. There was something so generous about it—it invited you to smile, too. And it suggested a calmness about him that she wanted to crawl inside. She thought that she could easily deal with anything going on in her life if she had someone around whose whole bearing offered that air of reassurance and rightness.

Oliver thanked the host and then extended his left arm, indicating that she could go ahead and he'd follow. They arrived at a small round table near the stone wall. The host pushed aside a planter, and suddenly they were overlooking the water. It felt like they were floating above the sea.

"This is so beautiful," she breathed.

The host handed them menus, and a few moments later, a server appeared for their drink order. Callie chose a local red wine, and Oliver suggested they get a bottle. But she told him that she feared if she had any more than one glass, she'd fall asleep right at the table. He laughed and ordered a glass for each of them.

"I was a little surprised to see you show up at the coffee bar tonight," Oliver said. "You've been awake, what? Thirty-six hours?"

She shrugged. "I don't feel tired. Actually, I never sleep well when I'm somewhere new. Even moving to Philadelphia, I had trouble sleeping. I think the best solution is just to get good and tired until I can't keep my eyes open anymore."

"Well, a delicious meal can help," he said. "And good wine. And a pretty setting. We have all three." He put his elbows on the table. "That's right, you said you live in Philadelphia. What do you do there?"

"I—" She stopped herself, suddenly remembering again that Oliver was under the impression that she was Pam. That seemed to be the reason Emilia was letting her stay there— because she liked the letter Pam had written. She didn't want to unravel her whole story right now. She didn't want to tell Oliver everything: how she'd moved to Philly, how she'd become estranged from her sister, how she'd discovered the jewelry box and Pam's planned trip only because Pam had died, and how she had called herself Pam just so she could meet Emilia. She didn't want to be that person, the one with all the drama, the one a new friend regrets having dinner with because the conversation is too intense. Oliver was a nice guy, and she hated deceiving him, but it seemed the best decision was to keep the fib going. She was leaving so soon. What did it matter?

"My sister's the one in Philadelphia," she said. "I'm in Connecticut. A small town called Little Bridge. About an hour's train ride from New York City."

"Oh. I thought you said it was you who lived in Philadelphia."

"Well... I did, but I came back. I'm hoping that my sister will move back, too."

"You don't like Philadelphia?"

"No, it's a great city. Lots of history. I just... I miss her. I don't quite know why she decided to move. It was kind of spur-of-the-moment. She didn't tell me..."

The waiter returned with the wine, which was a great relief. She was tying herself in knots, this crazy conversation.

"*Salute*," Oliver said as he clinked his glass with hers. They both took a sip, and she lowered her glass to the table.

"So what do you do in Little Bridge?" he asked.

"I'm a teacher," she said, continuing to be Pam. "Third grade."

"No kidding. And what got you interested in cooking?"

"Cooking?"

"Emilia's cooking classes. You must have made your reservation several months ago at least. She fills up pretty fast."

She paused. She had assumed Pam had booked the class just to get close to Emilia, but she didn't want to tell Oliver that.

"Although maybe you had special treatment because of the letter you wrote."

"Yes, the letter," she said. "I guess that helped..."

Again, the server saved her, this time to take their order. Oliver said something in Italian, and after the server responded, he nodded and looked at Callie. "We can get some antipasti, we can order a few pasta dishes, or maybe you'd like some meat or fish? What are you in the mood for?"

"Pasta would be good," she said. "For my first night in Italy."

"I think so, too," he said. "The specialty tonight is *spaghetti alla scoglio*, pasta with mixed seafood. Clams, mussels, squid. Or something simpler. What do you think about *cacio e pepe*—

that's pecorino Romano cheese and black peppercorns? It's a favorite in this part of Italy. A little spicy, if you're up for it."

"They both sound great," she said. "I wouldn't even know how to decide."

"Why don't we get both? And we can share? Unless you want to think about some other choices? I can translate more of the menu for you, if you'd like."

"No, this will be perfect," she said, appreciating his efforts to ensure she got what she wanted. It felt good to be included, even though she didn't know much about the regional cuisine.

Oliver exchanged a few more words with the server, and then turned back to her. "So how did you hear about Emilia's cooking school?"

Callie breathed in. It was going to be tricky, to tell him what she'd found without saying who she truly was. She started to think it was ridiculous to have lied in the first place. But telling the truth would mean revealing so much baggage. And she didn't have the courage to come clean right now. What if he got angry? What if he told Emilia what she said? What if Emilia kicked her out after all—when she had seen the picture of her grandmother on Emilia's desk and was now more driven to solve Pam's mystery than before?

But suddenly, she was aware of having a change of heart. Maybe it was the wine, the beautiful setting, the romantic sound of Italian, or simply Oliver's tender personality and irresistible smile. She wanted to reveal a little more. She trusted him. And maybe he could help her get to the bottom of her family's past. She thought she could reveal her grandmother's secret without necessarily admitting she wasn't Pam.

"Well, it's complicated," she said. "You see, I wrote to Emilia and got her response. I was excited about the cooking class. But mostly I wanted to come here because of my grandmother. Like I said, she didn't talk much about growing up in Italy, but she always talked about making a mistake, and being saved by someone. Someone she never got the chance to thank. We never knew what the mistake was or who the person was, but I do remember hearing her and my grandfather sometimes mention the name Emilia. And then I was going through some drawer... cleaning out a room, you know... and I came across some old things I didn't understand. There was a menu, like a recipe card, and a note written on the back in Italian. I think it may have been written by Emilia. And there also was mention of this town.

"Then things got even more complicated yesterday," she continued. "Because when I checked in, Emilia had some photos on the reception desk, and when I pointed them out, she said they were her sisters, and she was so angry at them. But there was another photo of Emilia with a young woman I'm sure was my grandmother. And Emilia... well, she seemed mad at her as well."

"A photo of Emilia with your grandmother? The one on the reception desk? With them hugging?"

Callie nodded. "Yes, that one. It's right next to the one with her sisters. They look like loving pictures, both of them, but Emilia told me she only keeps them there because guests like to see old pictures."

"But that picture—it's the one of the person who betrayed her. That's what Emilia has always said. If that's your grandmother, then she's the one Emilia has been angry at all these years." He looked like he thought he was imparting new information, but her expression must have told him she wasn't surprised. "Or did you know this already?"

"I didn't know anything—but what you're saying, it makes sense to me, too," she admitted. "And so this seems like the family secret our grandmother never wanted to talk about. The mistake she made. I think that whatever it is that my grandmother regretted, it had to do with Emilia. And whatever she did to make Emilia so angry—well, maybe she never wanted to return because she always felt so bad about it."

"And this is why you're here?" he asked. "More than the cooking class?"

She nodded and went on to tell him about the trip to California. "I mean, if this is the story that made her so sad and nervous her entire life, that made her cry when she thought about how old the trees were...

"And then, the strangest thing happened, just now," she added. "Maybe you can help me figure it out. My grandmother's name was Corinne. And when I went to the spot you mentioned, Memorial Square—one of the women mentioned on the memorial plaque was named Corinna..."

"Wait, you think your grandmother was Corinna Jorelini?" he asked, his eyes wide. "That would be something big. She's a hero around here. Emilia commissioned that memorial plaque, you know. Philippa and Corinna Jorelini helped feed all the Jews that were hiding here in town."

"Feeding the Jews?" Callie asked. "What does that mean?"

"I don't know all that much about it," Oliver said. "But evidently Corinna Jorelini and her mother ran a... a secret restaurant in their home. You see, there were many Jews who fled through this town when the Nazis invaded northern Italy. They'd stay here in town until they got the signal from the Resistance that it was safe to continue with their trip. And some families housed them and fed them when they arrived. Food was scarce then, and the local families would buy it on the black market and then pool whatever they could scrape together. And Corinna and Philippa would cook the food and help distribute it to the Jews who were fleeing."

"That sounds like my grandmother," Callie said. "She was an amazing cook. And a generous person. But she couldn't be the woman in the memorial. The plaque says she died in 1943, and my grandmother died decades later. Still, it's curious, isn't it? The photo of my grandmother on the desk. And the names being so similar. I know they can't be the same person. But still, I had this funny feeling when I saw the plaque. Like I was seeing something that felt familiar..."

She shook her head. "Maybe I'm thinking too much. Maybe it's not even my grandmother in that photo. Maybe I just want it to be. You see..."

She paused, frightened that the wine was loosening her tongue. But then she continued, sure that the train of thought was safe. "Sometimes in your life you want to learn more about who you are, you know? And I wanted to... I mean, I just thought this was a good time for me to see if I could find out more about who I am." She paused again. She was sure he had to be thinking she wasn't making sense. But then he surprised her.

"I know exactly what you mean," he told her.

Before she could ask him to explain, the server returned with the pasta, placing the seafood one in front of her and the cheese-and-pepper one in front of Oliver. The dishes smelled wonderful, a sweet blend of wine, tomatoes, and spices. And she loved how beautiful they each looked, how the colors and shapes created almost a work of art—the straw-colored pasta, the red cherry tomatoes and slices of pepper, the deep-green bits of parsley, the dark oblong mussels and light-shelled clams all arranged so precisely. Oliver put a portion of his dish onto one of the extra plates the waiter had left, and she did the same. They handed the plates to one another and both of them started to eat. Callie felt mesmerized by the taste of her seafood pasta.

"How is this so good?" she asked.

"The freshness of the ingredients, the spices—and also they do something very interesting here with the seafood dishes," Oliver said. "They use the seafood broth to boil the pasta. It gives it a very unusual taste, doesn't it? Extra flavor infused in the pasta, right? Just one of the little tricks you learn when you spend some time here."

At that moment, the music in the background changed. Callie recognized the melody—it was the same music she'd heard in the hotel. Haunting and hypnotic. Oliver sat back, fork in hand, and smiled at someone behind her. She turned to see the host giving him a thumbs-up.

Oliver shook his head and chuckled. "They do this all the time."

"Do what?"

"Do you hear that music?"

She nodded. "It's beautiful. It was playing at the hotel, too."

"My grandfather composed that," he said. "He was a brilliant composer. And he has a connection to Parissi Island. That's the story I mentioned before we sat down. He was there in the castle. When Emilia was there, actually. Unfortunately we didn't realize the connection until after he'd died. But he did know Emilia and her sisters."

"Really?" Callie asked.

"He composed this piece while he was there. Do you know the whole story about Parissi Castle? It was this unique place where artists and scientists and inventors went to do their work. It was owned by Emilia's uncle, Patricio Parissi, her mother's brother. And it was stormed by the Nazis and all but destroyed. Only a few people escaped."

"And your grandfather escaped?"

"Yes. He was one of the lucky ones. And Emilia escaped, too. She had been sent back days earlier to care for their sick father. But her sisters didn't survive. She was only a teenager when all this happened."

"Oh no," Callie said. "No wonder she's so hurt."

"So the rumor was that my grandfather was in love with her older sister," Oliver continued. "And that he composed this piece for her. He never talked about it directly, though. He was very secretive. You see, he had a good marriage to my grand-mother. He would never have hurt her by admitting that his first love was someone else. They had seven children. My father ended up in Baltimore, which is where I grew up."

They listened in silence to the melody.

"Everyone here knows who I am," Oliver said. "Everyone knows who my grandfather was. They play his music when I'm around. Not so well-known in America, but he's practically a household name in this part of Italy. He wrote an autobiogra-phy, too. But he never confirmed his love for Emilia's sister."

She looked at him. "So you do know exactly why I'm here," she said. "Is it crazy? We're both embracing ghosts. Sometimes I wonder if that's the best thing I could be doing right now. It's not like having the answers can change everything that happened before. So why are we doing it?"

"I don't think it's crazy at all," he told her. "I think it matters, knowing where we came from. Being surrounded by it, shaped by it. Even if the past can't be changed, the future can, don't you think? I can't help but believe that everything we do, everything we learn... well, it changes us a little. Hopefully for the better."

She nodded, grateful for what Oliver had just said. She hoped that being here would change her in a good way. So she could go home knowing what to do next. What would make her life more fulfilling than it had recently been.

"So you came here to find out more about your grandfa-ther?" she asked.

"Well, that and other things," he answered. "As I told you, I came here to study cooking with Emilia. I do have this plan to open a restaurant with some college buddies in Boston early next year."

"And what will happen to the coffee bar?" she asked. "Will you sell it?"

"Actually, I own it with my sister. She's lived here for

several years. Her husband is Italian—he's an anthropologist and teaches college classes remotely. They have a beautiful house up in the hills on the outskirts of town. They have three boys, and a little girl on the way. So it's a busy household."

"How nice, that you have your sister close," Callie said.

"It was a lifesaver," he said. "I came here after I'd broken up with someone. I wanted to settle down, and she—well, it's a long story. But that's another reason I came here—to get my head on straight after the break-up. It was so good to be with my sister and her family. I finally realized that Nina was never the right one for me."

Callie looked down at her plate. It struck her that when Oliver ended his relationship, he sought out family, while when she was in that position, she ran from family. What did that mean?

"Anyway, Emilia's classes are pretty amazing," he said. "People come from all over the world to take them. Sometimes she introduces them to local cheesemakers or fishmongers or vintners, and they talk about their craft. Everyone has a great time. I think you may have missed it, though. Tonight was the farewell dinner, I think."

"Oh, so that's what I saw," she said. "There was a big dinner going on in the dining room when I left. And they were all so happy and so engaged and talking and laughing as Emilia was serving. I would have sworn they'd all known each other forever, like they were old friends or something."

"Food does that. It brings people together."

They finished eating, and were soon on their way back to the town center, Oliver having insisted on paying the bill. They passed the train station and coffee bar, and Callie realized that he was walking her all the way back to the hotel. The moon was out, the sky was clear. It was a beautiful evening.

"So... so Emilia mentioned you have a daughter," he said as

they walked up the staircase to the hotel. "She said you wrote about it in your letter."

She nodded. "That's right. A little girl. Chloe. She's a little over a year old."

"And where is she now?"

"Back home. With her father." She paused. "My husband."

"Oh. And what does he do?"

"He's a lawyer."

"Very nice," he said.

They reached the hotel, and she stopped and looked at him. "Thank you for dinner," she said. "I hope I'll see you again before I leave."

"Sure," he said. "Stop by for coffee anytime."

He turned, and she watched him head back down the stairs to the cobblestone street, his figure a silhouette in the moonlight. Then she went inside. The lobby was quiet. She looked into the dining room. Most of the dishes had been cleared. She heard voices coming from the kitchen, water flowing, some laughter. The laughter of cleaning up, lovingly taking care of a home.

She listened to the sound, thinking of what Oliver had said, how food brings people together. She thought about the tradition of cooking and the role that it played in Emilia's life. She wished she could go into the kitchen and help out. But she didn't belong there.

So she went upstairs, thinking about Oliver. She'd been sorry to have to say she was married. She thought he'd looked disappointed when she said it. Still, she'd enjoyed their talk over dinner so much. She knew she would go back to the coffee bar to see him.

She only wished he knew who she really was.

SIXTEEN

OCTOBER, 1943

"I wanted to tell you myself," Corinna said to Emilia, as she entered the bedroom. "I know it must have been a big shock, what you saw just now in the garden behind the Possano house."

Emilia sat on her bed, her back against the wall and her arms wrapped around her bent knees. She wished she hadn't gone past the bushes behind the Possanos' house. She wished she hadn't thought the kitten was hurt. She should have left the basket on the table by the door, as she'd been told to do. It had all sounded so right when she left the house, basket in hand. There was a new Jewish boy in town to take care of. Signora Jorelini had made it clear that they needed to feed him and support him so he could leave safely when the time was right. Emilia had felt she was doing something good, delivering the basket with extra food for him.

All these weeks that she'd been part of the supper club, she'd felt a sense of purpose. It was important, being part of this household that was trying to help others. She knew it was precarious, but she believed that as long as she followed Signora Jorelini's rules, she would be safe. Feeding Jewish people as they made their way out of Italy felt right. It was something her father would want her to do, and a way of getting through this awful in-between time until her sisters came home and life could go on. And ultimately they'd get their home and their father's shop back.

She'd told herself that if she could stay put and do her work —write out the color-coded supper club cards each day and make the food deliveries each evening—she would be okay. With each day that passed, she was a day closer to when her sisters would arrive.

But now something huge had changed. Corinna was in love with the Jewish boy wanted by the Nazis. Corinna was sneaking off to be with him. How long could this go on? What would this lead to? Were they in more danger? After all, he was wanted by soldiers...

"Emilia, we need to talk," Corinna said. "Please look at me."

Emilia slowly lifted her head. Corinna had asked her to, and she always did what Corinna asked. She loved her. But she couldn't look at her now. She looked at the window instead. She didn't understand at all what she was feeling. Embarrassment? Anger? Fear? She wished Corinna would go away and leave her alone at this moment. All she knew was that love was dangerous. She'd seen her two older sisters fall in love at the castle—Annalisa with a handsome musician named Aldo; and Giulia, who had flirted so with the young boatman, Vincenzo, who delivered goods to the island. And now her sisters were missing. She assumed they were coming back for her, but she didn't know where they were or how much longer they would take.

Who knew what might have happened if they had not fallen for those boys? Maybe they'd have made wiser decisions. Maybe they'd be with her now. Or maybe the three of them would be on their way to America. She remembered how distracted Annalisa had been the closer she grew to Aldo, how being with him had seemed to become a bigger priority than getting Papa's medicine and bringing it home.

And yet that's what she'd seen today, once again. Two people in love. And she didn't want to have to seen it. The way Corinna and Tomas had held each other, their hands searching each other's hair, faces, arms. The way Corinna had lifted her chin and Tomas had pressed his lips to her neck and the curve that led to her shoulder. It had been both beautiful and terrifying, and Emilia had felt her face grow hot before she dropped the basket to the ground and ran away.

The last thing she'd seen was Corinna pull away from Tomas, evidently startled by the noise she made as she ran off. She hoped someone had found the basket of food on the ground and brought it to the house. She didn't want to have to explain to Signora Jorelini why the dinner hadn't been properly delivered.

Corinna sat on the bed. She pulled Emilia's arm gently, so her fingers around her legs unclasped. She held Emilia's hand between both of hers.

"I'm sorry I didn't tell you about him sooner," she said. "I hated keeping this secret from you. But when I left Rome, I didn't know when I'd see him again. And the thing is, Emilia—I love him. And he loves me, too. Our future is together. I'm sorry you were so surprised. But now you know. Now you're involved. And I need your help."

"But I don't want to help," Emilia said. "You can't be in love now. I watched my sisters fall in love and everything fell apart. And now they're missing, and I don't know how long it will be until they finally come back. We have work to do here, important work. The people who are fleeing need us. Being in love—it messes up everything."

"No, no, that's not true," Corinna said. "Love makes things better. The work we are doing, Tomas is a part of it. And he's Jewish. And he needs help, like the others do."

She went on to explain that she'd met him in Rome, through mutual friends. He was pursuing a degree in engineering at the university when he was forced to withdraw. He'd kept on studying with some other Jewish students and a few brave professors, but when the Nazis took over Rome, fewer and fewer teachers were willing to continue with them. The possibility of arrest was so high.

"He's so smart and so gentle, and so kind," Corinna said. "We spent one whole night sitting in the park near the school, just talking, just talking about the world we wanted to live in. He isn't like anyone I've ever met. He loves that I came to Rome to study, and that I want to be a teacher. He thinks I'm adventurous and brave. And beautiful." She blushed.

"Everyone thinks you're beautiful," Emilia said.

Corinna ignored her, lost in her memories. "And it broke my heart hearing his stories about his family. His mother and father and three younger brothers. He thinks they were probably sent to Poland. He's so scared of what may happen to them."

Emilia looked down. This she could relate to. She knew how it was to worry about family.

"And he has such dreams—of leaving Italy, of going to Switzerland, of being free," Corinna continued. "He believes that this will all end one day. He makes me hopeful. We both are sure that one day we'll live in a world that will be better, and we'll be better people for having lived through this. Oh, how can I make you understand, Emilia? You're only fifteen. But think about your father. Think of your parents, who loved each other and built a life together, even though your mother's family was against it..."

Emilia thought about her father, how gentle he was, how giving. How he never stopped loving her mother. Each year on the anniversary of her death, he'd tell her and her sisters the story of how he'd fallen in love with her while making clothes for her wealthy family. How he could never stop thinking about her. How she loved him so much, she was willing to walk away from her family, who never would accept her marriage to a lowly Jewish tailor. How their love was more important to them than anything.

"'I am my beloved's, my beloved is mine,'" Emilia murmured. It was the prayer her father would say each year on the anniversary of her death. The promise they'd made to each other, the sacred words he said they'd recited on their wedding day.

"Exactly," Corinna said. "'I am my beloved's, my beloved is mine.' That's all there is to say."

Emilia looked up. The memory of her father, and her father's love for her mother, never failed to move her. She was here in this world, waiting for her sisters, waiting for her future, because of that irrepressible love her parents had shared. Even after all those years without her, her papa never stopped loving her mother. How did you fight a feeling so strong?

"He started getting involved with the Resistance," Corinna said. "He could break codes so easily, his mind worked that way. They would show him messages from the Germans that they'd intercepted, and he was able to make sense of them. He would pass the messages to the fighters in the field who were orchestrating the attacks against the Nazis in Rome, which is how he became involved with the transfer of grenades. All we wanted to do was help keep the Nazi organization in disarray and fear, to buy time for the Allied forces to make their way north and finally win the war. I started to help, too. I delivered the messages. We were all so idealistic. We thought we could change everything."

"You could have been killed," Emilia said. "And your mother would have been so sad to lose you—"

"But I wasn't killed. It was a risk, but it was necessary. We were doing what's right. We were trying to make things better."

She looked down, letting go of Emilia's hand. "And then it happened," she said. "For so long his family—his parents, his brothers—had been living safely. The Germans demanded money at first, that's all, and his family contributed as much as they could. Lots of Jews were going into hiding, and his family was getting ready, too. There was a church that would hide them all. But the Nazis were after Tomas because of the intercepted messages. He just happened not to be home when they came.

"We'd both agreed we'd come here if things got bad," she said. "I'd told him about Caccipulia, how it's a beautiful little town with so much good. He sent word to me to leave. If he was in danger, then I was, too. That's why I left Rome."

The idea that Corinna had helped with the messages, and the Nazis could be after her, too, was too frightening to imagine. The thought of Nazis coming into Caccipulia, searching for Tomas, was unbearable. He had to go somewhere else. They had to search for him somewhere else. Every minute he was here was one minute too long. His being here put everyone in town at risk. Corinna. The Jews who were hiding. The people who were helping the Jews, like Signora Jorelini. *And maybe even me*, she thought.

"He has to leave," Emilia said. "He has to leave our town."

Corinna nodded. "You're right. He does. And he will leave. He's leaving for Switzerland as soon as he can. He just has to wait until he gets the go-ahead that it's safe. They'll be bringing him a new set of travel documents. He can't use his real name now."

"How long will that take?" Emilia asked, her voice trembling.

"I don't know. Hopefully not long. But the thing is, Emilia... when Tomas leaves for Switzerland, I'm going with him."

"What?" Emilia said. "No, you can't!" It struck her hard, the idea of being left behind again. The way her sisters had left her. Corinna was like a new sister. She couldn't lose another sister, not again.

"We plan to get married and build a good life together," Corinna said. "We both want a family, we both want to be surrounded by children, to grow old with each other, seeing our children grow up and start families of their own. And we will return, one day. We are young, Emilia. You and me and Tomas. We will make a better world. We will build a world that we can be proud of. It will happen."

Emilia got up and walked to the window to look in the direction of her home, the home that now housed others. She wanted to resist all that Corinna was saying. She wanted to beg Corinna not to leave her. But she saw the look in her eyes, the feelings she had when she said Tomas's name. And it touched her so deeply. She knew it was exactly what her father had seen when he looked into her mother's eyes. The odds had been stacked against Papa, too. Mama's family had wanted him gone. But Mama didn't care—that's what her father had said. They had a future together. And Emilia and her sisters were here because the two of them hadn't let anything stand in their way.

And maybe it wasn't love that had led her sisters to become separated from her, Emilia thought. Maybe it wasn't the connections they'd made. Maybe it was just this war, this awful war. Maybe love wasn't to blame. Maybe it was the solution. The cure to the sickness of the world. Maybe it was like the medicine her sisters had wanted to bring home to Papa. Maybe it was the antidote to everything that was bad.

"What is it you need me to do?" she asked Corinna.

"It's not safe for me to show up at the Possano house, as I did today," Corinna said. "We were lucky that it was only you who found us. There are people in this town who don't like what we're doing with the food, helping the Jewish people escape. They would hate knowing that we have Tomas here. They would be scared. And my mama would never let me see

Tomas, if she knew I loved him. She'd keep us apart. So we need to find ways to be with each other, secret places to make our plans. And you are a part of that."

"Me?"

"The supper club cards," she told her. "They are our ticket. You must put new codes that I will give you on the menu cards that go to the Possanos—drawings meant only for Tomas. They will tell him where I will be at midnight, so that he can come meet me. You have to be the one to make the drawings, and Mama has to see you do it, so she won't suspect that something unusual has happened. Just tell her you decided to decorate the cards with drawings. And it's just between you and me, okay? No one else can know anything about this."

Emilia took in all that Corinna had said. She could accept the idea of helping Corinna and Tomas be together. It reassured her, knowing they thought there was a better future ahead. She wanted to help people who loved one another as her parents had loved each other. *I am my beloved's, my beloved is mine.* If that was how Corinna and Tomas felt about each other, how could she stop them? Or fail to do anything she could to help them? She believed in love, too. She believed in love.

"Okay," she said. "I'll help. But promise me one thing."

"Yes?"

"Promise me you won't leave until you have to. Promise me to try to stay. And when you leave, promise me you'll tell me before you go. I couldn't bear it if I didn't get to say goodbye."

Corinna reached out and hugged her. "Don't worry," she said. "You will know."

That night, Emilia wrote a quick letter to her sisters.

I have a secret. I will tell you about it when I see you. When we leave this horrible world behind, I will tell you everything.

The next day as Signora Jorelini was doling out the

evening's meals, Emilia came into the kitchen and began writing out the supper club cards. When Signora Jorelini glanced her way, she began to sketch the "code" Corinna had given her that morning. She drew a stone fountain in the middle of a pool of water surrounded by stones. Tomas was good at breaking codes, Corinna had said. He'd quickly figure out that she'd be waiting at midnight at the fountain in the town square.

Emilia held up the supper club card for Signora Jorelini. "Do you like it?" she asked. "I thought it would be nice to add a decoration."

"Very pretty," Signora Jorelini said and went back to packing up the food. Corinna had been right. Signora Jorelini barely took note of the illustrations.

That night, Emilia heard Corinna get up and steal out of the house. Emilia waited, forcing herself to stay awake. After a half hour, when Corinna didn't come back, Emilia knew the code had worked.

She would find out tomorrow what code Corinna needed her to write next.

SEVENTEEN
OCTOBER 2019

Thursday

Callie came downstairs the next morning to find a crowd of
people in the lobby, all with suitcases and overnight bags. The
people were speaking a range of languages, and were hugging
each other and tapping on their phones. She thought she recognized some of them from the dinner last night. There was also a
middle-aged woman with a floral apron and sneakers walking
around with a clipboard. Callie remembered how Oliver had
said that the class Pam had enrolled in was finishing up last
night. She assumed that these were the students, all getting
ready to leave.

The woman saw her and came over. "Signora Crain?" she
said. "*Sono* Renata. I am Emilia's assistant. I'm sorry, my
English is not good. *Vorresti la colazione?* Breakfast? In the
dining room, please help yourself. I will be in soon when I have
everyone organized here. I can make you an espresso when I'm
finished here. Or we have filter coffee in the urn..."

"I'll pour myself coffee from the urn, that's fine. People
from the class are checking out?"

Renata nodded. "Yes, I am trying to help everyone make it back to the station to catch the right train."

"Where is Emilia?" Callie asked.

"Upstairs. Emilia doesn't like goodbyes." Renata turned to another guest who was waving in her direction. "*Si, mi despacio.* Let me check the schedule for you again..."

Callie went to the dining room. There was a beautiful display of meats, cheeses, and grapes on the dining room table, with a single lily in a vase as the centerpiece. Callie went to the breakfront and poured some coffee into a cup from a silver urn, then brought it to a small, heated sunroom just beyond the dining room. She put her cup there, then went back and filled a plate with cheese, bread, and grapes. Everything smelled delicious. She sat down and put some butter on her bread. She knew she couldn't keep eating like this, the way she'd eaten last night and now this morning. The food was so rich, and she didn't want to come back ten pounds heavier. Still, it was a pleasure to eat food so beautifully presented and prepared.

Emilia doesn't like goodbyes. She heard Renata's words echo in her ears. She was the same way. "Why can't you just come here before you move, if you really are determined to move?" Pam had said.

"I can't," Callie had answered. "I don't like goodbyes."

She thought back on that moment now. What was it about Emilia and her? Why did she feel this connection to this ninety-one-year-old woman she'd just met? Why did she want so badly for Emilia to like her, to trust her, to talk to her? She couldn't explain it now, just as she couldn't explain it last night to Oliver. But she knew that Emilia was unhappy beneath her toughness. And she wanted to get to the root of that unhappiness. Because for some inexplicable reason, she thought maybe she could get to the root of her own as well. She'd cut off her sister, although she'd never phrased it like that before. She'd cut Pam off when she moved, because she didn't want to see Pam until she felt good about herself. And yet in Philadelphia, she'd been lonely, a very deep kind of lonely, a loneliness that Emilia seemed to feel as well. Callie felt there might be a way through that if she and Emilia connected.

And of course, she wanted to know what her grandmother had done to make Emilia so mad.

She took a sip of coffee and a bite of the cheese. She didn't know what she was going to do today. She supposed she could go to town and shop for souvenirs for Joe and the baby, for when she finally told Joe what she'd found in Pam's drawer. She supposed she could bring home some packaged foods or coffees or a toy for Chloe. At least that would give her something productive to do if she didn't get a chance to see Emilia today.

A few moments later, though, she heard footsteps on the stairs, and then Emilia appeared in the doorway of the dining room. Renata approached her, and they spoke in Italian. The guests seemed to have all left, and Callie felt so strange, being the only one still checked into the hotel. As though she were trespassing. And she had the feeling Emilia thought of her that way. But she wasn't going to leave yet.

Emilia came into the sunroom. "*Buon giorno*," she said. She sounded tough, but once again Callie could see that vulnerability. As if she wanted to connect, too, but didn't know how.

"You want to cook with me?" she said.

"What?" Callie said.

"Cook! Learn to cook," Emilia repeated.

Callie nodded. "It's... why I came."

"You missed the class. You came late. I only give a few classes these days."

"I know. I messed up. I had some problems at home, and I was delayed. I'm very sorry." She paused. "I really wanted to meet you."

"I will cook something with you today," she said. "I have a

dinner guest. I will teach you if you want to help me. It's up to you. But we start now."

"Now?" she asked.

Emilia nodded.

Callie thought for a moment. It was so sudden, and she had barely touched her breakfast. But...

"Okay," she said, standing. She picked up her breakfast dishes. "Okay, now."

"Into the kitchen," Emilia said and led the way. Callie followed behind.

They went through the swinging doors. The kitchen was old and reminded her of the kitchen in her childhood house before Joe's mother remodeled it as a wedding present for Joe and Pam. The stove was large and squat, and the bulky refrigerator had rounded corners and horizontal, latch-type handles. There was no dishwasher. The floor and countertops were linoleum.

On the window were café curtains with yellow sunflowers. They were just like the curtains her grandmother had put on the windows back when she was young. Nonna would wash them every week and iron them tenderly. Callie pushed those thoughts from her mind, as Emilia handed her an apron off a hook on the wall, a white cloth covered in pink roses with bright-green leaves. Callie put her breakfast dishes into the sink and tied the apron around her waist.

Emilia moved to the countertop and began working with precision, lining up ingredients on the table: a large bowl of eggs, a canister of flour, a smaller bowl of lemons, a pitcher of cream, a plate of what looked to be breadcrumbs, a carafe of oil, a ceramic bowl covered with a dishtowel—Callie didn't know what it was covering—and glass cups of what looked like salt and spices. Emilia bent down to open a cabinet and pulled out a cast-iron Dutch oven and three sauté pans of different sizes and put them on the top of the stove. She went to the refrigerator and took out a pitcher with some clear liquid, which she poured into the pot. She adjusted the flame under the pot and then turned to Callie.

"We are making *coda alla vaccinara*," she said. "Do you know what that is?"

Callie shook her head.

"Braised oxtail stew."

Callie caught her breath. It didn't sound like anything she'd like to eat. Which probably didn't matter, because she hadn't been invited for dinner. It also didn't sound like anything she'd like to prepare. But that didn't matter either.

"Sounds delicious," she forced herself to say.

"And *pasta al limone*," she added. "Pasta with lemon."

Callie smiled. That sounded better.

"You can begin with the pasta," Emilia said. "Here, you work at the table. Measure about six cups of flour into the large bowl. Then make a *cratere*... what do you call it? A dip, a hole... a well, that's the word, right?"

Callie nodded.

"Yes, you make a well in the middle. Then you will crack an egg, the whole thing into the well..." She turned and looked at Callie. "What is it? What upsets you?"

Callie shook her head. She hadn't even realized that she was appearing a little emotional. "No, nothing, nothing. It's just... this reminds me of the kitchen in my house when I was little. This whole place looks just like it. It's so funny. The style of table, the chairs, the place mats you have... even the curtains on the windows. It was my grandmother's kitchen. She loved yellow. She loved sunflowers."

"Your grandmother was a cook?"

"Not professional. But yes... she was a wonderful cook. She loved it. I think cooking reminded her of when she was young. She was Italian, you know. She left Italy with my grandfather when she was maybe twenty, twenty-one. She took care of us, my sister and me, when we were little. I miss them so much."

"You had no parents?" Emilia asked.

Callie shook her head. "They died when I was very young. My grandparents moved into the house to take care of us."

"Here. Sit," Emilia said. Callie was surprised at how tender she was, how gentle, as she put her arm around Callie's waist and led her to a chair. "I lost my parents when I was very young, too," she said. "My mother when I was a baby. My father when I was a girl. Fifteen years old only."

"I'm sorry," Callie said. "Who took care of you?" She knew she was taking a risk asking Emilia such forward questions. She didn't want to push her. And yet she could feel Emilia was ready to open up a little. It was just as Oliver had said, that people loved Emilia when they got to know her. Callie was certainly leaning in that direction. Still, she wondered why Emilia was softening toward her. Was it because she also felt the kinship that Callie felt? That they were both alike, having lost parents, having lost so much so young?

"A woman who lived in our town," Emilia answered. "She was very kind. It was dangerous, you know. Because it was during the war. And my father was Jewish. It could have been very dangerous for her, having the daughter of a Jew in her home. But she was brave.

"So, your grandparents were from Italy," she said, changing the subject so abruptly that it took a moment for Callie to catch up. "Where in Italy?"

Callie hesitated, not sure if she was ready to admit who her grandmother was. "Well... I know they lived in this area for a time. And I know they also lived in Rome. That's where they met. My grandmother was a student there for a short time during the war."

"And who took care of you when your grandparents died?"

Callie paused again, this time remembering that she was

pretending to be Pam. "I was twenty-two then. It was my sister, my little sister, who was young. Only twelve. I raised her at that point. I was like a parent."

"Until you were... how old?"

"I never left. She left. For college, when she was eighteen. And she never lived at home again after that."

"And you never left for college?"

"No, I stayed home for college. I went part-time. So I could take care of her."

"You were a good sister," Emilia said. "You stayed because she needed you. You gave up much to be her parent all that time, didn't you?"

"Well, yes, I suppose," Callie said. She'd never really thought about what Pam might have given up to take care of her. She always thought Pam was living exactly the life she wanted.

"And now you have a daughter? You live in the town where you grew up?"

"Um..." Callie paused, thrown by the mention of Chloe. It was so strange, to pretend to be a mother. "Yes, I do live in the same town. In the same house, actually."

"That is nice. I live in my childhood house, too, you know," she said, pointing toward the floor.

"Oh?" Callie tried to sound surprised. She didn't want Emilia to know she and Oliver had been talking about her last night, that he'd explained how Emilia had returned home years ago and rebuilt the whole town. She didn't know if Emilia would appreciate that.

"Yes. I made it into a hotel. The small bakery in the front? My father was a tailor, that's where he did most of his work. It is nice, that your baby will grow up where you did. You will share memories of good food and love. That is a nice thing you are doing for her, your baby. She will appreciate it one day. You are a giving person."

"I... I try to be."

"And your younger sister? Is she a giving person?"

"Yes," Callie said. "Well, she tries to be."

"She lives in the same town too?"

Callie breathed in. Her only choice was to keep pretending. "No, she lives in Philadelphia. Do you know it? It's not too far. About a two-hour drive from New York."

"What is her name, your sister?"

"Callie. It's Callie."

"She didn't like your town?"

"She..." She paused. It was so strange, to be talking about herself as though she were someone else. "Callie's not the type to stay in one place," she said. "She likes to meet new people, go to new places. She was living in New York City, and then she quit her job and moved to Philadelphia."

"Maybe she is running away from something," Emilia said. "I was like that, too. Wanting to put my young life behind me after I'd left. So much heartache, so much pain. I lived all over Europe. London, Vienna, Marseilles for a time, Geneva, Amsterdam. I never wanted to stay put. Until one day I realized that running, it doesn't..."

She tapped her temple with her fingertips. "It doesn't free you from what is inside you. That's why I came back. It was better to be here, to stay here, than to always be running away."

Callie breathed in. "Well, I think Callie... she does have things that she wants to escape from. But she also... she's trying to straighten herself out. She loves to travel. She didn't want to stay put in one place all her life. Some people, you know... some people are like that. There's nothing wrong with it. We're all different."

"No, of course nothing wrong," Emilia said. "As long as she knows who she is. And understands that she doesn't have to reject her home to find somewhere else that touches... here." She tapped her chest.

"People who don't know what home is," she added. "They spend their lives searching and never get where they want to go. Ahhh, anyway, time to start. Make the dip, the hole," she said. "And crack three eggs into it."

Callie did as she was told, and Emilia picked up a fork. "You stir the eggs with one hand and push the flour in with the other, see?" she said, demonstrating. "Now, you." Callie did as Emilia had shown her, moving the flour into the eggs with the fingers of one hand as she used the fork in her other hand to keep beating. She'd never touched a raw egg before, at least not intentionally.

"Push," Emilia commanded. "Push it. Pasta isn't a timid dish. It demands a firm hand. Now you let go of the fork and keep pushing."

Callie nodded, jerked her hair away from her face, and dug into the well with both hands. She felt the ingredients start to combine to create dough. It was actually kind of pleasing. She pushed and pulled, enjoying the way the dough seemed to spring back against her hands.

"You knead until it feels smooth and not sticky," Emilia said. "Then roll it into a ball, and we leave it to rest."

Callie loved following Emilia's directions. She loved the expression on Emilia's face, the soft smile that lit up her eyes, the approving nod. That's what Oliver had said, that Emilia had a way of speaking that made you want to go along with her. She was direct and firm, but not nasty or bossy. Callie felt safe, following Emilia's instructions. She loved her confidence and her certainty, clearly obtained from years of experience and expertise. She couldn't help wishing she could have the same effect on someone someday. How did it feel to be so sure that what you had your hands on was exactly right? What was it like to make people feel confident just by being in your presence?

Callie continued on a few more moments, pressing her fingers into the dough, applying lots of pressure and being firm, as Emilia had told her to do. Then she looked up. Emilia was watching her, an expression on her wrinkled face that was somewhere between gentle and bemused.

"What?" Callie said. "Am I doing something wrong?"

"No, no, nothing wrong," Emilia said. "It's just... you make me remember learning to cook."

"You mean there was a time when you were as much of a beginner as I am?"

"Of course," she said. "Everyone starts off as a beginner. I was much younger than you. A child, really. But it was right here."

"Here? In this kitchen?"

Emilia shook her head. "No, not exactly. It was a house down the street. The home of the woman who took me in when my father died and my sisters abandoned me."

"They abandoned..." Callie started, then stopped herself. She didn't want to further invade Emilia's privacy, and she was scared that if she pushed her at all, Emilia might shut down. She seemed that volatile. And yet Callie also admired that she was so curt, so direct about her sisters. That she saw things so clearly, so black and white. If someone were to ask Callie to describe her relationship with Pam, she feared she could talk for hours and still not truly give a clear impression.

"That woman—she was so generous," Emilia said. "She taught me to cook. We cooked for other families. Oh, there were so many shortages then. But she made delicious food from nothing. She would go out every morning and barter and trade, sometimes to buy goods. What they call the black market. She sold her own jewelry, Signora Jorelini. What a generous woman."

"Signora Jorelini?" Callie said. She recognized the name from last night. "Wait, didn't I see a memorial to her? In that square, Memorial Square? Wasn't she—"

"What are you stopping for?" Emilia scolded. "Keep kneading!"

"I'm sorry," Callie said and started kneading again.

"It's the worst thing you can do, leaving someone you love behind," Emilia said, evidently back to talking about her sisters. "Someone who loves you. You remember that, you hear me? You never leave your little sister in the cold. You make sure that you do what she needs. That you are there for her. That's how you show you love her."

Callie nodded, keeping her head down. She couldn't help but relate to Emilia again. Because of how often she'd been left behind. By her parents, her grandparents, and Pam. It wasn't their fault that they'd died. But it felt like being abandoned. She wondered now about Emilia. Had her sisters actually abandoned her? Or was it just that they'd died? And did she blame them for that?

"I will," she said. "I'm always there for Callie. And I know she'll always be there for me.

"As much as she can, anyway," she added softly.

When Callie had formed the dough into a ball, Emilia nodded approvingly and picked it up. She put it into a deep bowl and covered it with the lid of a pot. "Come here," Emilia said and motioned Callie over to the other side of the table. She handed her a fat, oval lemon and a little metal tool with a line of small circles at the tip. "Here," she said and scraped the outside of the lemon. Small curlicues of peel rained down onto a cutting board.

"You try," she said. Callie took the tool and began scraping the lemon. The peel was thick as a callus, but the curlicues were delicate, like thin stalks of a flower or ribbon when you run the blade of a pair of scissors along it. The smell was wonderful, tangy and sweet at the same time. When she'd finished, Emilia motioned her over to the stove.

"Now we start the stew," she said. From the countertop, she

untied the string of a package wrapped in brown paper. Inside were round chunks of meat. Emboldened by her work so far, Callie picked up one chunk and examined it. Each chunk had a round piece of bone in the center and slim white strips of something—muscle? cartilage?—emanating outward, like spokes of a wheel. Emilia sprinkled a generous amount of salt on the chunks and then doused them in ground pepper. She poured olive oil from a decanter into a cast-iron pot on the stove, and when the oil had heated, she arranged the chunks inside. Soon they began to sizzle, the sound almost tuneful.

Callie watched the chunks brown, as Emilia rotated them with a pair of tongs. The smell was rich and earthy.

"So, tell me more," Emilia said.

"About my sister?" Callie asked. "Let me think. Oh, I know —the bakery in the front of the lobby—Pasticceria Sancino? Where your father had his tailor shop? It reminds me so much of my childhood. There was a snowstorm in our town one year, almost two feet of snow. There was a power outage on our block, and cars couldn't get through at all. My sister, Callie—she was only six. And we walked together, my sister and I, we walked in the snow all the way into town. We stopped at this wonderful Italian bakery, and we bought pignoli cookies and cannolis and custard-filled donuts. My grandmother loved that bakery, too. She said her mother would make desserts like that when she was little, but they didn't have enough flour and sugar for such treats during the war. Anyway, that was my favorite memory with my sister, when we came home with all those goodies and sat on the rug and covered ourselves with blankets, and split them up and tried everything.

"There was... a lot of sadness that came the next day," she added. "I often wish that night never had to end."

"You are lucky, for the good memories," Emilia said, as she began to remove the browned meat and put it on a plate. "And you are close, still? Even though she moved away?"

Callie hesitated. It was getting harder to talk about Pam. "Not so much lately, I'm afraid..."

Emilia put the tongs down and looked at her. "Don't you get so involved with your own life that you forget your little sister. Be the sister still who walked with her to that bakery. Do you understand?"

Emilia seemed to be accusing her of something. Something that pained her, something she couldn't let go of.

Callie looked directly at the woman. "Emilia," she said. "I don't know what happened to you and your family. But your sisters, in that picture on the desk in the lobby, all dressed up..."

"That was the summer we went to Parissi Island—"

"They look like they love you. And you love them. And the other picture," she added, thinking of the one with her grandmother. "You and she have your arms wrapped around each other, like you love each other, too—"

Emilia walked back to the table and began chopping the celery stalks. "That's it, the lesson is over," she said. "Enough cooking. You must go."

"But... I wanted to help. I'm sorry if I said something wrong—"

"We are done here," she said. "I will finish myself."

"Can't I even help clean up?"

"No. You must go. I need to work quickly. Supper club is tonight."

Callie remembered the menu card upstairs. "Supper club?"

"People will be waiting. That's all."

Callie watched her for a moment, her attention laser-focused on her chopping. Slowly, Callie removed her apron, draped it over a chair, and walked out of the kitchen—the room she had considered so warm, so welcoming, just a few minutes ago.

She walked through the dining room, where Renata was

putting the breakfast leftovers onto a tray. "You are finished cooking already?" Renata asked.

"No, she's still there working on it," Callie said. She was too embarrassed to say that she'd been kicked out. "She's making a lot of food. Is there another dinner party?"

"Dinner party? No, no," Renata said, chuckling. "Other than students, Emilia never feeds guests here. No, she cooks three times a week for the church in Terrasina. They give it to people in their area who need a meal. She calls it her supper club. And the sweets in the bakery"—she gestured toward the little shop in the lobby—"those go to the church, too, for the children."

"So nobody buys anything from the bakery?"

Renata shook her head. "Emilia doesn't sell what she makes. She prefers to give it away to people."

She carried the tray of breakfast leftovers into the kitchen, leaving Callie to contemplate this news. Callie couldn't help but wonder whether all of Emilia's efforts—the rebuilding of the town, the memorial to the Jorelini mother and daughter, the cooking school and now the meals and treats for the church—were some kind of attempt to make up for something. To be forgiven.

She wished she could know what Emilia felt guilty for.

But now that Emilia was mad at her, there seemed even less chance that she'd be able to find out.

EIGHTEEN

OCTOBER 1943

Within a few days, Emilia found it routine to add pictures to the supper club cards, so Tomas would know where to meet Corinna. It was just another task as she worked with Signora Jorelini to keep feeding the Jewish people making their way out of Italy. But food was getting scarcer. Often there was no meat at all when Signora Jorelini arrived home after venturing out in the early morning hours, the sky still dark as fall unfolded and the days grew shorter. Sometimes the vegetables Signora Jorelini brought home were all but inedible, the carrots and potatoes black with decay or the rice rancid. Emilia did her best to cut away the bad spots from the vegetables, and Signora Jorelini made soups or stews with what remained.

Still, she went out in the mornings and returned with as much as she could. Her stews and soups were thinner, less flavorful, and most of the time without any meat at all. But she never stopped cooking.

"I know it sounds strange... but I do feel lucky," she said one afternoon to Emilia and Corinna as she examined a head of cabbage. Emilia knew she was trying to decide whether there were enough edible spots to make it worthwhile to use. "We are still together, making food, and we are safe, the three of us. I pray every night that nothing more will change. That all will remain the same until this war is finally over."

Emilia had nodded as Signora Jorelini handed her the cabbage, gesturing that she should go ahead and start chopping. She kept her head down, hoping no one would notice the flush she felt rising up her neck and to her cheeks, or would just think she was reacting to the heat of the stove. Corinna stayed silent, too, her eyes focused on washing the utensils and soiled plates. She and Corinna both knew that things were not the same. The town was changing right beneath Signora Jorelini's nose, thanks to the daughter she loved. Corinna had brought Tomas to Caccipulia, and with it had come a new level of danger. Now it wasn't so simple to deliver food. As she went out every night to make deliveries, Emilia was terrified that this would be the night the Nazis would arrive, looking for Tomas. And maybe looking for other Jews, too. Jews being sheltered in houses around town or any Jew they happened to find—even Jews like her, with only one Jewish parent. Or maybe they'd be looking for people like Corinna, who had helped Tomas in Rome or were helping him now. Or other people—the ones hiding the Jews in town, the ones delivering food, the ones guiding them to the next safe location. Wonderful, brave people like Signora Jorelini.

And what made her fears even harder to bear was that she couldn't tell Signora Jorelini what was frightening her. Because she'd have to describe what Corinna had told her about Tomas, the level of his Resistance work. And she knew it would all come spilling out, how Corinna was in love with Tomas. And she'd sworn to Corinna she wouldn't tell.

Corinna had changed everything by urging Tomas to flee to Caccipulia, shaken things up like an earthquake deep beneath the ground. It was calm now, but the effects could soon be enormous.

Emilia hated being so secretive when Signora Jorelini was so good to her. But Corinna and Tomas's love for one another was an irresistible force. It was the only thing that made sense to Emilia, in this town where she'd lost her father and been abandoned by her sisters in just a few short weeks. What else was there to feel good about? Everything else was so awful. People fleeing their homes just because they were Jewish; her father being forced to sell his home and his shop; Signora Jorelini selling her keepsakes to get food... it was so wrong and so confusing. But this all-consuming love between two beautiful people—it alone made sense. And without it, Emilia didn't know how she could possibly believe that anything would ever be right again.

She knew Corinna would always love Tomas. It didn't matter that he was Jewish and she was not. Just like it hadn't mattered to her own parents, Papa and her beautiful Mama, whom she didn't even remember. But she knew how much they loved each other. How Papa had missed Mama every waking moment of the rest of his life, once he'd lost her. And now, the two of them, together, Corinna and Tomas, were Emilia's beacon, her touchstone, her way of being sure there was some good in the world after all. As long as they were together, there was hope.

So she drew the coded pictures that Corinna whispered to her each afternoon as she crafted Tomas's menu card, supporting Corinna's conviction that changing up the place where she and Tomas would meet was the only way to keep them safe and their secret hidden: a bunch of black olives, to indicate the olive grove alongside the Possano house; a gray, oval stone atop a field of green, if they were to meet by the boulder at the rear gate to the park; a whimsical array of books, to suggest the trees behind the library; a steeple, if they were to meet by the church. The pictures should look like idle doodles, Corinna had instructed, so that no one in the Possano house would pay them much mind except Tomas—the one person who'd be scouring the cards for their hidden message.

Tomas understood the codes, Emilia learned. Because he was always where he was meant to be.

Sometimes at night, Emilia would stay awake, keeping her eyes closed so Corinna wouldn't know. And a few minutes after Corinna left the bedroom, Emilia would follow her, closing the bedroom door softly and tiptoeing past Signora Jorelini's bedroom, the loud, rhythmic snores assuring Emilia that she was fast asleep. Downstairs, she'd throw on a coat and her shoes and steal across the front yard and down the street, knowing exactly where Corinna and Tomas would be. The fall was chilly but the moon was often bright, the sky clear and the darkness glowing, the night not nearly as dark as it could be. She'd find where the two lovers were and, hiding behind a tree or among thick shrubbery, she'd watch.

Because she couldn't turn away. There was something so entrancing about that moment when Tomas would open his arms and Corinna would run into them, and he'd lift her and twirl her around and around, her head thrown back and the bottom of her coat floating behind her. Sometimes Emilia would imagine that she was Corinna, being spun around by this lovely man who only had eyes for her. She'd watch the two of them sit on a rock or a bench, or on the grass with their backs against a tall tree, and they'd clasp their hands together on Corinna's lap, each one grasping and stroking and rubbing the other's fingers. Sometimes Emilia was close enough to see Corinna's eyes glistening, before Tomas reached out to sweep away a tear that had fallen to the top of her cheekbone.

Often, their conversation would be teasing. Like when they talked one night about the evening they met, and Emilia crept behind a nearby tree, close enough to hear their every word.

"Those chocolates you brought to the party—that clinched it for me," Tomas said. "I wanted to eat those chocolates every night for the rest of my life. I said to myself, this is the girl for me, a girl who can make something so heavenly."

She pushed him playfully with her shoulder. "That's the only reason?"

"They were delicious only because you made them. Your touch added the magic."

"I see," she said, kissing his fingers.

"And I couldn't believe when you agreed to dance with me," he added. "You could have had any boy in the room. They were all looking at you. The most beautiful girl by far."

"You know that's not true."

"Oh, yes. It is."

"And then you tripped when you went down the steps. I felt so bad for you."

"I couldn't stop looking at you. So I lost my footing."

"I was scared you were hurt. That scrape by your eye."

"I was glad it happened. It brought you over."

"I felt terrible after that, telling Antonio I wasn't leaving when he wanted to. So terrible to be stood up by your date at a party."

"*I* felt bad. Stealing his girl."

"He could see what was going on. He told me later he knew he'd lost me the minute you walked in."

"He saw the way I was looking at you?"

"And the way I was looking at you."

Emilia listened to their banter, their shared retelling of that evening. Nobody else these days reminisced about anything. There was no time. You had to always be on guard, glad at the end of each day that you could still lay your head on your pillows. Each night, Emilia knew, everyone in town slept with one eye open, one ear alert for the sound of a car engine, the slamming of car doors, the bark of German commands. Everyone had heard the stories, even Emilia. She'd overheard Signora Jorelini speaking with the neighbors, or she was told

things when she delivered the baskets, terrifying things. Someone's cousin in Rome had been arrested. Someone's friend had
disappeared. Whole families, Jewish families, were disappear-
ing, leaving their homes empty.

And sometimes Emilia would see Signora Jorelini look at
her with fear in her eyes. Emilia wondered if Signora Jorelini
would ever turn her out because of her Jewish father. If she'd
ever say it was too dangerous for her to stay, that she couldn't
risk it anymore. Then what would she do? Many of the neighbors knew Emilia was there. Would they keep her presence a
secret? Or would the promise of food or money cause them to
reveal that Emilia was there, right in Signora Jorelini's house,
right in that upstairs bedroom, helping other Jews escape the
country?

One day, Signora Jorelini took Emilia to the attic and led
her to a closet that was concealed by an old wardrobe. She
showed her a little bed she'd prepared on the ground, an old
wooden palette covered in sheets and blankets.

"Just in case," she said. "Just in case there comes a time
when you need to, when it's too dangerous... you know what I
mean, don't you? This is what all the Jews who are left in town
are doing. If you hear those cars, that language, you know where
to go—don't wait for me to tell you..."

But being here in the woods or the park, listening to
Corinna and Tomas talk about their memories, she could almost
imagine that life was different. That life was the way it was at
the castle when she was there with her sisters, that life was like
that around the world, all over the universe. Safety and calm
seemed to abound in the nature surrounding her, the sweet
beauty of the treetops against that glowing midnight-blue sky.
Corinna and Tomas's laughter, their melodic voices, swept her
back to the magical moment they first fell in love. They rose and
strolled to a tree, and as Emilia had ducked deeper into the
shadows, she saw Corinna press herself against the tree trunk

and Tomas move toward her. He ran his fingers through her hair, as she raised her chin and moved her lips toward his.

And sometimes their conversation was serious. One night when Emilia arrived at the courtyard behind the olive trees, the meeting spot she'd woven into that day's menu card, she'd found the two of them sitting on a curved marble bench on the stone patio. Tomas had his hands clasped between his knees, his chin down, and Corinna was seated beside him, one of her hands in his and the other stroking the back of his neck.

"Why did I run? Why did I leave them?" he said.

"You didn't have a choice," Corinna said.

"I left them alone. I left them there."

"It was you who were in danger. It was you the Nazis wanted. That's why you left, to protect them."

"But now they are missing..."

"Maybe just hiding..."

"My family. My family..."

He'd dropped his head lower and she'd pressed herself against him, their shoulders touching, stroking his neck. At one point he leaned his head on her shoulder and she kissed his forehead, his temple. "We'll all be together one day," she promised.

He kept his head down.

"We will," she said. "We will be back with the people we love. And it won't be necessary to hide anymore. This isn't the way it ends, Tomas. This isn't the way that our families' stories end."

He shook his head. "The Nazis broke into the house," he said. "My parents—they were pulled out, in their nightclothes. They didn't have coats. The people watched, and some cheered. That's all I was told."

"I know."

"My father would have taken my mother's hand," he said, his voice cracking. "To give her strength. I can't even think of them being tortured. Being humiliated and jeered. And ending up..."

"I know, my love," Corinna said, rubbing his back. "I know."

They sat that way for a long time, the two of them, Tomas's head on Corinna's shoulder. Emilia wondered if she'd ever know a love like that. It seemed so remote to her now. As if the two of them were here only in body, but really existed somewhere else, on some distant planet. Love seemed the perfect escape, the only escape. She envied them, but she also rooted for them. They'd found a solution to a problem that was haunting everyone. And she wanted that solution to prove long-lasting. To protect them always. If love like that existed in the world, then Corinna was right. Everything else was temporary. Everything else would finally be over.

Emilia watched them, captivated. This was the kind of love that overcame everything. She longed to enter their world, to be a part of their universe. But she didn't see how she ever could. They were floating on air, the two of them. And they belonged together on a planet far away from here. Because their kind of love couldn't thrive in this world. This world was too broken.

But they weren't on another planet. They were right here, trying to make something beautiful work in a world that could never bear anything beautiful. It suddenly seemed to Emilia that they were trying to do something impossible. Put a square peg in a round hole.

The breeze kicked up, chilly and strong. Emilia shivered and turned to go back to the house.

NINETEEN

OCTOBER 1943

One night as Emilia and Corinna were hurrying down a narrow, quiet street, baskets in hand, Emilia spotted a small group of people huddling beside a building. As they drew closer, it became clear that it was a family—a mother and father with a little boy and baby girl, the girl in the mother's arms. Emilia didn't know how, maybe because of their drawn, tired faces—but she could tell immediately that this was a Jewish family looking for shelter.

She tugged on Corinna's elbow, and the two of them approached the family. Emilia reached into her basket and gave a chunk of bread to the little boy. He glanced at his mother, then accepted it and took a bite.

"Are you lost?" Corinna whispered. "Can we help you?"

The parents looked at each other as if they didn't know whether to say anything, whether Corinna's kind words were a trap.

"It's okay, we are working with the Resistance," Corinna said softly. Emilia startled at Corinna's words. They were not supposed to say that anywhere in public. And yet, there seemed no doubt that this was a family who needed their help.

"We are trying to find the Abbates' house," the father said softly, evidently deciding to return the trust. "They are expecting us." It seemed he was wary to give much information. But Corinna looked at Emilia and nodded. The Abbates were on this evening's schedule.

"Yes, of course," Emilia said. "We are headed that way. Come with us. This food is for you."

"But we have to move fast," Corinna added. "It's not safe to stand out here all together like this."

They hurried down the street and soon reached the home of the Abbate family. Emilia knocked, and Corinna touched the man's elbow. "Where have you come from?" she whispered as they waited for Signora Abbate to answer the door.

"Rome," he told her.

"And how are things there? The same?"

The father shook his head. "We thought all the Nazis wanted was our money. But they started coming for the Jews last night."

"They were storming the houses, dragging them out of their homes," the mother said. "Women and men in night-clothes, no one with a coat. We were able to get to a church, and we hid in the basement before they reached our house. But we fled early this morning. It was too dangerous to stay longer."

"We're hoping to keep going south," the man said. "I have cousins in Argentina. We need to find a way to get on a ship to South America."

"You're safe tonight," Corinna told him. "And there are others who can help you tomorrow. See?" She lifted the menu card Emilia had made. "It's written in red, that means go to the train station tomorrow. Signor and Signora Abbate will tell you how to get there. Don't worry, there'll be people who will help you."

The door opened and Signora Abbate was there, surveying

the group. She motioned the family in, then took the basket from Emilia, and with a quick wave, shut the door.

Emilia looked at Corinna, unable to figure out the meaning of what this couple had told them. Was Caccipulia still safe? Were *they* still safe?

"What do we do?" she asked.

Corinna didn't answer.

By late that week, the news had grown even more grim. Coming back from one of her secret meetings and sitting down in the kitchen, Signora Jorelini reported that the Nazi roundups of Jews had intensified. And there were Italians rounding up Jews, too, to hand over to the Nazis. More and more towns were being stormed, more and more houses were being raided, more and more Jews were being taken away. There were reports of Resistance fighters orchestrating targeted attacks on Nazi soldiers, and Nazis retaliating with more arrests and killings. And reports, too, that earlier Nazi demands for money from the Jews of Rome had only been a ploy to learn where the Jews lived and how much cash they had.

Emilia thought of her father: What would Papa do if the Nazis had demanded money from him? How could he possibly put together enough to satisfy the Nazis? She thought of the ruby earrings that her mother had owned, which were upstairs in Giulia's dresser in the home that was no longer her own, at least not now. Would Papa have sold those earrings? Would he have asked friends for help? Would he have been able to swallow his pride enough to do that? It seemed the war was making enemies of people who used to care for each other. How could people who ordinarily would be so kind suddenly turn so evil?

She sighed, thinking of the people in town, neighbors, who

used to bring casseroles over to help her father, the poor widower with three young daughters. Did they blame her, with her Jewish father, for their trouble, their lack of food, their bleak life? How did people turn on people so quickly and so forcefully? One afternoon when she was little, she was running down the street with friends when she tripped and badly skinned her knee. Three women who lived nearby came running out of their homes with iodine and warm compresses and bandages. Would they do that now? Or would they let her limp back home, the trail of blood staining the cobblestone walkway?

Could she trust Corinna? Could she trust Signora Jorelini? She trusted them now. Signora Jorelini had made up that hidden bed in the attic just for her, if she needed to hide. But could she change her mind, too? Emilia had always thought trust was permanent, fixed; but was it actually fragile like a pencil, a piece of chalk, a crayon? At school, she and the other girls had promised one another that they'd be friends for life. And yet where were those friends now? She hadn't seen any of them in months. Did they hate her because her father was Jewish? Or were they just afraid to show that they still liked her? Did fear make you act differently toward people you used to love? Or did fear change your feelings?

"It's like we're just waiting for the worst to happen," Corinna said, interrupting Emilia's thoughts, when Signora Jorelini had finished relaying all she'd heard at the meeting. "What do we do?"

"We keep hoping that the Allied forces show up here soon," Signora Jorelini said. "And we take care of each other. And, my loves, we cook."

The next afternoon, after another secret meeting, Signora Jorelini called Corinna and Emilia to the kitchen table. "The Nazis reached the edge of town last night," she said. "They arrested all the Jews beyond the bridge, even some who were being hidden. It seems that people are getting desperate. They are accepting payment for telling the Nazi soldiers where the Jews are."

Emilia breathed in sharply, not knowing what to say. How did this happen? Would somebody tell the Nazis that she was in this house? Would the Nazis take her away? What would happen to her then?

Signora Jorelini took her hand. "Don't worry, *piccolina*," she said. "I will protect you. But things have to change around here. You can't go out anymore. You need to stay inside, and if anyone stops by, you need to be in the attic. I will tell people that you ran away and I don't know where you went. They will believe me because they won't see you anymore. You must promise me that you will do what I say. Because if they find you hiding, we will all get in trouble. The three of us will be in very real danger. Do you understand?"

Emilia nodded, thinking about the basket she'd delivered with Corinna yesterday. They'd gone to the Simona house, where a small Jewish family was staying, a couple and a small boy. The woman had a pretty name. Ariella. She'd warned Emilia that things were getting worse. Still, Emilia had never imagined that would be the last food delivery she'd make.

"But what about the supper club?" she asked softly. "Who will take my deliveries?"

"It may be time to end it," Signora Jorelini said.

"What? No!" Emilia cried out.

"Mama, you can't mean that," Corinna said.

"We'll take it day by day," Signora Jorelini told them. "But no matter what, Emilia can no longer deliver the food. It must be only Corinna and the others."

Emilia nodded. Then her thoughts went to the most important concern of all. "And my sisters?" she asked. "What about them? How will they find me if everyone thinks I ran away?"

She saw Signora Jorelini and Corinna exchange glances, and she felt her cheeks grow hot. "No..." she said. "No..." She shook her head and backed up against the wall. Her sisters were fine. They were coming for her, that's what they'd promised. How could it be anything different?

Emilia studied Signora Jorelini and Corinna's faces. There was no avoiding the sadness, the pity in their eyes. She sank onto her knees, shaking her head. Corinna came over to comfort her, sitting down next to her and holding out her arms. Emilia recoiled from the embrace. Yes, this was Corinna, who'd been so good to her. But she couldn't accept her hugs. Because that would mean that she believed what Corinna's sad eyes were trying to tell her.

Instead she rose and went upstairs. In the bedroom, she sat on the bed, holding tightly to the numbness she felt. She couldn't allow herself to feel any other way, because she was sure it would come out as screaming, as she faced the horror and fury now contained deep in her belly. And she couldn't scream, she couldn't shout here in this house that wasn't hers. How was she to handle all this? She was only a child.

She looked on the desk in Corinna's room. There were the drawings of the stars in the sky that her father had made for her. Go forth, the message had been. Persevere. But where was her courage now? She remembered the Abraham story, the one about the man who had to leave his home, the one with the message that wonderful things happen when you bravely move forward into the unknown. Go forth. She'd never clearly known what it meant. But now she understood. It was a battle cry, a command to remember that there are bigger concerns in the world than yourself.

"Papa," she whispered. "What would you expect of me now? How can I be the brave daughter you wanted me to be?"

A moment later, Corinna entered the room. She shut the door and pressed her back against it.

"My sweet Emilia, I can't put you and my mother in extra danger any longer," she said. "By being here, Tomas and I put you at risk. So you must write one last code for Tomas, and I'll get Signora De Luca to deliver the basket. We have to tell him to pack up all his things and come here tomorrow night. So he and I can leave for Switzerland."

TWENTY

OCTOBER 2019

Thursday

That afternoon, with the disastrous cooking lesson still on her mind, Callie left the hotel and went down the street to the coffee bar. She wanted to tell Oliver what had happened. She was anxious to share what Emilia had said, how much she'd pressed Callie to talk about her sister, and how angry she'd become when Callie mentioned the photos in the lobby. And she wanted to ask, too, about what Renata had revealed, the food donations to the church. She wondered how much of this Oliver had known, and if anything would be new to him. And she wondered if he'd have any advice for her.

Yes, he had urged her not to question Emilia about anything, and she'd been hopeful that if she spent some time with Emilia, more information would come out. She still didn't know how Pam had ended up with the menu card, or the story behind her grandmother's photo in the lobby.

She still felt bad about lying to Oliver, making him think she was Pam. But she didn't think that should stop her from talking to him. After all, he cared about Emilia, too.

She reached the coffee bar and stepped inside. But when she looked around, she didn't see Oliver anywhere—not behind the bar and not out among the tables. She waited in the entryway for a few minutes, hoping he'd emerge from the kitchen. But when he didn't, she went to the bar and caught the attention of the girl with blue hair she'd seen yesterday.

"*Scusi...* Oliver?" she asked. "Is he here?" She pointed toward the floor, hoping that would help convey her meaning.

"Oliver? No, *mi dispiace*," the girl said. "Not today. Tomorrow, yes."

"Tomorrow? Thank you. *Grazie*," she said, and the girl nodded and went back to her work. Callie sighed. She was disappointed that she wouldn't be seeing him today. Now she wouldn't be able to talk to him until tomorrow—and her flight home was Sunday, three days away. Time was passing quickly. And yet, there was more to her disappointment than the fact that she'd have to wait another day to talk with him about Emilia. She had enjoyed his company last night, and wanted to see him again. She was lonely here all by herself—and her loneliness was intensified by the fact that nobody back home knew she was gone. She truly was all alone.

She left the coffee bar, determined not to spend the day feeling sorry for herself. After all, it was a lovely autumn day, the temperature perfect for the jacket she was wearing, the sunshine brilliant, the sky blue and cloudless. She decided she'd explore every inch of this beautiful little town. She went back to the train station and up the stairs where she'd been yesterday, stopping again at the memorial to the Jorelinis. In the light of day, she could see the intricate carving. She looked at the bronze etchings of the two women, and the younger one's cascading hair reminded her anew of her grandmother. It was so reminiscent of her grandmother's beautiful hair in the picture Emilia kept on the reception desk. But how could this be her grandmother, if this young woman—Corinna Jorelini—died in 1943?

Putting that mystery aside, she stared at the plaque a bit longer. The workmanship was so beautiful. She had to believe that these women meant so much to Emilia, for her to commission this work of art.

There were some food trucks parked near the train station, and Callie stopped there for lunch. The vendor, who spoke only a little English, suggested a *trapizzino con parmigiana di melanzane*—a triangular-shaped pocket made of pizza dough and filled with baked eggplant and cheese. Callie found a small table on the square and dug in, hardly believing how delicious it was. She followed it up with pistachio *gelato*. It was rich and creamy, and served with a little waffle cookie, which the vendor called a *pizzelle*. She went back to the hotel when the town closed down during the afternoon hours, but returned to the town center later to stroll through the clothing and gift shops. She also spent some time at a small historical museum, which had photographs of Caccipulia through the decades. It was remarkable to see how similar the layout was today to what it had been like back in the 1930s and 1940s—and to think about what Emilia had gone through as a young girl. It was a story the pictures didn't tell.

Still full from lunch, she stopped in a café in the early evening for a coffee and a bowl of *burrida*, which she learned was a traditional Italian seafood soup. Then she made her way back to the hotel. She was surprised to realize that even though she'd been alone, it had turned out to be an enjoyable afternoon. It struck her, the thought that you could be alone but not be lonely. And the converse was also true—you could be lonely when you were with others.

The next morning after a quick breakfast at the hotel, she made her way back to the coffee bar. When she walked inside,

Oliver was coming out of the kitchen, wiping his hands on a towel. He looked disheveled, his curls wild and his face flushed.

"Hey," he said as he crossed behind the bar and stood opposite her.

"Wow, you look like you've been working hard. Coffee is a tough business."

He laughed. "You're telling me. Actually, one of the dishwashers sprang a leak, and I was trying to fix it so we wouldn't have to call in a plumber. We try to save a buck when we can here."

He put the towel on the bar. "I heard you were looking for me yesterday," he said. "Sorry, it was my day off. My sister went to a coffee trade show in Rome, and I was taking care of my three nephews. They're a handful. I guess you know what it's like. Although maybe it's different with a baby. But if she's anything like my nephews, you will have your hands full before long."

"Oh. Yes, my daughter." She'd forgotten for a moment about her lie. She felt her cheeks flush and looked down.

"Was there something you needed?" he asked.

"Yes... I mean, yes." She was glad for the change of subject. "I wanted to tell you that I spent some time with Emilia. She gave me a cooking lesson after all."

"Nice. How did that go?"

"Well, good at first. But then she started talking about her sisters again. And how they abandoned her. Is that true—did they abandon her? From what I read online, they didn't abandon her at all. They died on Parissi Island when the Nazis invaded it, didn't they?"

"There's no direct proof that they died," Oliver said. "But hardly anyone escaped, and those who did, there's information about what happened to them. Like my grandfather. From what I understand, her sisters sent her back here to tell her sick father that they'd be returning soon with medicine for him."

"It's like she doesn't want to believe that they're dead," Callie said. "It's easier for her to think they just never came back. And to be mad at them." She paused. "You know, it's strange," she said. "I was at the historical center yesterday, and I saw photos of how the town looked in the '30s and '40s. And the way you said she rebuilt the town to look exactly like it used to—I feel like maybe she did that because she's still waiting for her sisters. That she wanted to make the town familiar to them when they finally returned. You said she came back here thirty years ago? I bet she still thought back then there was a chance they'd return."

"Hmm. Could be," he said. "Wow. Sounds like she's made an impression on you."

"I guess it's because I know what it's like to be a sister," she said. A younger sister who's been left behind way too early, she added to herself. A younger sister who didn't expect to be alone so soon.

"You okay?" Oliver asked. "I feel like I said something wrong."

"No, no." She shook her head and raised her palms, trying to acknowledge that she'd overreacted. "But you're right—she did make a big impression on me. I want to know more."

"Hey, I have an idea," he said. "I'm having dinner at my sister's tonight—why don't you come? She's a great cook, and she knows a lot about Emilia. And my brother-in-law is actually studying the culture of these small Mediterranean towns for a book he's writing. It'll be fun."

"Dinner?" Callie said. "Oh, that's so nice of you, but..." She was overwhelmed by the invitation. It didn't seem right—she was a stranger, no one to these people. She didn't belong here. Would they really want to have her?

But then she saw how hopeful Oliver looked. It seemed that he genuinely wanted her to come.

"Are you sure I wouldn't be imposing?" she asked.

"Imposing? No! My sister will love it. She always worries that I don't have enough friends here. You'll be doing me a favor."

"Okay, then," she said. "I'd love to."

They agreed that she'd return later that afternoon, after he'd finished work and gone to his apartment above the bar to change his clothes. With the rest of the afternoon free, she wandered around the town, stopping at the food trucks again for lunch. As the day went on, she felt more and more strongly that she was looking forward to going to Oliver's sister's house. Having dinner in someone's home seemed the most wonderful opportunity in the world. It had been such a long time since she'd had an invitation like that. The last time was probably when she'd gone home last Thanksgiving. But it hadn't felt so welcoming. Pam had been so happy with her little baby and her husband and her in-laws. Such a sweet little world they had. And Callie had felt like an outsider.

She thought now of what Thanksgiving would be like this year without Pam. No doubt Joe would try to make things good for the baby. No doubt his parents would help. Yes, there would be tears. Of course, there would be tears. And Pam's seat would be empty. They would continue with smiles of pain, with smiles for the baby, who would need them to think of Pam with joy.

At the hotel, she took a shower and changed into one of her favorite dresses, a short-sleeved floral dress, belted at the waist. Then she headed back to the coffee bar. Oliver was outside waiting for her. He was wearing a pair of khaki trousers and a black pullover sweater. He was really quite lovely, she thought. And he seemed older, more mature, than when she'd first met him in the coffee shop.

They walked down to the train station and to the town's one parking lot, where he kept his car. A few minutes later they were on their way. They drove up a hillside overlooking a deep span of water.

"So tell me about your sister," she said. "How did you both end up here?"

"Well, like I said, I was a teacher in Boston. And a good one. I liked it. I liked the kids. Anyway, I had a sabbatical coming up, just around the time that my sister and I inherited a little money from our grandfather. I was trying to think what to do with it. And the more soul-searching I did, the more I realized that I wanted to open a restaurant. A great place where people could come and stay and hang and feel just plain great."

"So you found out that this was the place to learn about cooking?"

He nodded, his eyes on the road. "My sister studied at the Culinary Institute in New York, which is where she met her husband. He's from this area, but he was living in that part of New York after getting a Ph.D. in anthropology from Syracuse. They married and decided to live here for a while. That was about eight years ago. Well, I had visited them from time to time, but last winter, with my relationship over and my sabbatical starting, it was a chance for me to get away and think about my future.

"And now I have to decide what I'm going to do," he said. "Like I told you, my sabbatical ends in December."

"What are you thinking?" she asked.

"I honestly don't know," he said. "My buddies are ready to move forward with a restaurant. But I do like it here. Italy agrees with me. Still, it may be time to go home. If Boston is still home. I don't know anymore."

She looked down at her lap. She, too, was no longer sure where home was. She hoped she and Oliver could still be friends after she left on Sunday. No matter where he ended up.

She watched the sun setting behind the hills ahead.

TWENTY-ONE

OCTOBER 2019

Friday

They continued driving higher, past houses that became increasingly far apart and set back from the road. Eventually they came to a two-story stone farmhouse set against a range of trees—sycamore, maple and tall pines, all still lush despite the inevitability of fall weather ahead. The facade of the house was a mosaic of warm brownish shades—sand, cappuccino, camel, chestnut. The roof was terracotta, adding to the sense of grounding and rootedness. Callie was enchanted by the structure. It looked like it dated back centuries, and she imagined how wonderful it would be to live in such a place. To feel the embrace of generations of history, generations of people. To embrace the responsibility of caring for a home where so much life had been lived before.

Oliver turned and drove down the winding driveway. They parked along the side of the house, which had tall windows on the upper floor and a series of wide windows on the ground floor, rimmed with open wooden shutters.

"Remote, I know. But it's cozy and really pretty. They're so happy here. Come on."

They got out of the car, and Oliver led her past a covered patio with a long wooden table and black metal chairs, which looked like the perfect spot for a family dinner on a warm summer evening. Past the patio, she could see a small olive grove and multiple vegetable gardens, although it looked like all the crops had been harvested. No surprise, it was already October. There was something sad about that, but also inspiring. A season well lived. The promise of another growing season next year.

Oliver knocked on the door and then opened it. Callie was surprised and charmed by the inside of the house, which had a light, airy quality to it. The floors were a gleaming honey-brown wood, and the white vaulted ceiling was high and vast. To her right was a cozy living room, with a large, arched window and skylight that let in the evening sun. There was a stone fireplace fronted by a long, tan sofa and a couple of deep tan armchairs, with a glazed wooden chest as the coffee table. There was a modern air to the furnishings, and a little whimsy, too—especially in the series of four square paintings of individual irises in bloom, set above the fireplace. Callie loved this blend of styles, this combination of the past with a nod to the present moment.

Just after they'd stepped inside, a boy who looked around seven came running down the stairs. "Uncle Oliver!" he called. "We're going to play soccer!"

A woman's voice sounded from deeper within the house. "Oh, no you're not!" she said. "It's dinnertime. Now go wash up and tell your brothers to as well." A moment later, the woman came out from the kitchen, drying her hands on a dishtowel. She looked to be in her late thirties, and had an undeniable family resemblance to Oliver, with thick dark curls and a small, delicate nose and mouth, and long, beautiful eyelashes. She was wearing a denim dress and a full-length apron that cradled her pregnant belly. Behind her was a tall man with short-cropped graying hair and a neat, salt-and-pepper beard.

"Pam, this is my sister, Meg, and her husband, Gustavo," Oliver said as he helped Callie off with her jacket. Callie startled a little, still not used to being called by her sister's name. "And this is my friend Pam."

"Hello," Meg said, as she held out her hand. "Welcome."

Callie shook her hand. "Thank you for having me," she said.

"The pleasure is ours," Gustavo said, his English embellished with a slight but distinct Italian accent. "We are so glad to see someone who's staying with our Emilia. We can't wait to hear all you've learned."

Callie smiled, charmed at how he referred to her as "our" Emilia.

"Something smells awfully good," Oliver said as he kissed his sister's cheek. He took off his own jacket and draped them both over the banister.

"Wait until you taste it before you say any more," Meg said. "I'm experimenting with some new fall dishes. I hope you don't mind being a guinea pig, Pam."

"Not at all," she said.

"Well, I'm sorry to rush you two, but everything's ready," Meg said. "Come inside and have a seat at the table."

Callie followed the others into a large dining room, contemporary in feel, with a glass-topped table and slender, upholstered chairs. She and Oliver sat on one side of the table, as the three boys—the older one and twins who looked maybe five or six—clamored into the room and found their seats on the other side. In front of them all were steaming bowls of soup, the red broth filled with beans, vegetables, and chunks of toasted bread.

"This is *ribollita*," Meg said. "It means 'reboiled' because traditionally it's a soup that uses leftover bread and vegetables.

It's a traditional soup for fall, rich and dense. We'll be eating this all winter to help stave off any colds."

Gustavo poured the adults some red wine from a crystal decanter. He sat back down and lifted his glass. "*Salute!*" he said. Oliver waited for Callie to lift her glass and then clinked his with hers.

They started on the soup, and Callie found she was entranced with this family. They all seemed at home, the boys eating politely and chattering about school and sports. Callie noticed how Gustavo would look lovingly at Meg when she talked more about where she'd found the *ribollita* recipe and the way she'd varied the ingredients to make it a little more flavorful. Callie could see why Oliver wanted to be here with his sister and her family as he healed from his break-up. There was so much to enjoy in this gathering of people who loved one another. She supposed it had been that way between Pam and Joe, too. But she feared she'd been too self-involved, too defensive about her lifestyle, to notice.

When they'd finished their soup, Meg and the children cleared the bowls. Callie rose to help, but Meg insisted that she and Oliver stay put at the table. A moment later she came back out with a large, shallow serving bowl, the food inside steaming.

"This is *pici al ragu di cinghiale*," she said. "*Pici* is like a thick spaghetti, and *cinghiale* is wild boar. It's all simmered with onions, carrots, tomatoes, and celery. Another hearty meal for the upcoming winter."

"You don't have to like it," Oliver said to Callie. "That's the rule here. I'm sure there's plain pasta in the refrigerator that we can warm up."

"Yes, please don't be shy," Meg said. "I can be too adventurous for some with the dishes and the recipes I choose. You wouldn't be the first guest to opt for something else."

But there was no need to do that. Callie found the meat

tasty, the consistency soft and chewy, and the spices a perfect blend of sweet and tangy. Still, she was touched by Meg's kindness and loved hearing how she'd changed up the seasonings to make the dish more her own. She wondered how she'd have liked Emilia's oxtail stew, if she'd had the chance to taste it.

"So how long are you here, Pam?" Meg asked as they all continued to eat.

"Just until Sunday," Callie said.

"She has a daughter to get back to," Oliver said. "She's about one, right?"

"A little older," Callie said. "Almost... well, a little older." She felt bad that she didn't immediately recall her niece's exact age. "Her birthday was in August," she added.

"Oh, a little girl!" Meg said. "What's her name?"

"Chloe," Callie answered.

"How pretty," Meg said. "We're undecided here. Leaning toward Alexandra or Alicia, but it's a work in progress."

"So what brings you to Caccipulia?" Gustavo asked.

"Pam is investigating a family mystery," Oliver said. "It involves Emilia."

"Please tell us," Meg said. "There's so much history in this town. How are you connected to it?"

Callie looked down. She wanted very much to share her life with this family. She was drawn to Meg, who was so friendly and nurturing. She was drawn to Gustavo, who was so warm and friendly, and to the sweet boys. And, of course, she liked Oliver very much. But it was hard to be open, given the lies she'd told. And she also felt guilty. This was a happy family, this was what family was supposed to be. Why had she turned her back on her own family, her own sister? Why had she stayed away, when she was enjoying this family dinner so much?

She pushed those thoughts out of her head so she could answer Meg's question. "Like I told Oliver, I found some things in my home when I was cleaning. There was something that looked like a menu, and there was a picture that looked to be from a newspaper, with Emilia and her sisters. It was the same picture that Emilia has on the reception desk of the hotel. And there was also the name of this town and the address of Emilia's hotel."

"Do you know who put those items in the box? Your grandmother, maybe?"

"Um... maybe," Callie said, not wanting to reveal the true story.

"Were your grandparents from Italy?" Meg asked.

"Yes, both of them. They left here in the 1940s. My grandfather was Jewish and living in Rome when the Nazis invaded. But neither one of them ever wanted to talk about Italy."

"Your grandfather was lucky," Gustavo said. "The Italians were allied with Germany at first, but in 1943 Italy surrendered to the Allies in Sicily. And as soon as the armistice was signed Germany declared war on Italy. That's when the Nazis occupied Rome and began rounding up Jews to take to Auschwitz or other camps. By October they were working their way south, while the Allies were pushing northward. For a while, the front was just a bit south of here."

"Oh, this town suffered terribly during the war," Meg said. "The Nazis invaded our pretty Caccipulia on October 27th. There were a number of Jews being hidden here at that time. Including Emilia."

"As you've probably heard by now, Emilia was Jewish on her father's side," Gustavo said. "Her mother was part of the rich Parissi family, which owned an island and a castle in the Mediterranean, but they disowned her for marrying a Jewish man."

"Emilia survived because her sisters sent her home," Oliver told her. "They stayed on at Parissi Island to get medicine for their father."

"Yes, apparently," Gustavo said. "Although she was in

danger here, too. She ran off before the Nazis arrived. It was a good thing, because the Nazis killed or arrested all the Jews hiding here in Caccipulia, and all the people helping them."

"So why is she still so angry with her sisters?" Callie asked.

"I think she feels guilty that she survived and they didn't," Oliver said. "And also angry that they didn't come home with her. She thinks they'd still be alive if they left when she did. Even though they had a good reason for staying."

"So, Pam—your grandmother knew Emilia?" Meg asked.

"I'm pretty sure of it," Callie said. "Pretty sure that she lived here in Caccipulia when she was young. Emilia has a picture of herself with my grandmother at the hotel. At least, I'm all but certain it's my grandmother. They look like close friends. They're hugging each other in the picture."

"Did your grandmother ever say anything about Emilia?" Gustavo said.

"A little. I remember hearing her mention Emilia's name sometimes. She was very troubled by something that happened when she was here. She would say she made a big mistake, and she regretted it very much. That's why I came here when I found those things. I wanted to see if Emilia could tell me the story of my grandparents—if they actually lived here and what mistake my grandmother made.

"It's something I promised I'd do for my... for Chloe," she added. "I think it made it hard on my sister and me, not ever knowing my grandmother's past. I think... well, I think my sister in particular... my sister, Callie... might have had an easier time growing up if we had known more."

Callie looked down. She didn't know why she'd said what she just said. But as she was talking, she'd started to think about that thing Emilia had said to her in the kitchen yesterday. About how people who don't know where home is spend their whole lives searching for it. Was Emilia suggesting that's what Callie had been doing? Had she spent her whole life searching for home? She supposed now that maybe home was more than an address. Maybe it was a state of mind, too. Maybe she'd never stayed anywhere for long because she never knew what it meant to feel like you were home.

"I asked Pam not to confront Emilia," Oliver said. "But to wait until Emilia trusted her and wanted to talk to her."

"Yes, we all leave Emilia alone," Gustavo said with a smile.

"And I understand that now," Callie said. "I spent some time with her yesterday morning. She seems kind of tortured by her memories."

"She's holding a lot of hurt, and it comes out as bitterness," Meg said. "She never wanted to believe that her sisters died. Some say she recreated the town so they'd come back and find her. And they'd feel at home once they returned, and have delicious food to eat. Others say she's waiting to learn the truth about her sisters. Something that will bring her peace."

Callie nodded. She couldn't help but think about her own grandmother's cooking, too. Had she, too, been trying to recreate her home, the home she'd left, through food?

The boys were getting restless, and Meg asked them to clear their dishes and go play for a little bit before dessert. Meg got up to finish clearing, and Callie rose to help her, while Oliver and Gustavo went to make a fire in the fireplace in the living room.

In the kitchen, Callie brought plates to the sink and loaded the dishwasher as Meg started the coffee and reached into a cabinet for plates, cups and saucers. On the table was a golden-brown cake dusted with powdered sugar.

"That looks amazing," Callie said.

"*Torta Caprese* with white chocolate and lemon," she said. "We get lemons from Naples that are just delicious."

"The food here is so good. Every meal I've had."

"It's one of the reasons why we love it here," Meg said. "Everything is made with such care. This is a value I've learned so much here. I'll be sorry when we go back."

"You're leaving?"

Meg nodded. "At some point, yes. Once Gustavo's done with his book, he will be up for a very important academic seat at Stanford University. It's too good an opportunity to pass up."

"It'll be hard to leave, I'm sure," Callie said. "Especially for your boys, I would think. This is their home."

"I suppose. But I think home is where you make it, don't you? Place is less important than the feeling you get when you walk in the door. I like to think that by having spent some happy years here, my boys will always know that you don't expect home. It's not that simple. You make a home."

"That's a beautiful thought," Callie said. She stood still for a moment, absorbing those words. She'd never thought of home that way. She'd never thought about home the way Emilia had yesterday in the kitchen. How did Emilia and Meg know so much about home? How had she never before figured it out?

Callie took the dishes out to the living room, where a fire was roaring. Meg brought out the cake and set it on the coffee table. A moment later, Gustavo and Oliver came into the living room from down the hall. Gustavo was wearing wire-rimmed glasses and carrying a large book.

"What's up?" Meg asked.

"We were just doing a little investigative work," Gustavo said. "Pam, did anyone ever tell you about the Caccipulia Supper Club?"

"Isn't that what we were talking about yesterday?" Callie asked Oliver. "The plaque at Memorial Square?"

Oliver nodded. "I was mentioning how the town helped feed and hide Jewish families trying to escape."

"Evidently the woman Emilia lived with was a talented cook who owned a restaurant before the war," Gustavo said. "That was Signora Jorelini, who is on the memorial plaque. When the Nazis came and food was so scarce, she started the supper club."

He sat down beside her and showed her a page from the book. "A local historian published this not too long ago," he said. "Pam, you mentioned a card that you found earlier, with a menu on it. Is this what your menu card looks like?"

Callie felt her jaw drop and her back stiffen as she looked at the photo in the book. "Yes, that's just like the card I have. *Club della cena*—that's what it says! It's back in the hotel."

"That's quite a gift your grandmother left you," Gustavo said. "There weren't many of them. See here what it says?" He read the paragraph out loud, translating from Italian:

The supper club was a way the Caccipulia community came together—by helping families feed the Jewish people hiding in their homes. The menu cards were part of what was distributed to the families. While the number varied, there were likely five or six families hiding Jews when the Nazis arrived in town on October 27th.

"And if your grandmother had one of those cards, then she must have known Emilia pretty well," Meg said.

Gustavo looked at Callie. "Could your grandmother have been one of the Jews hiding out? Is that how she would have gotten the supper club menu?"

"No," Callie said. "My grandmother wasn't Jewish. My grandfather was, but not my grandmother."

"Well, that doesn't help us much," Gustavo said. "But... wait," he said, pointing to the page. Here's more."

The club was run by Philippa Jorelini, her daughter, Corinna, and their young neighbor, Emilia Sancino, who lived with them in the closing months of 1943. It's believed that the club helped feed somewhere between four and six dozen Jewish people as they fled from the Nazis. Subsequently, Sancino was forced into hiding in the Jorelini house, due to her Jewish parentage.

Among the Jews surviving thanks to the supper club was Tomas Sachsel, a Jewish scholar from Rome who was rumored to have worked with the Resistance. It is believed that Corinna Jorelini and Sachsel perished when they tried to flee to Switzerland together...

Callie put her hand to her mouth.

"What is it?" Oliver asked.

She shook her head. "I can't believe this," she said. "You know, when I saw the memorial, I wondered if that was my grandmother. But now I think it must be. My grandfather was called Tom but his full name was Tomas. Tom Sackes. We always knew they changed their last name slightly when they left Italy."

"Then Corinna Jorelini must be your grandmother," Meg said.

"But they didn't go to Switzerland," Callie said. "They didn't die escaping. They went to the United States instead."

There was silence in the room, as everyone took in Callie's words.

"Then the book is wrong," Oliver finally said. "And the memorial plaque in the square, too."

Gustavo nodded. "A lot of Jews from this area did try to escape to Switzerland. And many of them made it. But it's entirely possible that your grandparents changed course while they were on the run. Maybe they encountered a problem at the border. Maybe it was safer to go south instead of north. Otherwise you'd be Swiss instead of American."

"So the girl in the picture at the hotel really is my grandmother," Callie said. She felt as though it would take a few times repeating it for her to believe it without any doubt. "My grandmother really did know Emilia."

Gustavo closed the book and went to sit next to Callie. "It's so much bigger than that," he said. "Pam, Emilia's father was

Jewish. And Emilia was all alone, the daughter of a Jew at a very dangerous time. And your grandmother and great-grandmother took her in and fed her and hid her.

"Your grandmother and great-grandmother didn't just know Emilia," he said. "They are the ones who saved her."

TWENTY-TWO

OCTOBER 1943

Emilia stared at Corinna. "Switzerland? Tomorrow? But what about the Resistance group in Milan that's supposed to help him?"

"We can't wait here any longer. We have to set out on our own." Corinna tilted her head. "Come on, Emilia. Don't make this any harder. You knew this day was coming."

"But I didn't want it to." Emilia shook her head. "I thought there would be more time, that you'd be with me at least until my sisters came back. I don't want to be here without you."

She rose up on her knees on the bed. "Let's just tell your mother the truth. She's smart, she'll figure out something better. Let's tell her about you and Tomas. Let's talk to her now—"

"No," she said. "Mama would want me to stay here. She would try to stop me."

"And that's not okay? If she could keep you both safe?"

"She can't," Corinna said. "She will want to, but she can't."

"So you're just going to leave? Leave your home, your mother?"

"Emilia, we have to," she said. "If she tries to save us, she will put herself in danger. He is wanted by the Nazis. Please try to understand. There are whole worlds out there. Places where we can start fresh."

Emilia sighed. She'd heard Tomas say that very thing. That night when she was hiding behind the tree.

"We'll come back here someday," Corinna said. "When all this is over.

"Oh, Emilia," she said sitting down next to her on the bed. "I love him so much. When I look in his eyes, I feel that it's okay to leave my home, because I've found my home. He's my home. I don't even feel at home here the way I feel it when I'm with him. It's like he is the person I was born to find. And he makes me become the person I want to be. I just..."

She shook her head. "I don't know why I'm telling you this. You're so young and you've been through so much. I don't mean to make you listen to all this. But one day I hope you'll find someone like him, too. That you'll feel what I'm feeling..."

Corinna walked to the window, and Emilia watched her look outside. She didn't want Corinna to feel bad. Corinna's thoughts about Tomas were the one positive thing she'd heard lately. Corinna's faith that she could escape with Tomas and go somewhere else, find a new home, build a new life, make something wonderful from this horror that was the world now... it elevated Emilia, because it made her believe there was a way out. Go forth, her father would say. That was the lesson he had taught her all those years ago.

"You don't have to be sorry," Emilia said. "I love to hear you talk about him. It makes the world feel a little less... awful..."

Corinna came over and hugged her. "So will you do this for us? Will you draw the last code?"

Emilia paused. "Can't you?" she begged Corinna. "Can't you go to the Possano house and talk to him yourself? The other codes were fun, romantic. But this is too big for me to take on—"

She stopped because Corinna was shaking her head. "If I went there to see him, they would suspect why, and they would send for Mama. And they would make him leave, right then, right at that moment. Emilia, he is Jewish and a Resistance fighter, he is an outsider, and as much as they care about him, they all want him gone. They have been kind and they have been generous. But now they are scared. And people behave badly when they are scared, I'm afraid.

"Your sisters would want you to do this for me," she said. "And your papa would, too. They would want you to have courage."

Emilia nodded. Courage.

Courage, she repeated to herself late that night, sitting up in bed, her knees drawn up to her chest and her arms wrapped around them. A fierce wind kicked up outside, rattling the window. Her summer on Parissi Island felt years and years in the past; the draft was an ominous reminder that winter was barely a stone's throw away.

Across the room, Corinna slept soundly. Emilia could hear her breathing. The steadiness of the sound had proven comforting on so many nights. It had helped Emilia sleep on even the most terrible nights, the sad nights right after her father had died, the desperate nights when she longed for her sisters so hard that her chest ached. She was surprised that Corinna could sleep so peacefully—although the more she thought about it, the more she knew it made sense. Corinna was sleeping the sleep of someone with a settled conscience. Someone who felt no indecision at all.

And yet, Emilia felt nothing but indecision. What was she going to do? By tomorrow she would have to decide: either she would draw the code Corinna would give her so the menu card would be carried to the Possano household, the deliverer unknowingly setting the stage for Corinna's departure; or she would draw something else, and Tomas would leave on his own, believing that Corinna had changed her mind when she didn't show up at the specified place.

"*Lech L'cha*," Emilia whispered, remembering the Hebrew name of the Abraham story her father had told her, the one with the command to go forth. She could hear her father saying it, that funny, guttural "ha" sound of Hebrew that always made her think of someone clearing their throat. He always loved those sacred stories. It came so naturally to him, the words, the Hebrew words, the pronunciation. But to her, the words were strange, and they didn't sound right when she tried to imitate them. She was not a Jew. She was not raised to be a Jew. And yet, she was her father's daughter. And it meant something to her, the stories he'd shared, the way he'd prayed each year on the anniversary of her mother's death and the death of the baby who would have been her little sister. She would not have been the family's baby, if that baby had lived. She would have been an older sister, like her own two older sisters.

But that's not what happened. She was the youngest. She was only fifteen. How could they not be here, Annalisa and Giulia, to tell her what to do?

She felt the tears burn in her eyes as she clutched her hands together around her knees and shook her head, her eyes closed, Corinna's breathing in the background. "How could you do this to me?" she whispered in her mind to her sisters. "How could you have sent me back without you? What secret promise did you make to each other to stay together but make me leave? You're my sisters! How could you leave me alone?" She pursed her lips together, trying to hold back the words that were in her mind and needed to come out. She held them as long as she could, and then took a deep breath and let them emerge.

"I hate you!" she hissed into the air. "I hate you both!"

She listened, hoping the hiss would echo in her ears for a long time, for the rest of the night, even. It had felt good to say that, and she wanted the moment to last. But too soon, the sound had disappeared, and she was back to where she'd started. Alone in the chilly silence. Unable to sleep, unable to decide, unable to accept that this night would end and things would need to move forward, one way or another. Closing her eyes, she wrote a letter to her sisters in her head:

Dear Annalisa and Giulia,

I don't understand. How is it possible for the world to be like this? How do you make the world be the way it should be? How do you do that? How can I do that?

I wish you were here to explain it all to me.

She considered getting up and writing out the words on paper. But she knew she didn't have to send this letter. She knew what her sisters would say.

They'd tell her to side with love.

She thought of what Corinna had said, the words that were too disturbing to have focused on before. But now she had to face them. *He is Jewish and he is an outsider... they all want him gone... his mere existence puts them in danger.* Was that what Corinna actually thought? Was that what this whole town had always felt? The neighbors who had cared for her and her sisters so completely and wholeheartedly when they were young. Who had sympathized with her father and made sure he always had food for his young motherless daughters, who had trusted them with their delicate table linens handed down from generations, who trusted him to repair and remake the most important garments of their lives, wedding dresses and baptismal gowns. Was he always an outsider? Were the four of them—her father, herself, and her sisters—always outsiders?

Or was Corinna right? Was it fear at this horrible moment in history that was confusing everyone, making them say things they didn't mean, feel things they didn't really feel? She looked over at Corinna again. The moonlight lit up Corinna's face, painting stripes across her forehead reflecting the slats of the window blinds. The thoughts she had were terrifying, awful, scary.

But it was the image in her mind that was the most powerful, more powerful than the thoughts. The image she'd seen the first night Tomas had arrived in town and Corinna had gone to meet him. How he'd gripped her shoulders, how she'd held his face, how he'd pressed his lips against hers, how she'd let her body sink against his. The world was crazy, falling apart, and yet for a moment all that mattered was the two of them together. He'd moved his hands to her head, one on each side, while her fingers stayed pressed against his cheeks. He'd leaned forward, pressing his forehead to hers, using his thumbs to wipe the tears falling from her eyes. They'd been breathless—she'd seen Corinna's chest heaving up and down, she'd heard Corinna's heavy exhales. She'd heard Tomas's quiet, soothing voice, knew he was saying something beautiful and wonderful and reassuring. He'd uttered something that she couldn't make out, but she'd seen Corinna nod—again and again as Tomas soothed her.

What was it she'd been watching? She didn't have the words to describe it. She didn't have the experience to know it, to understand it. It was love, maybe, but it was more. They were a force, the two of them. They were something new, something bigger than just two people embracing. There was an energy, a private energy, a huge field of will and determination and inevitability that existed when they were together. It was something that couldn't be broken, or shouldn't be broken.

It's what they are together, she thought now. It's what they make as a pair. It's what they will bring to the future. She didn't know why, but she suddenly felt that the future of the world depended on Corinna and Tomas becoming one. They had to go forth. That was the message of her father's story.

And that was the message Papa was giving her now. He had fallen in love with her mother—he a lowly tailor, she an heiress. Two people who never should have been together. And yet they couldn't be separated. And the family they made was here. Her. And maybe, maybe she had been created fifteen years ago, created from the love between her parents, so that she would be here at this very moment. So that she could make sure that another love, another pairing, could happen.

She slid down in her bed. Now she knew what she would do. She would write the code. And she would enable Corinna to leave.

It would all happen tomorrow.

TWENTY-THREE

OCTOBER 2019

Friday

The drive back to the parking lot behind the train station was quiet, and Callie was grateful for that. She knew that Oliver was staying silent intentionally. She knew he thought she needed time to work through all she had discovered at Meg's house. It was a shock, to finally learn the connection between her family and Emilia. Her grandmother, along with her great-grandmother, had helped care for Emilia when she had no one. And Emilia had helped nourish her grandfather while he was hiding at the neighbor's house.

The connection between them all was so close. And it gave her a deep sense of contentment. She'd grown fond of Emilia over these last few days, and loved that her grandmother had taken care of Emilia. But at the same time, she was so confused. Why had they all never reconnected? Why had her grandparents never gone back to Italy to try to find Emilia? And why had Emilia never searched for Callie's grandparents? What had happened to keep them apart when they could have been reunited? Was there more tension, a misunderstanding that

Callie hadn't yet discovered? Emilia was still so angry, so hurt, that her grandmother had never returned. Why hadn't she come back once the war was over?

It all led Callie back to the original question she'd had on the day of Pam's funeral. How had Pam come to collect the objects in the box? Why had she left them there, locked with a code only Callie knew, in the drawer where they kept all their mutual secrets? Why had this story never been explored until now?

It frustrated her, because this wasn't just Pam's story. It was her story, too. She had a right to have been involved when Pam was alive and could have explained everything. And could have included her. Callie thought about how ashamed she'd been these last several months—too ashamed to come home, too ashamed to tell Pam the truth. She'd sent herself to Philadelphia, believing she needed to reclaim her life, to start a new life she could be proud of, before ever returning home to see her sister again. She'd spent her life being the troubled sister, the wild sister, trying to be good and always failing. And Pam had been the golden girl. Everyone at the funeral had talked about how selfless Pam was, how giving, how nurturing, how devoted to others. What a wonderful mother, what a wonderful wife. But if that was so—if she was such a good person—why had she shut out her own sister from this family secret? She and Pam had promised to discover the truth together.

They arrived at the parking lot. Oliver turned off the motor, and they climbed out of the car and walked to the cobblestone street. Callie knew that Oliver was walking her back to the hotel, and she again marveled at how sweet and decent he was. And here she was, lying to him, so that he didn't even know her real name.

She wondered if she'd ever deserve a guy as nice as Oliver. Maybe she'd end up alone. That would be fine, if that was how she wanted to live her life. But she didn't want to be alone. She wondered if Emilia had decided she was too independent to connect with another person. Or if she'd been so damaged by the war, so disappointed by the people she'd loved who'd abandoned her—people like her sisters and Callie's grandmother. She wondered if that had left her unable to trust anyone fully.

The streetlamps were lit, the golden and orange flames dancing in their glass cases. The weather was still warm for late fall, especially by New York standards. But there was a chill in the air, in the breeze that kicked up and shuffled the leaves on the walkway. The sky was a deep indigo, seeming to go on forever and ever. It was the kind of night that could make you hope it would never, ever end. They passed the coffee bar and went through the archway, then up the steep staircase that had nearly sent her turning back around a few days ago. It was hard to believe all that had happened to her since then—all the people she'd met and the things she'd discovered. She wondered if this was the end, and if she'd go back home with some answers but plenty of questions still left.

"Want to talk about any of this?" Oliver said softly as the hotel came into view.

Callie shrugged.

Oliver sighed. "I feel terrible," he said. "I invited you over for a nice dinner with my family. I never meant for you to go home feeling so... actually, I don't know what you're feeling. Shouldn't you be feeling good, knowing that your grandmother saved Emilia?"

She stayed quiet, not knowing what to say.

"At any rate," he added. "I'm sorry to have caused you to wrestle with all these deep, hard thoughts."

She shook her head. "No, you didn't do anything wrong," she said. "I told you that I came here looking for answers. You were right to bring that up with your family. I'm glad you did. I mean, I could have gone home with nothing. You did me a favor. Gustavo was wonderful, pulling out that book. I'm glad."

Oliver chuckled. "Yeah, you look very glad."

"No, I am. It's just..." She paused. How could she explain what she was feeling? She had come here like gangbusters, determined to bully her way into the town, get the information she needed, and then go home, satisfied that despite Pam's secrets, she'd gotten to the truth on her own. And yet being here, she'd met the most wonderful people. People who were giving and kind. Even Emilia, bitter old Emilia—Emilia who made food to bring to the church three times a week. It was eye-opening, how you never really knew what people were going through, you never really knew their suffering. Because lots of times people don't talk about suffering. They keep it to themselves. And those who love them never know why. Even she had kept secrets from those she loved. She'd kept her secret because she was embarrassed.

She had come here thinking that she and Emilia were alike. And she'd discovered they were even more alike than she'd suspected. Too proud to open up. But alone. And suffering in silence because of it.

She and Oliver continued in silence to the hotel's entrance. "I wish there was something I could say to get you to smile," Oliver said. "Or talk to me. Or confront me, the way you did when you first got here, when I demanded that you not confront Emilia." He smiled.

She smiled. "I'm sorry. I have a lot to think about."

"Then I should let you go."

He turned, and she grabbed his arm. "Wait," she said. "The least I could do is show you that supper club menu. If you'd like to see it."

He nodded. "Yeah. I really would."

They went into the hotel, and she led him up to her room. She unlocked the door and they stepped inside. The moon sent a shaft of gleaming white light across the room. She turned on a lamp, while he sat on one of the two armchairs. She opened the bottom drawer of the dresser and took out the box, then lifted the lid and removed the menu card. It had the Italian dishes she'd translated back home.

"Wow," Oliver said as he took it and ran his fingertips over the words. "*Caccipulia Club Della Cena.* The Caccipulia Supper Club." She knew what he was feeling. It was so strange to be touching history like this.

"So sad," she said. "This little piece of good they were trying to do. Feeding others. As Emilia waited for her sisters to come back."

Oliver nodded. "It's hard to think of Emilia as a young girl. Yet there's that piece of her personality that was there even then. Trying to do something to have control. Through food. This is the one thing that spelled... sanity to her. This is the one thing that gave some meaning to a world falling apart."

"No wonder she cares so much about cooking," Callie said. "I found out yesterday that she makes meals for the church three times a week, to distribute to anyone in need. And she sends sweets, too, for the children."

He nodded and lifted the card to read it again, and that's when she saw the handwritten note. She hadn't thought about it all that much since the day she found the box in Pam's room.

"There's something you don't know," she said. She turned the card over so he could see it. "I translated it before I came. I didn't know for sure who wrote it, or if it was to my grandmother. Now I think I understand."

He took the card and read the meaning aloud in English. "'You must return this to me. I will be waiting for you.'"

"It has to be from Emilia," Callie said. "It's clear to me now that she wrote it to my grandmother. She knew my grandmother was leaving, and she wanted her to promise to come back. But my grandmother never did. She's just one of a whole list of people who left Emilia behind. No wonder she's so mad. She must have hated my grandmother."

He smiled and shook his head. "She didn't hate your grand-mother. She loved her."

"Why would you say that?"

"Didn't you see the memorial to her and her mother? Your great-grandmother?"

"Yes, but—"

"Come on," he said. "You need to see it again, to really absorb what's there. Get your jacket, we're going back."

He took her hand and led her back down the stairs, out of the hotel, and past the coffee bar to Memorial Square. She couldn't believe how quickly they got there. He was a man on a mission, and she was happy to trust him. They passed a few people who were standing around, until they were directly in front of the plaque. He pointed toward the bottom.

"Did you see the inscription? Did you translate it?"

Callie shook her head. She hadn't noticed that the inscrip-tion was embedded in the engraved vines at the bottom of the memorial. It looked as if someone had tried to hide the words. Like a secret message, a code.

"*Nei ricordi amorosi degli angeli che mi hanno preso,*" Oliver said. "'In memory of the angels who took me in.'"

Callie caught her breath. It was overwhelming. So giving. So much love. "But that doesn't make sense," Callie said when she started to breathe again. "She didn't think of my grand-mother as an angel. She's furious with her."

"So?" Oliver said. "People aren't machines. They don't need to be consistent. They rarely are. I'm in the restaurant business, and before that, I was a teacher. I'm around people all the time, so I see this. Emilia could have been angry, she could have been disappointed, she could have been downright mad. She clearly was. But she also could have recognized that your grandmother saved her life. In fact, I suspect she felt so angry especially because she loved your grandmother so much."

"But my grandmother never came back," Callie said. "I

can't get that out of my head. Why didn't they ever return here?"

"Who's to know?" Oliver said. "Maybe they had a good reason. Maybe they still intended to, someday. Or maybe the memories were too painful. Maybe Emilia knows the reason. Maybe that's a piece of the puzzle she'll tell you before you leave. But she loved your grandmother, Pam. Corinna saved her. With food. Maybe *that's* one of the reasons Emilia became a cook. And why she cooks for others. That's probably also why she came back herself, and she rebuilt the town. She felt anger, but more than that, she felt love. That's why she commissioned this memorial."

Callie sighed. It suddenly seemed as though Oliver had explained not only Emilia to her, but herself to her as well. Yes, she'd been angry at Pam for judging her so harshly, for looking down on her choices—but she'd always loved Pam. Oliver was right; people were complicated. And it was possible for her to feel both. Being angry with Pam didn't mean she didn't love Pam. She adored Pam. Pam was her sister.

She only wished she had learned all this while Pam was still around.

She looked up at Oliver, with the moon and the vast sky framing him like a beautiful piece of art. "Thank you. For saying that. I don't know if I can explain it, but you just handed me a gift, your words."

He took her hand and squeezed it. "I think it's great that you came all the way here to discover this," he said. "That you went to such lengths to learn about your family. Not everyone would upend their lives to do that.

"I'm sorry you're leaving in a few days," he said. "I've enjoyed getting to know you."

"You've been a real friend this week," she told him. "I'm going to miss you."

"Yeah. Well." He dropped her hand and looked down. "I'll

bet you'll be glad to get back to your husband and daughter. My sister misses her boys so much when she and Gustavo go away even just overnight."

Callie looked at him, then shook her head and went to sit down on the stone bench. She knew she couldn't go home without telling him the truth. And it gave her a little reassurance, thinking about what he'd just said. Yes, he'd be angry. But maybe he could still remember that he liked her, too.

He sat down next to her. "What is it?"

She sighed. "Oliver... there is no husband and daughter. Well, there is, but it's my sister's family. She's the one with the baby. I'm not Pam, I'm Callie." She went on to explain how she'd come home when she'd gotten the awful news that Pam had died, and how she'd found the box in Pam's desk drawer with the two boarding passes.

"I hadn't been home in a long time," she said. "And so when I got there, I found out that Pam had this whole trip planned that I knew nothing about. That she'd planned to travel with me, assuming I'd just up and go when I found out what she wanted to do. She was right, I would have. I wanted to know what my grandparents had hidden from us. There was something about our family we were always trying to unravel, something that made us always a little insecure, I think. But I waited too long to come home.

"So I came myself. I owed that to her. I had to find out what our grandparents had been keeping from us. And then that first day, you told me that the only reason Emilia let Pam into the cooking class was because of the nice letter she wrote. I thought that if I wanted to connect with Emilia, I'd have to pretend to be Pam. And once I said it... I had to keep the lie going."

"Oh. Well." He looked stunned. She knew this was so unexpected. "Wow," he said. "That's a little crazy."

"I know. But I didn't realize... it was a spur-of-the-moment decision. I didn't expect to... I mean, can you possibly understand?"

He sighed. "I guess. I mean, sure. And I'm sorry about your sister. I only wish you'd told me sooner. We were becoming friends, you know?"

"I know," she said. "And I'm sorry. But it was more than just wanting to trick Emilia. It's hard for me to talk about Pam. I still don't fully believe she's gone. I guess I've been thinking a lot about her lately. Being here, it was almost as if I could pretend that she wasn't gone. Not for good. And that I could come back and patch things up with her. Like I said, I hadn't been home for a while."

"And why is that?" he asked. "If you don't mind my asking."

She sighed again. "Ugh," she groaned. "Here's the really terrible thing I did. I..." She took a breath and continued. "I was... well, I was involved with a married man from my work. I met him on a business trip to New Orleans last winter. It lasted for way too long. He didn't tell me he was married, but there were clues, and I should have known. I don't know why I did it. It's just I'd spent so many years growing up being the wild girl, the undisciplined girl, and Pam was the golden one. And it was such a tough childhood—Pam was mainly the one who raised me. She was ten years older than I was and gave up everything to take care of me. Maybe I was finally embracing that bad girl reputation I'd fought for so long. Or maybe it was because he was older and wealthy and made me feel secure. That was a feeling I never had before.

"Anyway, I caught sight of him in New York one afternoon when I thought he was out of town," she added. "They were on Columbus Avenue, going to the circus at Lincoln Center. He was with his wife and their three little kids, and she looked so happy to be with him, and I just felt horrible. I felt ashamed. That week I left my apartment, quit my job, and moved to Philadelphia to try to start over. I honestly didn't feel I could ever face my sister until I had a life I could be proud of."

Oliver breathed in deeply, as though he needed to make a physical effort to take in all she'd said. "Well, lots of people fall in love with the wrong person," he said. "I did. And honestly, I don't think you were the only one at fault. I mean, he's the one who was married."

"But I'm not responsible for him," she said. "I'm responsible for me. I should have known better. Sometimes I think that if I had come home like Pam wanted me to instead of hiding out in Philadelphia, things would be so different now. She wanted me to come home because she had this trip planned. I know she thought it could make us close again. Maybe I could have saved her when she fell."

They were silent for a moment. Then Oliver took her hand in his. "Callie... it's Callie, right?"

She smiled and nodded.

"Callie, I don't know you very well," he said. "We only met a few days ago. But what I've seen... I like. You're kind and warm, and smart. Funny. You care about people. You... you seem to me to be a very loving person. I mean, you fell in love with Emilia. Very quickly. You saw her for who she is, and you loved her, warts and all. And truly, anyone can make a mistake. You made a mistake with that guy. It's not the end of the world. You broke it off. And you punished yourself. Harshly. Banished yourself from your own home.

"So I have one question," he said. "Don't you think it's time to forgive yourself?"

She considered this, then shook her head. "I don't know," she said. "I don't know if I can ever forgive myself. For not being there for Pam. For the night she died, and also for all the months that came before. For not appreciating how much she sacrificed for me."

"You didn't know Pam was going to fall. You would have

been there if you'd known. And as for raising you—she did it because she loved you. You were her sister. Families don't come with scorecards. Or at least, they shouldn't."

"She was so mad at me. For never coming home. And I was so mad at her for making me think I didn't deserve to."

"And the tragedy is that you didn't have enough time to talk it out," he said. "But the love—that's never going away. Just like with Emilia and your grandmother."

She looked at him. "Thank you," she said. "This was, I think, the most valuable conversation of my life." She held his gaze for a moment, looking into his dark eyes.

"Oh, and wait a minute," Oliver said. "I have one more question." He rose and pulled her to her feet.

"Yes?"

"Just to be clear," he said, still holding her hands. "You don't have a husband and a daughter? You're not married?"

She shook her head. "Joe is my brother-in-law. Chloe is my niece."

He stayed still for a moment, then lifted his chin and rolled his eyes. "Thank God," he said.

She started to laugh. But then she stopped herself. Because that would have delayed the kiss she wanted so much.

She felt him take her shoulders, and she moved in toward him, until her lips touched his. They were soft, and the kiss was tender and sweet. And when she ran her hands up his shirt and around his neck, she felt something she'd been missing for a long time.

In a strange but real way, it felt like she'd finally come home.

TWENTY-FOUR

OCTOBER 1943

The next morning, Emilia came downstairs, where Signora Jorelini was already cooking the day's meal. It smelled heavenly.

"I was able to get some chicken today and some beautiful greens," she said. "We'll be able to feed everyone well tonight. The scallions look tough, but parts of them can be salvaged."

Emilia nodded.

"So don't just stand there, *piccolina*. Chop up the scallions, throw away the rotten parts, and I'll keep things going here with the sauce."

Emilia nodded again.

"So quiet, today," Signora Jorelini said, studying her.

"I'm okay," Emilia said.

"I know it's a lot for you to take in, about Tomas and about the bed in the attic," she said, returning her attention to the pot. "But let's keep our heads together. This is all precaution. This war can't go on forever, and with any luck, Tomas will be on his way soon and the Nazis will have no interest in our little town."

Emilia kept her gaze down, focused on her chopping. It was a huge betrayal, what she was about to do. This woman, who had been so welcoming to her and so good to her family all these years, was about to lose her daughter. And Emilia was the one who would enable that to happen. She was the key to the whole escape. She didn't know if she'd be able to live with herself after Corinna left. She hated being thrust into this position, hated her role in Corinna and Tomas's plan. As she began to chop the scallions, she composed in her head a new note that she'd put down on paper later today:

Dear Annalisa and Giulia,

I am lost and I am afraid. I don't know what to do. I am more alone than I ever imagined. Where are you? I dream of seeing you both coming around the corner. I hope you come soon enough. I don't know what to do...

Then she shook her head, knife still in hand. No, she wouldn't write this letter down. She was so far removed from them now, she barely remembered what they looked like. She could hardly imagine the sound of their voices. She knew Annalisa's was lower, Giulia's was higher and musical. She knew these things, but that was all she remembered. She couldn't hear them anymore. She could only think about what they used to sound like. And wish she could hear them one more time.

She watched Signora Jorelini stirring the sauce. Yes, she hated herself for what she was about to do to this poor woman. But she couldn't shake the images in her memory of Corinna and Tomas together, planning their future, loving each other, loving the life they envisioned for themselves. That love, their physical expression of love, their courage and faith in the possibilities ahead—it needed to be honored. And heeded. It was the manifestation of her father's beautiful words—Go forth. It was the only way to live.

That afternoon, she took a handful of blank cards from the desk in the kitchen and carried them upstairs.

"Going to make the menus?" Signora Jorelini asked. "The color is red today."

She nodded.

Upstairs in her bedroom, Emilia sat at the desk and took out her red pencil. She sharpened it until there was a tip so pointy that it would surely sting if she were to stab her palm or accidentally insert it beneath her fingernail, touching the delicate skin there. She wrote *Caccipulia Supper Club* in her best handwriting, erasing the letters that weren't perfect and trying again. She listed the foods Signora Jorelini was cooking. She spent more time than she ever had before on the words. She copied the same words onto five more menu cards, one more than she needed. And then, on Tomas's card, she drew a set of steps against a building with two tall windows and a small flower garden. It was the code Corinna had given her last night, the picture that would tell Tomas to meet Corinna here this evening, on the steps at the side of the house beneath their tall white bedroom windows.

When she was done, she put the extra card in her pocket and brought the others down to the kitchen to place in the baskets. For now, only Tomas would understand the drawing. Even if someone else in the Possano house noticed it, they wouldn't know what it meant. At least not tonight. Maybe in time others would understand. Maybe someone would figure it out. Maybe next week, next month, next year, a million years. But not tonight. Not tonight, when it mattered. Tonight only she, Corinna, and Tomas would know.

"*Grazie*, my darling," Signora Jorelini said. "Why don't you go upstairs? You look a little pale. Are you feeling okay? I'll finish with the baskets, and I'll make the deliveries with the other women. Then I'll get dinner ready for us, okay? Corinna should be home from tutoring very soon."

She put on her coat and wrapped her scarf around her neck. "My, it's getting colder, isn't it?" she said, almost to herself. "It's nearly winter. It's darkening early. My, my. The change of the seasons. It tells us that life has some normalcy, doesn't it?"

Emilia closed the door after her, then watched through the window, standing back so no one could see her. She watched Signora Jorelini until the growing darkness enveloped her.

Then she went back inside and upstairs, where she removed the menu card from her pocket, the extra one. She turned it over, and on the blank side, she wrote a new message.

You must return this to me. I will be waiting for you.

She hid it in the suitcase Corinna was planning to take, beneath some clothes she'd already packed.

Dinner was silent that night. Emilia was consumed with her own thoughts, and Corinna and Signora Jorelini seemed to be, too. They finished eating, and the three of them silently cleaned the dishes and then went upstairs to bed. Emilia watched Corinna kiss her mother goodnight, same as always, although maybe her hug was a little tighter, a little longer. But not different enough to make her mother sense that anything was amiss. It must have taken such willpower, she thought, for Corinna to behave so normally, not to cry or tell her mother the truth. But she had her mother's best interests at heart. She knew her mother would try to stop her from leaving. And if she were delayed, Tomas might wait, too. And that could put them all in danger, the whole town in danger, if Tomas were found hiding in the Possano's house. It was safer for everyone this way.

In their bedroom just before midnight, Corinna switched on the small table lamp on the desk. She put some additional clothes into her suitcase, and then tossed in a toothbrush, a hairbrush, some face cream. Emilia sat up in bed and watched.

Then Corinna turned to Emilia. "You should start packing,

too," she said. "Not too much. Warm clothes for sure. But you'll need to carry your own suitcase, so don't make it too heavy. I don't know how long we'll be walking each day. Come on, hurry up now. Midnight will be here before we know it."

Emilia looked at her. "What are you saying?"

Corinna paused, a partly folded sweater in her hand. "I couldn't tell you before. I thought it would be too hard for you to keep it from Mama. But Tomas and I—we want you to come with us."

Emilia was sure she'd misunderstood. "Wait... what?"

"You have to come," Corinna said. "It's not safe for you here. Hiding in the attic won't protect you."

"But your mother said I'd be safe."

"I don't think she's right. You are the daughter of a Jew. I love you too much to let you stay. We will start a new life somewhere. You can be part of it."

Emilia looked at her, then shook her head. "I can't," she said. "I'm not going."

"Yes, you are. You have to." Corinna came over and, kneeling in front of her, gripped her shoulders. "It's time to go," she whispered. "Start to pack. Now."

"But I can't."

"And why not?"

"Because of my sisters."

Corinna stared at her. "What?"

Emilia breathed in. "I have to wait for my sisters. I have to be here when they arrive. They will risk everything for me. They would never abandon me. They'll get here when they can. Even if it's months from now. I can't not be here when they arrive. I told them I'd wait. I told them in the letters you sent them."

Corinna paused, then rose and went to the desk. "I didn't want to have to show you this." She opened the desk drawer and pulled out the stack of letters she'd addressed to her sisters at the castle. "I never sent these," Corinna said. "There was nowhere to send them. The castle was invaded and everyone there was killed. They're gone. I'm your sister now. You must come with me."

Emilia looked at the stack, her eyes filling. How was this possible? "You never sent them?"

"There was no one there to receive them. Only Nazi soldiers. Emilia... your sisters—"

"No, you're wrong!" she cried, and Corinna ran over, putting her hand over Emilia's mouth to quiet her.

"You have to be quiet, you can't wake up Mama—"

Emilia pushed the hand away. "It doesn't matter," she whispered. "It doesn't matter if they never received them. They know where to find me. They're coming back."

Corinna drew her close for a hug. "Please don't be foolish. You will be found here. They will take you away. Or they will kill you right here. You will die if you stay."

"Your mother has a place for me in the attic—"

"They will find you there. And when they do, they will arrest her, too. Please come tonight. It's the only way to keep everyone safe..."

There was the sound of footsteps outside, crunching on gravel, just beneath the window.

"That's Tomas," Corinna whispered. "We have to go. Now."

Emilia stayed still.

"Please, Emilia. Please."

Emilia looked up. "I love you, Corinna."

Corinna sat back down on the bed, and Emilia wrapped her arms around Corinna's long neck.

"This is the last chance," Corinna said. "Come with us, Emilia, I beg of you."

Emilia pushed herself away.

"I will come back for you," she said. "And for Mama. Stay safe. Stay hidden. I will be back for you."

Corinna lowered the lid of the suitcase and snapped it shut. Then she went to the bedroom door. She hesitated, and for a fraction of a second Emilia thought she would get her wish. That Corinna would stay. That they would continue as they had been.

Corinna turned to her and took a breath. Emilia held hers. The silence seemed endless. Then finally Corinna spoke. But they weren't the words Emilia wanted to hear.

"Please tell my mother I'm so sorry," she said.

Emilia nodded.

Corinna stepped into the hall and then closed the door behind her. Emilia went to the window to look outside. Below, dimly lit by the moon, she could see the silhouette of a man in a heavy coat waiting on the pathway. She knew it was Tomas and breathed a sigh of relief that he had indeed understood the last code. Although she hadn't seriously doubted that he would, she still felt a tinge of satisfaction that her codes had worked, that they'd kept Corinna and Tomas together and would help them build a future. But that feeling lasted just a moment, and before long, the weight of all that had happened settled down on her again. She saw then Corinna's silhouette appear from around the corner of the house. She placed her suitcase down, and the two silhouettes merged into one. It was an embrace, a beautiful embrace, an embrace full of joy and promise. Then, slowly, the figures retreated from one another. Corinna picked her valise back up with one hand, and Tomas grasped her other hand. They stole away, and soon they were invisible.

Emilia crawled back into her bed but couldn't fall asleep. She kept picturing Tomas and Corinna as they looked from the window, two shadows taking off into total darkness. Sometimes she imagined that she was the one Tomas was running with, that he was holding her hand and leading her away, out of town, far from everything that frightened her. And sometimes she imagined it was Corinna guiding her to safety. A part of her yearned to jump out of bed and run downstairs, even in her nightdress, to run after them and say she'd changed her mind. There was so much uncertainty here, so much terror.

Would the Nazis come to Caccipulia and find her and whatever other Jews were hiding? Would the danger ultimately prove too much for Signora Jorelini? If push came to shove, would she turn Emilia in? What did it even mean to be taken by the Nazis? Where would they take her? And how would it happen? Would those awful soldiers do what she'd heard? Would they come in and take her, at night, from her bed, while she was sleeping even? Would they let her get dressed? Would they let her bring something with her, maybe pictures of her father, her sisters? Would anyone say goodbye? Would Corinna and Tomas ever think about what had happened to her? Would they ever find out? Where would she eventually end up?

I did my best, Papa, she whispered. *I thought this was what you'd want. For me to wait for Annalisa and Giulia. To be here when they finally came back. So we can be a family again.*

At some point she must have fallen asleep because the next thing she knew, the sun was up. She climbed out of bed and dressed quickly. Then she sat on the edge of her bed, waiting to hear sounds from downstairs, Signora Jorelini entering the house with the food she'd been able to obtain and starting to prepare breakfast. She wondered how long it would take for Signora Jorelini to notice that Corinna wasn't coming downstairs for breakfast. Maybe she would think Corinna left early for school today. Or maybe she would think Corinna had decided to sleep late. Maybe she'd think Corinna wasn't feeling well. Surely she'd ask Emilia to explain where Corinna was when they didn't come downstairs for breakfast as usual.

What would Emilia say? Had Corinna and Tomas left her with the job of breaking the news of their escape to Signora

Jorelini? When Corinna had mentioned her mother last night, all she'd done was ask Emilia to say she was sorry. Had she meant for Emilia to also explain what she was sorry for?

Her questions were suddenly answered—with a loud gut-wrenching wail. "Nooo!" It was Signora Jorelini crying out, her voice harsh and hoarse. "*Nooo!*"

Emilia threw off her covers and ran downstairs in her bare feet. The kitchen door was ajar. Emilia ran to the window with the pretty sunflower curtains and looked outside. Signora Jorelini was still wailing, holding a sheet of paper in her hands. Signora Possano was nearby, and she and two other women came running over.

"What is it? What is it?" Signora Possano said, waving the others off and pushing her friend back inside.

"She's run off!" Signora Jorelini cried. "She's run off with the boy from your house."

"Tomas?" Signora Possano said. "Our Tomas? All his things are gone. He left last night."

"Did he say goodbye? Did he tell you Corinna was going with him?"

"Corinna is gone too?"

Signora Jorelini crumpled down onto the step. "No…" she wailed. "No. My baby. They are after him. They will find him, and they will take her too."

Emilia continued to watch as Signora Possano put her arm around her friend. The two women swayed and rocked, Signora Jorelini's cries turning into quiet, heartfelt sobs. Emilia stayed still, surprised and yet grateful that Corinna had left the note. She wouldn't have wanted to say the words that would cause Signora Jorelini such anguish. She went to the oven to warm some bread. The least she could do now was make breakfast for the poor woman who had taken her in.

A few moments later, Signora Jorelini walked her friend outside, then came back into the kitchen. Her eyes were sunken and her shoulders were stooped. She looked like she had aged ten years from when Emilia had seen her yesterday morning. She put the note on the table and sat down heavily on a chair, dropping her chin down, her hands clasped between her knees.

Emilia wiped her hands on a towel and went to the table to pick up the note. She unfolded it and read:

Dear Mama,

I am leaving with Tomas to start a new life together. I love him and I must be with him. I am so sorry to leave you, but I don't have a choice. I didn't want to tell you, because I knew you'd try to stop me, and I didn't want our last time together to be filled with fighting and bitter words. I will think of you now in the kitchen, making delicious meals for others, putting such love and care into your food. I will miss you and think of you always. I will be back one day when everything is safe again, and we can all be happy. I am confident I will be back and we will be a bigger, happier family. Please know how much I love you.

Your loving daughter,

Corinna

P.S. Please don't blame Emilia. She didn't know a thing.

Emilia folded the note up again and handed it back to Signora Jorelini. "I'm so sorry," she said.

"You didn't hear her leave?"

Emilia shook her head. She couldn't bring herself to admit that she'd known what was going to happen. Corinna had said in her note that Emilia knew nothing. It was easy to go along with the lie. It seemed somehow the kindest thing to do. "She only said last night to tell you she was very sorry," Emilia said. "I agreed to tell you that this morning. But I... I didn't know why."

Signora Jorelini dropped her head again.

"Can I bring you something, Signora Jorelini? Something to drink? Some warm bread? Cheese?" Without waiting for an answer, she went to take a coffee cup from the cupboard.

"I've lost everything now," Signora Jorelini said. "How do I go on?"

Emilia stood helplessly, not knowing what to say. Tomas had talked about how many people had lost everything. His own family had been taken away. He didn't know their fate, but she'd heard him tell Corinna that he thought they'd likely be killed. And she, too, had lost everything. Her father and her sisters. If Corinna was to be believed, Annalisa and Giulia were dead, too.

Although she didn't want to believe it. She couldn't believe it. Her heart wouldn't let her.

But this was different, Corinna's escape. Because Emilia had helped in the escape. She had enabled Tomas and Corinna to leave. With her codes. And that's what had broken Signora Jorelini's heart. She was accountable for that.

"Her note sounds hopeful," Emilia said. "Maybe she's right. Maybe she and Tomas will get to safety. And they will return one day. And everyone will be happy again..."

"Emilia, please," Signora Jorelini said, holding up a hand. She paused for a moment. "Anyway, it's time to start cooking," she said. "We need to get started. It's a green day today for the menu cards. The woods."

Emilia looked up. "The supper club?" she asked. "We aren't ending it?"

Signora Jorelini shook her head. "No. We aren't ending it yet."

Emilia stood in the kitchen for a few moments. She felt

horrible. She had betrayed the woman who had cared for her father, who had nursed him when his daughters were gone, who had taken her in and fed her and given her a place to live when she had none. And by not speaking up, she had broken this poor woman's heart.

And yet, if she had the chance to do it all again, she didn't think she'd do anything different. Corinna and Tomas belonged together, even she could see that. What they felt for each other, it was stronger than any other need, it was more important than any other want. They deserved a chance for happiness. The kind of happiness her father had had with her mother.

And that's when she knew that this was part of war, the part that accompanied the killing and the torture. It left you with no good answers. No way forward beyond what was bad and what was worse. Everyone was scared and everyone was alone and everyone was searching for peace and safety. And love. And finding substitutes only in things that didn't last, that weren't yours. A bed that belonged to another. A meal made from ingredients scrounged together, with no guarantee that there'd be another one tomorrow. A home that wasn't your home at all. Because it was missing the people who made it a home.

She was like Tomas. She was Jewish. She was the outsider.

And there was only one thing to do for Signora Jorelini, the woman who'd saved her.

She would save her in return.

That night after Signora Jorelini was asleep, Emilia packed a small bag and tiptoed downstairs. She'd written the menus that day in green, for the woods. Now it was her turn to follow the code. She wished she didn't have to leave. She wished she could stay for her sisters. She didn't want to believe they were dead. But she didn't have the luxury of waiting any longer. She had betrayed Signora Jorelini by keeping Corinna's plans from her.

The least she could do was protect her now. Signora Jorelini would be arrested or worse if the Nazis came and found out she'd been hiding Emilia. She had to leave so Signora Jorelini would not suffer that fate.

She stepped outside and took a breath. The way to the woods, to the outskirts of town, led right past the house where she'd grown up. She was glad. She'd stop and look at it for a moment if it felt safe to pause. She would need to hold onto that memory possibly for a very long time.

But she would be back.

She thought of her father's Abraham story, the story about the man who left his home assured by the stars in the sky that he would live on, that there would be generations and generations to come. *Go forth*, that was the story's entreaty. She stepped outside and looked upward, hoping to see a skyful of stars. But the night sky was gray and overcast. There were no stars above.

Maybe tomorrow, she told herself. At some point, there'd be stars. And she would be happy to see them. And they would spur her on. For now, she thought, she'd have to make do with whatever lighting the members of the Resistance had out there in the woods. A flashlight, maybe? A torch or candles?

Whatever light there was, she would pretend it was a star. And she would follow it and be grateful for it. And wait for the sky to brighten and the real stars to appear once more.

TWENTY-FIVE
OCTOBER 2019

Saturday

It was way past midnight, and Callie was still awake in her hotel room, sitting on the rug with her back against the bed, thinking about that kiss in the courtyard a few hours ago. It had felt so honest, so genuine. Like Oliver was. He'd listened to her when she told him why she was in town, and he'd introduced her to his family because he thought they could help. And in one short evening, he'd taught her so much about life and family, and getting along in the world. And liking herself. She felt as though she'd been holding her breath for so long, waiting to hear that she was the failure she always thought she was. But she didn't need to hold her breath any longer. She wasn't a failure. She didn't need to punish herself further. Oliver was smart and thoughtful. And he was able to see the good person she was, despite the mistakes she'd made.

Of course, there was no telling where things with Oliver could go. It was just a few days since they'd met, just one kiss they'd shared. But now she felt a kind of safety. The safety that came with knowing she didn't have to try so hard or worry so much. She could just be.

She looked over, then reached to the table and picked up the note that Emilia had written to her grandmother, where she'd left it when she came back to the room, after their romantic walk along the cobblestone street. She looked at Emilia's writing and then held the note to her chest, remembering the sound of Oliver's voice as he'd read the words in English. It seemed unbelievable that her grandmother had received this card from Emilia, had held it in her hands back in 1943, when she would have been so young, a girl really, twenty-one. Callie knew so little about her grandparents. Only that they'd met in Italy, escaped the Nazis, and married in New York. And that they loved each other so much. Although maybe that was the most important thing she needed to know. She remembered how Nonna had spent every day alongside Nonno in his hospital room while he lingered after his stroke. How her cancer progressed so quickly and she'd died just months after him. Pam and the neighbors had said she couldn't live without him. That she wanted to be with him.

They were together for fifty-five years. They'd made a life for themselves. They'd chosen each other, and everything else was the outcome of that choice, that promise, that belief that things could be better. She was the outcome of all that—she and her parents, and Pam. And Chloe. That little girl that Callie now saw had her great-grandmother's light eyes and her great-grandfather's long lashes. She was the next hope of this family, the unknown little person so full of promise. Who knew what she would create, build, do or become?

Callie thought now of that day her grandfather died. She remembered that the call from the nurse at the hospital had come while Nonna was driving home from grocery shopping to change her clothes and get some sleep before returning to Nonno. Pam had taken the message. She remembered sitting across the kitchen table from Pam as they waited for their grandmother to come home. Pam was twenty-two, a grown-up by all accounts; Callie knew this was a huge responsibility on Pam's shoulders. How do you break the news to your grandmother that the love of her life has just died?

Nonna came in and saw immediately from their faces that something was very, very wrong. "Is it Nonno?" she said, putting the grocery bags on the table.

Pam nodded. "The hospital just called. I'm so sorry," she'd said, her voice trembling but her body still. Callie knew she was trying so hard to be an adult, to take charge of the situation, knowing her grandmother's heart would be broken. But it had to be so hard, being the one to say this horrible news out loud.

Nonna came over, her arms open, and Pam ran into them. Nonna hugged her, and then motioned for Callie to join them. Callie got up and pressed her face against Nonna's soft dress. Pam was sobbing now, and Nonna was kissing her head.

"I hate that I had to tell you that," Pam said. "I hated that you were coming home from shopping and I was the one to make you sad. I didn't even tell you to sit down or prepare you. I just blurted it out. You were still holding the groceries."

"Oh, my darling Pam," Nonna said. "You did it perfectly."

"No, I didn't. I just blurted it out. I didn't even tell you to sit down or anything."

"Sweetheart, it wasn't that much of a surprise," Nonna said. "He was very sick. I knew it was coming. I'm sorry you had to take the call."

"I didn't care about taking the call," Pam said. "I only wish I didn't have to tell you the news."

"I'm glad you were the one to tell me," Nonna said. "It made it easier for me, hearing the news from someone I love so much."

Callie thought now of that conversation. She imagined that Nonna was telling the truth. It did make it easier to learn bad news from someone you loved. Someone who cared about you, someone who cared how you felt. She thought now of how she had come to town, mad at her sister, embarrassed about her love life, determined to drag information out of Emilia at any cost. She'd been so strong, so selfish, so self-protective. And yet, here she'd met Oliver, who showed her there was a better way to move forward. And when he'd kissed her, he'd made her feel he was totally open, with no agenda, just affection. She wanted to be someone like that, too, someone who gave affection and care.

And Emilia was certainly deserving of that.

What happened between her grandmother and Pam made all the sense in the world. And now, she wanted to be the person to do it perfectly, as Pam had. To deliver the information that Emilia needed to know. Oliver had convinced her that she needed to forgive herself. And now she realized that maybe Emilia needed to do the same thing.

It was funny, she thought. She'd come here determined to get information from Emilia. But now she knew it was Emilia who needed the full story.

The next morning she got up, put on a pair of pants and a sweater, packed her suitcase, and went downstairs, the jewelry box in her hands. Another beautiful breakfast was on the table, breads and pastries, cheese and meats and fruit. All for Callie, as the other guests had left. Callie supposed that Emilia would bring these leftovers to the church as well.

She picked up a plate and put some fruit and cheese on it, along with one of Emilia's delicious *cornetti*. Just then Renata walked into the room. "Cappuccino, Signorina?" she asked.

"*Si, grazie,*" Callie said. "And also, Renata, can you tell Emilia I'd like to speak with her? *Per favore?*"

She finished putting food on her plate, and Renata returned with coffee. A moment later, Emilia walked into the dining room from the kitchen, wearing a simple, straight skirt and blouse, her gray hair tied in a knot.

"You asked to see me?"

Callie nodded. "I have something to tell you."

Emilia paused, expressionless.

"I know you're mad at your sisters," Callie said. "And yesterday I was with Oliver from the coffee bar and his family. And I found out more about why. And I know you're convinced they abandoned you. But Emilia... you understand they didn't make it off the island, don't you? You know the Nazi soldiers arrived there and killed everyone.

"I know it's easier sometimes to be mad at a sister than to admit how much you love her," she continued. "And how guilty you feel for what happened to them, when bad things happen. I've felt the same way. But Emilia, you don't have to feel bad that you survived. You don't have to feel guilty that they were stuck on the island and you weren't. You didn't do anything wrong. And neither did they. And whatever happened to them —you have to know they'd be glad that you lived. Even if they didn't."

Emilia pulled out a chair from the table and sat down, leaning heavily with her arm on the table. "This is what you wanted to tell me? You don't know my story. You don't know about my sisters. Or about Corinna, the other one, my dear friend. You don't know that she left, too, when I asked her not to. You don't know that she fled and died in the woods. She should have stayed—"

"No, Emilia, no," Callie said. "She didn't die in the woods."

"She never made it to Switzerland. This I know—"

"Because they went to America instead. They lived good lives—"

"And how do you know this?"

"I know this because... Corinna and Tomas are my grandparents," she said. "They married when they got to New York.

See?" She pulled out the wedding photo from the jewelry box. "This is them on their wedding day."

Emilia took the photo in her hands. "Corinna," she murmured. Then she looked up. "Your grandparents?"

"They made it safely to America," she said. "And they had a son who married my mother. And then came my sister and me. And now... now there's a little baby in the world. My niece, Chloe."

"They lived?" Emilia asked. "They had a son?"

Callie nodded.

"But why did they never come back?" she said. "Why did they never return? As they promised they would? They said they'd come back for me. Your grandmother said she'd return. She promised. This was wrong. This was cruel."

"And this is why you're so angry at her?" Callie said.

"Of course. Of course it is!" Emilia raised her voice, and her cheeks grew red.

"But there's a reason," Callie said. "And I think I just figured out why. She told us when we were kids, my sister and me, that she made a terrible mistake. And she would mention your name. You. And she said, so often she said, that she couldn't go back, because the town where you lived was destroyed. She must have known the Nazis came and killed all the people and leveled the town.

"That's why she never came back," Callie said. "She thought you had been killed with the others. I think that was the mistake—that she left you and never saw you again."

Emilia shook her head. "They thought I was dead?"

"Yes. There was no way she could know differently."

Emilia paused, then let out a sad chuckle. "They thought I was dead. And I thought they were dead. I was mad at them for leaving me and getting themselves killed. I thought they could have escaped with me if they'd stayed."

"I'm sorry you never saw them again," Callie said. She

reached into the box again and pulled out the menu card. "But this was among the things they left behind."

Emilia took the card and looked over the menu, then turned it over and read the note she'd written to Corinna.

"It's my handwriting," Emilia said. "I wrote this. Oh, my Corinna. How I loved her. She saved my life. She and her mother. They took me in when I had no one. They fed me."

"She loved you, too," Callie said. "She never forgot you."

Emilia blinked, and Callie waited. It was a sight she'd never have thought she'd see. Emilia crying. But then Emilia rubbed her eyes and stood, apparently never one to show emotion for long. Although when she spoke, Callie knew she was expressing love as best she knew how.

"You must be very hungry, you haven't touched your break-fast yet," Emilia said. "Come. Let's eat."

And so Callie had breakfast with Emilia in Caccipulia. It was a long breakfast, more than two hours. And as they ate, they talked. Emilia told her about her father, the Jewish tailor, and her mother, the Italian heiress, who had, against all odds, fallen in love and married. She told her about how her mother had died giving birth to a fourth sister who'd also died, and how her father's broken heart had never mended.

And then she told her what ultimately happened during that rainy October of 1943. How Tomas had come to town after working for the Resistance, and how she'd discovered that Corinna and Tomas were in love, and how the sight of Corinna and Tomas late at night together, planning their future, was what gave her strength and hope during those frightening days. She told her all about the codes, how she'd written the codes on the menu cards, and how that was the way Callie's grandpar-ents were able to escape.

"So you saved their lives," Callie said. "My grandmother told me that once, that you saved them. One day when we were on vacation in California and she was crying. They survived because of you.

"Which means I'm here because of you," Callie said. "My whole family. We owe our lives to you."

"I saved them as your grandmother and her mother saved me," Emilia said. "That, I suppose, is how love wins."

She went on to explain that the night after Corinna and Tomas left, she left Caccipulia too. As the daughter of a Jewish father, she knew she would be taken away by the Nazis as soon as they arrived. And that she'd be putting Corinna's mother in danger. She didn't think her hiding place in the attic would work for long. She described how she'd left town in the middle of the night and headed for the woods, and from there she'd made her way to Switzerland. Where she thought she'd find Corinna and Tomas, but never did.

And she explained that Philippa—Callie's great-grand-mother—was not killed when the Nazis stormed Caccipulia. No, Emilia had heard later that Philippa died of a heart attack just hours before the Nazis arrived. So she never had to see her beautiful town destroyed or her friends killed. She died believing that her daughter and her daughter's love were safe and on their way to a better life.

"It was a blessing, the way she died," Emilia said.

And then it was Callie's turn. Callie told her all about Pam and Joe. She explained that she was the younger sister, and she apologized for lying. She said that like Emilia, she had often been annoyed or mad at her older sister. She hadn't always liked her, in fact. But she'd always loved her and would miss her for the rest of her life. "Pam always used to say that sisters are the closest relative there is," she'd said. "And while I didn't always believe it, now I think it's true."

And she explained her move to Philadelphia, and described the conversation she'd had with Oliver last night that had proved so meaningful. And how much he meant to her, even though they'd only met a few days ago. How she hoped they could stay in touch. She even mentioned the kiss, which made Emilia smile.

"So when are you leaving?" Emilia asked.

"I'm scheduled to fly back tomorrow," Callie said.

"And what will you do today?"

"Walk around town. I'm meeting Oliver for dinner when he finishes work at the coffee bar."

Emilia looked at her watch. "Dinner is a long way off," she said. "Come into the kitchen. I'll make a little snack for you to take on your walk."

Callie smiled and followed Emilia into the kitchen. There was no better way for the two of them to end their conversation, she thought. No better way than with food.

EPILOGUE

SEPTEMBER 2022

"Pamela," Callie cooed as she bent over the crib, tickling the baby's round belly. "It's time to wake up. We have a big day."

She reached into the crib and lifted up her eight-month-old daughter, whose fine, brown hair resembled those of her namesake. But those long eyelashes—those were her father's all the way.

Callie brought Pamela over to the dressing table in her sunlight-filled room and changed her into the dress she'd bought especially for today, a pale-yellow dress dotted with pink and purple carnations. Pam's favorite flowers.

Just then she heard footsteps from down the hall. "Daddy's coming," she said.

A moment later Oliver walked into the room, looking so handsome in his jeans and blue button-down shirt. Marriage and parenthood agreed with him, she thought. As it agreed with her.

He put his arm around Callie's waist and leaned over to plant a kiss on Pamela's nose. "Ready?" he asked Callie.

"I feel like I've been ready forever," she said.

Oliver scooped up the baby and they walked downstairs to

the expansive living room. Callie never would have believed it, but she loved living in this farmhouse. Not too long ago, she would have thought it too remote. In fact, that's exactly what she'd believed when she first saw it, back when Meg and her family were living here. But when they'd returned to the States last year so Gustavo could accept his new position at Stanford and were looking for someone to rent the house, she and Oliver were quick to grab it. They'd been living in Oliver's small apartment over the coffee bar in Caccipulia since they'd married a few months earlier, and with a baby on the way, they needed to move. They didn't know how long they were planning to stay in Italy, but for now, it suited them perfectly.

Callie didn't want to be anywhere else but close to Emilia. She wanted to take care of her, for as many years as Emilia had left. She'd felt that way as soon as she'd finished breakfast with her that morning in Caccipulia. At dinner that night, she'd told Oliver all about it.

"Emilia told me her whole story, and I told her mine," she'd said. "And I don't think I'm ready to put her story behind me."

"I don't think I'm ready to put *our* story behind me," he'd said.

She'd nodded. She, too, had thought there could be so much more to come.

She took Pamela from Oliver and brought her to the living room, where Joe and Chloe, now four, were working on a puzzle. She was so glad Joe had wanted to take some time off from work to visit. Joe had been wonderful to her from the moment she came home from Italy three years ago. She'd had surprises for him—the story of her grandparents and Emilia. And it turned out that he had surprises for her as well.

"Of course, I knew Pam had that trip planned," he'd told her as they sat down in the living room the evening she returned, after putting Chloe to bed. "I helped her plan it. I didn't tell you when you came home for the funeral because... well, I was a wreck that week. I barely remember any of it. It was the last thing I was thinking about, that trip. But if you had shown me what you found that day up in the bedroom, I would have told you all about it."

"I didn't think that you knew," she said. "I was sure you would have talked about the trip with me at some point if it wasn't a secret."

"We found the supper club card and the old photos when we were remodeling the bedroom for Chloe," he said. "Pam learned that Emilia taught cooking, and she wanted to go there to learn and also to find out more about your grandparents. She wrote Emilia a letter all about us and Chloe and how your grandparents were from Italy and came here during the war. And that's how it all started."

"But she hated to travel. She never left home."

"She didn't hate to travel. She just loved being here. She wasn't as much of an adventurer as you, but she wasn't a hermit, either."

"But if you knew all about it, why did she hide the stuff in the box with the code that only I would know?"

"She thought it was the right thing to do," he said. "After all, it was your story too."

"Then why didn't she tell me what she was doing?"

"Callie, she wanted to tell you. She wanted to invite you to go with her. But you seemed to be avoiding her, especially when you decided to move to Philadelphia. She didn't understand, but she thought that if she got you to come home, she could entice you to take the trip to Italy on the spur of the moment. You were pretty spontaneous in those days. And, you know, she did have your passport."

Callie looked away. "I was horrible to her. I just couldn't face her back then. But it never occurred to me I'd never see her again. We were on such bad terms when she died."

"I guess," Joe said. "But Callie, she loved you. You were her sister."

Callie put Pamela in her infant seat on the floor to watch her cousin and her uncle finish the puzzle. She watched Oliver give Pamela her bottle, then went into the kitchen.

Emilia was there, preparing the most glorious feast imaginable. She'd closed the hotel last week so she could be here preparing for five full days. She'd been up since before dawn to complete the spread. There was fish and chicken and pasta and all kinds of savory vegetable dishes, with plenty of cakes, cookies, and pastries for dessert. Enough to feed a small army. Which was just about the size of the crowd they were expecting. Oliver had helped her all week as well. He still loved Italian cooking, although he'd never made it back to Boston to open a restaurant with his friends. Because a better opportunity had come up. He and Meg had decided to open a new restaurant in Caccipulia on the site of Callie's great-grandmother's restaurant—the one Philippa had closed back in 1943, due to the war. The one that Callie now knew was pictured among the photographs she'd found in Pam's locked box.

And Callie had gotten a dream job, too. She'd learned that the Parissi Museum—the historical museum on the site of Parissi Castle, where Emilia and her sisters had spent that fateful summer of 1943—was looking for apprentice curators to help with its painting and sculpture wing, devoted to artists who'd spent time at Parissi Castle. She was working remotely part-time as she completed a degree in art history at the University of Rome.

And when she started working for the Parissi Museum, that's when Callie learned how Emilia came to have enough money to rebuild the town of Caccipulia. Many years after the war, she'd been identified by the Italian authorities as the sole living heir to Parissi Island. She'd gone there to look around, but had found she wanted nothing to do with the island or the castle. The memories were just too sad. So she'd accepted a settlement to turn the whole island over to a nonprofit company with plans to develop a museum there. And she'd used the settlement to recreate the town she loved so much.

Callie watched Emilia at work, her big, white apron reaching almost to the floor, protecting her new blue dress. Her hair was combed into a beautiful, sleek bun, and she'd put lipstick and eye shadow on. She was so excited about today. Everyone was. Including Meg and Gustavo, who had arrived a few days ago with their boys and two-and-a-half-year-old daughter named Gabriella, to help with the preparations.

Suddenly, Oliver called from the living room. "They're here, they're here!" And Callie and Emilia ran to the window where he was. It had taken many, many months of research, but finally Callie and Oliver had traced what had happened for sure to Emilia's sisters. And while they'd both been on Parissi Island when the Nazis arrived, it turned out neither of them had been killed in the ambush that had taken the lives of so many. The eldest sister, Annalisa—the sister that Oliver's grand-father had fallen in love with on Parissi Island long ago—had eventually made it to the United States, married, and settled on Long Island. Sadly, she'd passed away but she'd left behind a granddaughter named Mia, a researcher with a Ph.D. in cardiol-ogy, who lived in New York with her history professor husband and two small children. And remarkably, Mia's husband, Leo, was also a grandson of that famous composer who had fallen in love with Annalisa. He and Oliver were distant cousins. They'd even met a few times when they were children.

As for the middle sister, Giulia, she was still alive, and had moved with her husband to New York just as the pandemic hit. They'd wanted to be closer to their granddaughter, Tori, a dress-maker, and her family—a musician husband, a teenage daugh-ter, and a pair of young twins.

The pandemic had delayed the reunion, but finally, the

entire family had arrived from the United States that morning. There had been so many of them that Callie had chartered a coach to transport them from the airport.

Now as she looked out, she saw all the people—women, men, children, babies—start to descend from the coach onto the driveway. And then she saw a young man hold out his hand— and a very old woman slowly make her way down the steps.

It was Emilia's sister, Giulia. A beauty, just as Emilia had described her. With wavy white hair and large eyes, and a sweet, heart-shaped face. Here to see her younger sister. After almost eighty years.

Emilia, her hands trembling, removed her apron and slowly made her way out through the front door. Callie and Oliver followed, along with Meg, Gustavo, and their children. Outside, everyone fell silent. It was as though time stood still, while the two sisters made their way to one another. They paused for a moment and then embraced, their arms tightly around each other, their bodies swaying. At one point Giulia took her baby sister's face in her hands and shook her head, as though she couldn't believe they were together again. And then they hugged some more.

Callie felt herself start to cry, as Oliver came up behind her and wrapped his arms around her. She sniffled and looked up at him. "It's unbelievable," she whispered, and he nodded and held her.

And it was unbelievable. A lowly Jewish tailor and an Italian heiress had fallen in love and married against all odds. And look what they had created, she thought. Look what came of those two lives—this crowd of families, these people who had fallen in love and made babies and were pursuing great careers, sharing with the world their talents and expertise. Living with hope and purpose and love. Embracing happiness despite the horror that had sadly consumed their ancestors—or maybe because of the dreams they'd never given up on. And Callie, too

—Callie was a product of that brave couple from long ago. She was here thanks to their youngest surviving daughter, Emilia, who'd helped her grandparents start afresh.

Joe came out just then with Chloe and Pamela, and he handed Pamela to Callie. Callie adjusted her position so Pamela could watch the sisters embrace. She hoped that in some way, her baby would remember this moment. Or just absorb it deep inside of her.

Yes, this was a day for family. But it was mostly a day for sisters.

Callie thought of Pam as she watched Emilia and Giulia hold onto one another. *Sisters are the closest relative there is,* Pam had always said.

"You were right, Pam," she whispered. "You were so right."

A LETTER FROM BARBARA

I want to say a huge thank you for choosing to read *The Forgotten Italian Restaurant*. If you enjoyed it, and want to keep up to date with all my latest releases, just sign up at the following link. Your email address will never be shared and you can unsubscribe at any time.

www.bookouture.com/barbara-josselsohn

While I've loved writing each of the books in my Sisters of War series, I must admit that Emilia's story was especially poignant. My heart ached for this fifteen-year-old heroine who returns alone to her hometown as the Nazi threat in Italy intensifies, and seeks purpose in a world on the brink of disaster.

It's a funny thing about novel writing—you often base characters on people from your past, many times without realizing it until you've finished the story. That's what happened to me this time around, when I was imagining Corinna, the young aspiring teacher who shows Emilia where hope lies and what it means to put love first.

Even before I knew her name, I knew Corinna would have fair skin, honey-colored hair, a passionate personality, and an insatiable zest for life. I knew, too, that teaching would be her profession. There was nothing that suited her more.

Later, I came to understand that I'd been mining my memories to create this pivotal character.

Corinna is based on my fourth-grade teacher, Miss Clarson.

Young and energetic, she had an astonishing ability to own the room, so that even the most rambunctious of students grew silent when she spoke. She was artistic and imaginative and had a mischievous sense of humor—but she could be serious, too. One day, through tears, she told us the story of someone close to her who'd perished in the Vietnam War. I think she was trying to help us understand that people carry invisible hurts, and that we care best for them when we see beneath the masks they use to hide their pain. It was a talk I never forgot.

In our school on the last day of class, the sixth graders would carry around small autograph books for teachers and friends to sign and add their well wishes. When I was in sixth grade, I made sure to find Miss Clarson and offer her my book. She knew I wanted to be a writer, and in her note, she implored me to "not let obstacles stand in your way." I have that book still, and I look at those words often.

It's bittersweet to reach the conclusion of the Sisters of War series. I have come to think of these three sisters—Annalisa, Giulia, and Emilia—as close friends. I don't want to say good-bye, but I'm happy to send them into the world. I hope they will make an imprint on your heart, as they have on mine.

I hope you loved *The Forgotten Italian Restaurant* and if you did, I would be very grateful if you could write a review. I'd love to hear what you think, and it makes such a difference helping new readers to discover one of my books for the first time.

I love hearing from my readers—you can get in touch on my Facebook page, through Instagram, Goodreads or my website.

Thanks,

Barbara

KEEP IN TOUCH WITH BARBARA

www.BarbaraJosselsohn.com

 facebook.com/BarbaraJosselsohnAuthor

x.com/BarbaraJoss

 instagram.com/Barbara_Josselsohn_Author

REFERENCES

Below is a handful of books and resources I found most helpful in my research about Italy during the Second World War.

Benevolence and Betrayal: Five Italian Jewish Families Under Fascism by Alexander Stille (Summit Books, January 1991)

The Other Italy – The Italian Resistance in World War II by Maria de Blasio Wilhelm (Norton, January 1988)

The Italian Refuge: Rescue of Jews During the Holocaust, edited by Ivo Herzer (Catholic University of America Press, 1989)

Italy's Jews from Emancipation to Fascism by Shira Klein (Cambridge University Press, 2018)

The Bicycle Runner: A Memoir of Love, Loyalty, and the Italian Resistance by G. Franco Romagnoli (Thomas Dunne Books, August 2009)

The Italians and the Holocaust: Persecution, Rescue and Survival by Susan Zuccotti (University of Nebraska Press Reprint Edition, January 1996)

And finally... about the sacred texts mentioned in the novel...

The story Emilia remembers about Abraham and the stars is from the Book of Genesis

ACKNOWLEDGMENTS

Writing a historical novel can feel like walking into a dark cave without even a candle. I'm so grateful to all the people in my life who've shown up to offer some light along the way.

With the third and final book of my Sisters of War series now finished, it's a great time to take stock of all the people who helped me reach this point—and to express my heartfelt gratitude.

As always, I am so grateful to agent, Cynthia Manson, who has been my advocate, advisor, rock, and cherished friend for almost ten years! Cynthia is a pro in every sense of the word, as well as a wonderful human being. It's not overstating things to say I could never have reached this point in my career without her. The more we work together, the more I realize how lucky I am and how much I benefit from her wisdom each and every day, and I look forward to working with her over many, many more years to come!

Thanks, too, to my brilliant editor, Jennifer Hunt—the editor every writer dreams of! Her insight into what a story can be is beyond exceptional. After working together for several years, I was so happy to finally make it to London this past winter so we could meet in person—and what a special day that was! I'm exactly where I always wanted to be as a writer, and Jennifer is a huge part of the reason why!

Thanks so much to all the publishing, editorial, marketing, rights, and sales professionals at Bookouture—what a remarkable team! And a special shout-out to the PR crew led by Kim

Nash, Digital Publicity Director, and to Sarah Hardy, the Bookouture publicist who has worked with me on all three books in the Sisters of War series. I don't know how you both find time in the day to do all that you do for us Bookouture authors. And speaking of Bookouture authors, let me just add that you are all such talented writers. I love reading your books and I'm delighted to be part of the community!

I am so lucky to have a wonderful circle of author friends, who are as generous and kind as they are talented and accomplished. Thanks to Jimin Han, Patricia Dunn, Marcia Bradley, Jennifer Manocherian, Diane Cohen Schneider, Ines Rodrigues, Linda Avellar, Gosia Nealon, and Diana Asher—I am awed by you all!

And an extra shout-out to Ines Rodrigues for reviewing the Italian words and phrases in the book. Ines is both an expert in languages and a beautiful writer—so how lucky was I to be able to draw on her talents?

I'm deeply appreciative once again to Kerry Schafer, who continues to be an Author Genie—what better name for her business? Kerry's such a great person, and I love working with her (and reading her novels—check out her books at allthingskerry.com). Thanks, too, to Jessica Sorentino, a talented branding professional. What fun, working with you!

Thanks to Westchester Reform Temple in Scarsdale, N.Y., and to the entire clergy team, led by the always-inspiring Rabbi Jonathan Blake. I am moved by your words and elevated by your teachings. And thanks so much to the Scarsdale Adult School for its fascinating and important class, "Italian Jews Under Fascism," which helped immeasurably with the writing of each of the books in the series. I've come to appreciate the Scarsdale Adult School, led by Jill Serling, so much—and am thrilled to have started teaching writing classes there!

To all the wonderful writers affiliated with the Women's Fiction Writers Association, the Writing Institute at Sarah

Lawrence, the Scarsdale Library and its Writers Center, and Westport Writers Workshop, and all those students who have trusted me with their work: thank you for sharing your stories, your inspirations, and your love of writing with me. I learn from you all every day.

And a special thanks to all the online bloggers and reviewers I've come to know over the last several years, including Lisa, Bea, Elaine, Annie, Reena, Lori, Jennifer, Denise, Dorothy, and many, many more—I am so appreciative of what you do and how you do it! You have all become cherished friends.

Like *Secrets of the Italian Island* and *The Lost Gift to the Italian Island*, much of *The Forgotten Italian Restaurant* was inspired partly by the beautiful North Fork of Long Island. Thanks to Scott Raulsome of Burton's Books of Greenport, Jessica Montgomery and Liz Larsen of Shelter Island Public Library, and Janet Olinkiewicz of Floyd Memorial Library in Greenport for being so welcoming. And much appreciation to Rosemary Nickerson for opening her beautiful home to us. What a beautiful place to write! Thanks, too, to Mark Fowler and Jessica Kaplan, owners of Bronx River Books in Scarsdale, N.Y., my hometown bookstore. What a special place and a special couple!

Thanks to Dr. Brittany Glassberg and to Ben Pall for your continued enthusiasm, and expertise on aspects ranging from travel to technology to medicine!

And finally, I am beyond grateful for my wonderful family: my husband, Bennett; our three children—David, Rachel and Alyssa; and our mini schnauzer Albie. Thanks for always teaching me what home truly is. I love you guys so much!